HIGH PRAISE FOR KELLEY ARMSTRONG AND
FINDING MR. WRITE

"Smart characters, tender romance, outdoor adventures, and comedic moments make this delightful rom-com a sure pick."

—*Booklist*, starred review

"Armstrong packs in plenty of laugh-out-loud moments while driving home her point about gendered expectations and inequities in genre publishing. Add in believable chemistry between the leads, and the result is sure to please fans of meta rom-coms."

—*Publishers Weekly*

"Fans of Melissa Ferguson will be delighted to read Armstrong's rom-com that dives into the publishing world in a new way."

—*Library Journal*

Also by Kelley Armstrong

Finding Mr. Write

WRITING MR. WRONG

KELLEY ARMSTRONG

FOREVER

New York   Boston

Copyright © 2024 by K.L.A. Fricke Inc.

Cover art and design by Elizabeth M. Oliver
Cover copyright © 2025 by Hachette Book Group, Inc.

Forever
Hachette Book Group
1290 Avenue of the Americas, New York, NY 10104
read-forever.com
@readforeverpub

First Edition: June 2025

Forever is an imprint of Grand Central Publishing. The Forever name and logo are registered trademarks of Hachette Book Group, Inc.

The publisher is not responsible for websites (or their content) that are not owned by the publisher.

The Hachette Speakers Bureau provides a wide range of authors for speaking events. To find out more, go to hachettespeakersbureau.com or email HachetteSpeakers@hbgusa.com.

Forever books may be purchased in bulk for business, educational, or promotional use. For information, please contact your local bookseller or the Hachette Book Group Special Markets Department at special.markets@hbgusa.com.

Library of Congress Cataloging-in-Publication Data

Names: Armstrong, Kelley, author.
Title: Writing Mr. Wrong / Kelley Armstrong.
Other titles: Writing Mister Wrong
Description: First edition. | New York : Forever, 2025.
Identifiers: LCCN 2024059821 | ISBN 9781538742761 (trade paperback) | ISBN 9781538742778 (ebook)
Subjects: LCGFT: Romance fiction. | Novels.
Classification: LCC PR9199.4.A8777 W75 2025 | DDC 813/.6—dc23/eng/20241213
LC record available at https://lccn.loc.gov/2024059821

ISBN: 9781538742761 (trade paperback), 9781538742778 (ebook)

Printed in the United States of America

CCR

10 9 8 7 6 5 4 3 2 1

CHAPTER ONE

GEMMA

Gemma Stanton stared down at her newly released first novel and told herself—for the hundredth time—that the kilted Highland laird on the front did *not* look like Mason Moretti and absolutely *no one* would realize she'd used the pro hockey player as her inspiration. While she was sure many sports stars had inspired romance heroes, in this case, it was not a compliment.

Fucking Mason Moretti.

She shook her head, set the book on her lap, and looked around the tiny green room. In the corner, a TV was tuned to *Vancouver This Morning*. The cheery title card showed a skyline backdrop of a ridiculously blue ocean and a blinding sun that reminded people November would not last forever.

Gemma's interview would open the show…which wasn't stressful at all.

She took a few deep breaths. She'd do fine. Just fine.

If only she could stop fretting about her dress. She should have worn jeans and a sweater. That's what she'd picked out and paired with a new pair of boots, and it'd looked good, damn it. But then the doubt crept in, and she'd grabbed a dress instead. Now she fretted that she was filling a stereotype—the romance author in a flowery dress and heels.

She hated this anxious version of herself. She'd written a romance? Deal with it. The book had sex scenes? It sure did. If she risked being labeled a lonely middle-aged divorcée who poured her most torrid fantasies into a book, she didn't give a damn. Anyone who'd spent a decade married to a two-minute champ was entitled to a stockpile of unfulfilled erotic fantasies.

"Gemma?"

She instinctively tensed as a woman slipped into the room. Ashley Porter. Head cheerleader and certified mean girl—

No, Gemma mentally corrected. That had been high school. Ashley was now host of Vancouver's hottest morning show, where she was renowned for being a total sweetheart. When Gemma's publicist asked about local media contacts, Gemma hadn't dared include Ashley on the list. It'd been Ashley who reached out and offered this. The prime morning show slot on Gemma's release day.

Now Ashley breezed in wearing jeans and a cashmere sweater that could have been the twin of the one Gemma almost wore. Ashley's sable hair gleamed under the lights, and her tan whispered of a recent trip south. The sapphire sweater perfectly matched Ashley's eyes, and the boots had to have cost triple Gemma's bargain bin find. Also, Gemma didn't fill out her sweater like that. Or her jeans.

Yep, switching to the dress had been a very good call.

As Ashley enveloped Gemma in a hug, the sweet scent of apple and water lily washed over Gemma, and she tensed so hard it was practically a spasm.

Princess by Vera Wang—the same perfume Ashley wore in high school. The same scent she'd worn on the last day of school, when she'd cornered Gemma and leaned in to whisper, "*You really thought Mason would look twice at you, Gemma? Mason Moretti?*"

Present-day Gemma gritted her teeth and admitted that she hadn't exactly been a ray of sunshine at that age either. All teeth and attitude, as one boy had muttered when she'd flipped him off for smacking her ass.

Ashley released her from the noxious cloud of perfume. "I am *so* happy for you, Gem. I remember what an amazing writer you were. I always knew I'd see your name on a book someday."

Gemma tensed again, braced for some snarky comment slammed in on the knifepoint of a cheerful chirp. Twenty years ago, she'd have been ready with a comeback. But she wasn't that confident and smart-mouthed girl anymore, as much as she was desperately trying to find her again.

Ashley continued, "I'll admit I couldn't believe you'd written a *romance*." Here it came… "But I'm so glad you did. I love historical fiction, and Laird Argyle is…" Ashley made a swooning noise, hand to her forehead.

Huh. Apparently her writing group had been right. Readers did go for asshole romantic leads.

The first romance Gemma had written featured the kind of guy *she* liked—sweet and considerate. When it hadn't sold, her writing group had talked her into penning what the market seemed to want. An alpha hero. A self-absorbed, egotistical, inconsiderate, talks-with-his-fists asshole. So she'd dipped into her past and pulled up the perfect guy for the role.

Mason Moretti had been her school's golden boy. The kind of athlete who comes around once in a century. He'd gone on to play enforcer for the Vancouver Growlers, because of course he did. To be an enforcer, you had to be an asshole, and Mason was the best. Or the worst, depending on how you looked at it.

The worst. Mason Moretti was definitely the worst.

MASON

Mason Moretti didn't need anyone to show him to the TV studio green room. Ashley wrangled him on her show every chance she could, and his damned publicist wouldn't let him say no. But this time was different. He smiled to himself as he reached for the green room door.

"Whoops!" Ashley appeared from nowhere and held the door shut. "Gemma's in there. Let's take you down here."

Ashley led him down the hall, chattering away. Mason would never say he liked Ashley as a person, but she was useful, and she knew it and used it to her full advantage. He couldn't fault her for that, because he used her right back. Not like *that*. Never like that. Oh, Ashley had been letting him know *that* was on the table since high school, but you don't grow up in the spotlight without being able to smell a baited trap at a hundred paces.

Speaking of baited traps, this whole interview felt a little... unsettling. Suspicious. Ashley said Gemma knew he'd be here, but what if...?

"How's Gemma?" he asked. "Is she—?"

"She's fine. Just fine." Ashley steered him into the makeup room. "Stay in here. Makeup will be in shortly."

After Ashley left, Mason glanced around the tiny room, with its three salon-style swivel chairs and massive mirrors. He settled into the middle chair and shrugged off his unease like an ill-fitting shirt. Worrying didn't suit him. In this case, it only reminded him of all those years he'd spent worrying that Gemma Stanton hated his guts.

But she obviously didn't hate him, because she'd written a romance novel with him as the hero. If Gemma had been pissed off, she wouldn't have hesitated to let him know—with both barrels.

Gemma Stanton…

As Mason propped his feet on the adjoining chair, he remembered the first time he'd spoken to Gemma. Kindergarten. The cloakroom. It'd been October, the little room overflowing with Halloween decorations. He'd arrived late, after an early morning lesson, and he'd been hanging up his skates when Gemma walked in from the classroom.

She'd looked from the skates to him. "You skate?"

Under her level gaze, he couldn't help puffing up. He knew who she was, this little pixie of a girl with freckles and eyes the color of fresh grass and hair that reminded him of a wheat field in fall.

"I play hockey," he'd said.

"You any good?"

"I'm the best."

She'd rolled those green eyes and taken something from her cubby. She'd been about to walk away, and he'd been struggling for something to say, when she turned back. Her gaze dropped to his shoes, and she lowered her voice.

"Miss Wang's sick. We have someone else, and she made Jay sit in the corner for tracking in dirt."

"Oh. Okay."

He reached down to switch to his indoor shoes and then looked up to thank her. But she was already gone, leaving him hanging there, wishing he hadn't been so flustered that he'd forgotten to say *thank you*.

Gemma had always been nice to him. Even when he didn't deserve it.

He shook that off. The point was that she didn't hate him. You don't write a romance novel about a guy you hate, right?

"Mason Moretti," a voice said from the doorway.

He looked to see a young woman carrying a makeup case. Late twenties, with a jet-black bob and powdered white skin. She always did his makeup. Which meant he should know her name, but he was so bad at that. Too many names, he told himself. Too many people who flitted in and out of his life. He couldn't be expected to remember them all...and yet he was expected to, and when he forgot, it made something in his stomach twist, and his brain shout that he needed to fix this *now*.

He knew he had had the makeup artist's name in his contact info for Ashley so he could refresh his memory. It was one of his many tricks for coping in a life where he briefly connected with endless people. But he'd been so focused on seeing Gemma again that he'd forgotten to check his notes.

He glanced at the young woman. When he hadn't responded, she'd started taking out the little pots, snapping each down with a clack.

He tried to fix it with a broad smile. He might not be the hottest player on the team, but he had all his teeth, which was kind of a miracle, all things considered.

The woman's eyes narrowed. "You don't remember me, do you?"

"Of course I do. The best makeup artist in Vancouver." He smiled again.

"If you don't remember my name, just admit it."

"I—"

"It's Nadia," she said. "Not that it matters to you."

Mason's gut twisted. He *did* remember her. He'd just temporarily forgotten her name. But it was too late to fix that. It was always too late.

Do better.

They were finishing up when someone rapped on the door. "Two minutes," a man called.

Nadia studied Mason, hands on her hips. "Can't work miracles with that mug. How many times have you been hit in the face?"

"It adds character."

She sighed. Deeply. "It does, damn you. Get up. Let's go."

Nadia ushered him into the hall, where a woman waited with a printed photo, pen outstretched. Mason reached for it automatically, only at the last moment remembering to confirm it was a photo of him.

"My daughter is such a fan," the woman gushed. "She plays hockey, too."

"Good for her." He signed the photo as he walked, the woman jogging along beside him. "Maybe she'll be the first woman in the NHL."

He always said that. He meant it, but the words sounded hollow, a sentiment repeated too often to have any meaning.

"Hey, Moretti," a voice called.

Still walking, Mason turned and lifted a hand in automatic greeting.

"I hear Denny is still in the hospital." A middle-aged guy appeared, face set in an expression Mason knew only too well these days. "You got anything to say about that?"

Mason shrugged. "Hockey's a rough game."

He hated the words, but that's what he'd been told to say. *Don't apologize. Don't get flustered.* Mason wasn't the one who put the Growlers' young star center in the hospital. Not his fault the kid got hurt.

Not his fault…unless his actual job was protecting his teammates. Unless he'd seen the guy going for Denny and…

And what, Mason? What happened out there?

He pushed the thought aside as staff members elbowed his accuser away. The guy would get a talking-to later. This was supposed to be a safe space for Mason. No one would mention the incident with Denny. No one would ask what happened out there.

Which was good, because Mason had no fucking idea what happened.

He only knew that he hadn't done his job, and a brilliant young player went to the hospital. People were pissed off.

And he didn't blame them.

Didn't blame them at all.

CHAPTER TWO

GEMMA

The set was arranged like a café, with a love seat and chair to the left and a little breakfast counter to the right. When Ashley had led Gemma in, Gemma had eyed the love seat longingly, only to be directed to one of the ridiculously high stools at the counter. As she waited for the show to begin, she perched on the stool, keenly aware of how her legs swung like a toddler's. She went to cross her legs, only to feel her skirt ride up.

Do not flash the audience, Gem.

Might sell more books.

Mmm, no, that's not really your target audience.

Focus on her target audience. Women like her, a lifelong romance novel reader. What would convince her to pick up *A Highland Fling?*

The hot guy in a kilt.

Except the hot guy...She glanced at the cover filling the floor-to-ceiling screen. When she'd completed the publisher form, she'd thought her description of Laird Argyle was vague enough. Dark, wavy hair. Square face. Wide forehead. Strong jawline. Rough looking, as if he knew his way around a bar brawl. An average face but with a body that meant your gaze never rose above his neck. Broad shoulders. Bulging biceps. Perfectly defined pecs and abs. All that...in a kilt.

She hadn't specified eye color, let alone mentioned dark beard scruff and a nose that'd been broken a few times. Maybe the last part seemed obvious to the cover designer. It was a romance trope after all—hot bruisers always had crooked noses.

The designer took all that and...Gemma glanced at the cover again. Damn. It really did look like Mason Moretti.

The only reason Gemma saw it was that she knew who the inspiration had been. No one else would spot any resemblance between a Scottish Highland laird and a Canadian hockey player.

The camera operator counted down as Ashley hopped onto the adjoining stool. Not only did *her* feet touch the ground, but wearing jeans meant she could cross her legs.

Gemma focused on keeping her knees closed and prayed she didn't get carried off by nervous enthusiasm and start swinging her feet. Although that might win her the pity vote. She'd totally buy a book from any author who made a fool of themselves on live television.

She should have asked her publicist about that. As marketing strategies went, how many sales could she win by making a total fool—

"Happy Tuesday!" Ashley trilled as the cameras rolled. "We have *such* a treat for you today. Get ready for a morning jam-*packed* with goodies. Later, I'll introduce you to a man who trains capuchin monkeys as seeing-eye pets. Monkeys! They are the cutest things ever! And I promised to share that recipe for nonfat sugar-free caramel corn. First, though, local author Gemma Stanton's debut novel came out today."

Ashley spokesmodel-waved. Gemma straightened, ready to say hello, when she realized Ashley was indicating the screen instead. They'd taken down the book cover during the intro. Now, out of the corner of her eye, Gemma saw it return. And when it did, peals of laughter rang out from the crew.

Gemma froze.

Romance covers had always been a source of mockery, but this wasn't one of those old-school clinch covers with the heroine practically humping the hero's leg. Sure, Laird Argyle had apparently lost his shirt in battle, but it happened.

"Oh, I don't think that's the right one." Ashley's voice took on a tee-hee singsong. "Someone in the art department seems to have done a little facial reconstruction."

Oh, shit. Gemma turned to the screen...and saw Mason Moretti's face over the cover model's. And just to clarify who Mason was, they'd replaced Laird Argyle's sword with a hockey stick.

"Hmm," Ashley said, with a thoughtful finger to her lips. "Let's see the real cover."

Both versions appeared side by side.

"That is a *striking* similarity," Ashley said. "Now, I should mention that Gemma and I went to high school together...the same high school as a certain local star player."

The blood drained out of Gemma as the temperature in the room plummeted.

Play along. Just play along.

Gemma forced a laugh. "I guess that does look a little like Mason. I'd love to take credit for giving our old classmate a shout-out, but authors don't design their covers or pick their cover models."

"But they do write the book, and that looks an awful lot like the guy you describe."

Ashley picked up the novel and started to read, her words drowned out by the crashing in Gemma's ears.

She'd been set up.

Was she actually shocked? In school, Ashley and Gemma had always sparred—the polished cheerleader and the smart-mouthed valedictorian, circling each other. Now Ashley was mocking Gemma on live TV? What a surprise.

But they weren't teenagers anymore. Gemma hadn't seen Ashley in over a decade. Why would she do this?

Because she could. Because some girls never get past high school.

Ashley closed the book and wagged her finger at Gemma. "Sounds to me like someone had a crush."

Gemma opened her mouth to laugh it off, to say something, anything, salvage this—

"Oh!" Ashley gracefully hopped from her chair. "Look who just walked into the studio."

Ashley threw open her arms, and Gemma turned slowly as the piped-in hockey announcer's gravelly voice rolled out a familiar intro.

"And here he is, folks, the one, the only, the Growlers' not-so-secret weapon. Give it up for . . . the Mace!"

Gemma patiently waited for the nightmare to end. It was fine. Just fine. A bad dream, that was all. A bad dream where Ashley invited Mason Moretti himself to join them, plunking him and Gemma both down on that cozy little love seat, with his arm around her shoulders and that grin on his face.

Gemma hated that grin. Always had. She'd even told him so, after his English teacher said he could earn a passing grade by volunteering for the school paper, where the editor would write his articles for him. Except the editor was Gemma, who sure as hell was not writing Mason's articles for him. He'd shown up at the tiny newspaper office an hour before he was due to deliver his first article and said his computer ate it, while giving Gemma that ridiculous grin.

"Does that usually work?" she'd said.

"Does what usually work?"

"That smile."

"What smile?" he'd said, managing to keep grinning while saying it.

She'd sighed. "That is not your real smile, Mason."

"I don't know what you mean." Still grinning.

"I've known you since kindergarten, Moretti. That is the smile you use to get what you want, and what you want is for me to write your article. I'm not. I know you're failing English. I know you're dyslexic. I also know that only means you need some accommodations, which I am willing to give. The problem isn't your dyslexia. It's that no one makes you do shit because you're a star."

She'd leaned over her editor's desk. "You are capable of writing that article, so you'll have it to me by morning. Got it?"

Now, as the interview rolled on, Mason had that smile firmly in place. He also had his arm around her shoulders. Well, not exactly around them. It would look that way to the viewer, but his arm was resting against the love seat back, with his fingertips not quite touching her. Seemed he remembered her well enough to know that he risked losing any fingers that made contact without permission.

This wasn't a nightmare, was it?

This was actually Mason Moretti sitting beside her with his shit-eating grin, certain that she'd based her romantic lead off him because he was such an amazing guy and she'd never gotten over him. That one kiss they shared had obviously been seared into her brain. As for the utter humiliation that came after it, well, that was water under the bridge. Didn't stop little Gemma Stanton from secretly pining for him, writing smutty scenes about the two of them—

Oh God, she was going to puke.

That's what he'd think, wasn't it? That's what everyone would think. That she'd published a sex fantasy featuring herself with her high school hockey star crush. It wouldn't matter that her heroine bore no resemblance to Gemma—in appearance or personality— and was just a character she'd created who seemed a good match for someone like Moretti, a starry-eyed simpering girl who took his bullshit and told herself she was special when he stopped aiming his assholery her way.

"So what do you think, Mason?" Ashley waved at the screen. "You're on a romance cover."

He gave a hearty laugh that Gemma knew was also fake. "I'm flattered. Kinda makes me want to run out and buy a kilt."

Tittering laughter from Ashley, who continued with "And you're a romance hero between the covers, too."

"So I've been told."

Ashley slapped her hand to her mouth, eyes widening, just in case anyone missed the double entendre.

Ashley reached out to rap Mason's arm. "You are so bad."

Was Gemma really sure this wasn't an actual nightmare, with her trapped as Ashley flirted with Mason on live TV?

"But seriously, Mason," Ashley said. "Gemma based her romance-novel hero on you. What does that feel like?"

"Great. How else would it feel?" He aimed that inane grin Gemma's way. "It's really flattering."

"Yes, but Gemma isn't just a random author writing you as a hero. We knew each other in high school. Seems *someone* had a secret crush."

Gemma stiffened. She was very aware of how she must look right now, frozen under the studio lights, unable to flee the locomotive bearing down on her.

"Speaking of high school," Mason said. "Gemma was always a great writer. Editor of the school newspaper."

"But she obviously had a crush—" Ashley pushed.

"And you did the video announcements, right?" he said to Ashley. "So we all ended up where we were heading. Me with hockey, you with TV, Gem with writing. That's cool." He turned to Gemma. "When did you start the novel?"

Her brain spun, frantically searching for the trap. This must be a trap. But it wasn't. Mason might be an ass, but he wasn't Ashley. He'd never been vicious or mean-spirited. He didn't need to be.

Gemma realized what he was doing. Throwing her a life preserver. Acting like a decent guy. Because he could be one, when he wanted to. The problem was when you started believing he *was* a decent guy and lowered your defenses, and then he reminded you what he really was, what he'd been all along.

Not a slithering snake, but king of the jungle, master of all he surveyed. Even a king could be magnanimous now and then.

She found her own fake smile. "I stopped writing after university, but I got back into it a couple of years ago and remembered how much I loved it."

Ashley opened her mouth, but Mason plowed on.

"So you're making up for lost time now?" he asked.

"I am. I'm working on book two, which is due out next year."

He asked what it was about, and she relaxed and joked that it was a secret, and they continued on like that, Mason taking over the interview and Gemma gratefully letting him.

CHAPTER THREE

MASON

Mason was *not* lying in wait to ambush Gemma. Sure, it felt a bit like that. Sure, he was just outside the building exit, tucked behind a pillar, waiting to hear the click of her heels—

"I can see you there, Mason."

He peeked out at her.

She shook her head. "If you're trying to hide, you need a bigger pillar."

"I was just getting some air."

Damn, she looked good. He hadn't known what to expect, whether he'd even still recognize her, but that was silly. No matter how much she'd changed, he'd have known her in an instant. And he had.

In the studio, he'd taken one look and seen the Gemma who'd rolled her eyes at him in the kindergarten cloakroom, the Gemma who'd told him she was not writing his school newspaper article, the Gemma he'd kissed behind the school just before graduation.

Oh, she was older now. They both were, but she wore it a hell of a lot better. Eyes like summer grass. Hair like autumn wheat. Teeth that could snap you nearly in two and a tongue sharp enough to finish the job.

Okay, so the last part wasn't quite so poetic, but he remembered how it felt when she'd give him a look that said she saw right through him and wasn't putting up with his bullshit.

He used to remember how that felt, and think it'd been hot. Maybe a little bit "schoolboy and teacher." Except now, seeing her again, it reminded him that he'd liked her attitude long before he'd been old enough to even think like that.

He'd liked that she'd called him on his bullshit because it meant he didn't need it around her. She looked at him and said, *I see you.* And what she saw wasn't a kid on his way to stardom. It was just a boy with a girl. A girl he wanted to be with. A girl who'd sometimes seemed like she wanted to be with him too—be with *him*, not "the Mace."

He shook that off. He was getting sentimental. Too much going on in his life, upsetting the smooth flow he fought so hard to keep. Seeing Gemma again was good. Great even. Seeing her again when she clearly didn't harbor any ill will? Fucking amazing. But that was all. No need to analyze it and get all maudlin, like he'd lost something all those years ago. They'd connected, briefly. It hadn't worked out. They'd moved on, him to his career and…

His career. What more did he need? An incredible career, good friends, women when he wanted them. Life was a little rocky right now, but in general, it was all anyone could want. Right?

He pulled away from those thoughts and focused on the woman in front of him. He'd moved on to the NHL, and Gemma moved on to being an author. What had she been doing with her life? He suddenly felt desperate to know.

"I'm sorry about all that," she said. "Ashley clearly thought it was hilarious. You shouldn't have gotten dragged into it."

"There's no such thing as bad publicity, and being the inspiration for a romance hero is definitely not bad publicity. I really am flattered. I can't wait to read the book."

She hesitated. "You don't need to do that."

"No, seriously, I want to." And he did. He'd just need to wait for it to come out in audio, which is how he read, never having really gotten comfortable with words on a page.

A look flitted over her face. Something almost like panic. "Really, Mason. Don't read it, okay?"

He smiled. Gemma Stanton, nervous about people reading her stuff? That was new. Or was she just nervous about him reading a book where she was the heroine and he was the hero?

"We should catch up," he said. "Let's go grab a coffee."

She shook her head. "Thanks, but I'm under deadline."

"All the more reason why you need coffee. Or brunch? There's a little place just around the corner."

"I really can't."

"It's literally on the corner. We can see it from here." He smiled wider. "My treat."

"It was great seeing you again, Mason, and I appreciate that you were decent about this whole mess." She looked up at him. "Really. Thank you."

A bead of sweat trickled down his temple, despite the autumn chill. He was doing this wrong. *What* was he doing wrong? He needed to figure out what she expected and change course.

"You don't like coffee? There's a bubble tea place just—"

"I really need to go, Mason. Again, it was good to see you, but the deadline for this second book is kicking my ass. I'm already late."

Ah, that was it. Gemma had always been super responsible, and the missed deadline was stressing her out.

"Give me your number then," he said. "I'll call later, and we can celebrate after you finish the book. Go for dinner. Catch up."

"That isn't necessary, Mason." Gemma reached out and squeezed his forearm. "Again, thank you. It's good to see you, and I'm glad to see you got where you wanted to be."

He found his grin. "Was there ever any doubt?"

That slight roll of her eyes, the old Gemma surging, and then she turned and walked away, and it was only as she disappeared that he realized what he should have said.

I'm glad to see you got where you wanted to be, too, Gem.

Mason skated backward as fast as he could and then executed a perfect stop, feeling a rush of satisfaction at the shower of shaved ice. That never got old.

He had most of the suburban rink to himself, a weekly treat. It wasn't about practice. It was about just getting out and skating, like he had when he was a kid. He'd barely been old enough to lace his skates before he was sneaking out of the apartment at dawn to skate alone on the pond behind their subdivision.

At thirty-six, Mason had hit his NHL senior years. Hell, for an enforcer, he was a freaking dinosaur. "Enforcer" wasn't his formal position, of course. After the 2004 lockout, the rules changed to emphasize speed and scoring, and there wasn't as much room for guys whose primary role was fighting. Also, the game had changed—for the better, Mason thought—with less of the dirty play of slashing, hooking, checking, high-sticking and the like. Oh,

Mason liked a good brawl, but he'd always been exceedingly careful with his health and safety, terrified of ending up like the old-school enforcers, with CTE from too many blows to the head.

Mason didn't mind spending time in the penalty box if it helped his team. Nor did he mind getting cursed out by fans of the opposite team. He was supposed to be an asshole. That was his job description. A professional asshole who'd do whatever it took to protect his team and help them get the goal. It meant he was one of the lowest scoring players on the Growlers, but he had a wall full of MVP awards to make up for it, and when it came time to meet the fans, he had the longest line for photos and autographs.

Or he used to have the longest line. For the past month, he'd been skipping those meet and greets, at the coach's insistence. No one on the team blamed Mason for what happened. Not even Denny.

Except...

He heard his coach's voice. *Maybe you should speak to Dr. Colbourne about this one, Mace.*

That'd been three weeks ago. When he'd ignored the hint, the coach obviously took the direct route because Mason now had two voicemails from the psychologist herself.

Two unreturned voicemails, which really wasn't like him. He might be the designated asshole on the ice, but in real life, he didn't do shit like ignoring calls from someone who was just trying to help. That was rude.

But it's also exactly what he was doing.

Mason shook it off and skated faster. He had no problem speaking to the team shrink, but he didn't need her this time. He'd get past this on his own, and he'd tell her that. Soon. When, you know, he remembered to return the call off-hours so she wouldn't pick up and he could just leave a message.

People thought Mason had intentionally failed to protect Denny because he was jealous of the young and popular player. Dr. Colbourne would know that wasn't like Mason. At all.

You didn't agree to be an enforcer unless you were a team player. Mason liked Denny. The last thing he wanted was for the kid to bounce on and off the injury list until he finally had to quit hockey. That happened too often with the rising stars, and Mason didn't want it happening to a good kid—and a good player—like Denny.

So what had gone wrong that night?

Mason had seen what was coming, started to intercede and… froze. He still didn't know why.

Mason pushed into a hard skate, and his right knee whimpered. He glared down, as if he could shame it into submission. After thirty years of hockey, he pretty much *had* to expect a bum knee, but it still frustrated him.

A girlish shriek pulled his attention to the far left. He always shared his ice time with a figure-skating group who couldn't afford the rental. The kids were wee ones, none coming past his waist, all of them zipping around, shrieking and giggling. He was glad to see a few boys in the group. There'd been a time when he'd wanted to figure skate. Hockey was his passion, but he'd seen girls whirling and zigging and zagging in figure skating, and it had always looked like fun. He'd asked his dad, who nearly had a heart attack.

"You want to do *what?*" his father had said with that same look he'd given when Mason had said he wanted to go to college.

"You want to do *what?*"

"Get a college degree," Mason had said. "Maybe kinesiology. Something to fall back on when I retire from hockey."

"And how the hell will you get into college?" his father had said. "You're barely passing high school."

"The recruiter said they can get me in. On a scholarship even. I could get my grades up, if I tried harder—"

"No, you couldn't." His father had planted his hands on Mason's shoulders, though he had to reach up to do it. "I've said it before, and I'll keep saying it until it gets through that thick skull of yours. God gave you one gift. One incredible gift. That is what you are good at. Focus on hockey, and don't embarrass yourself by trying to do more." Dad had shaken his head. "College. You can barely read."

Mason skated faster to banish the memory. He executed a perfect set of crossovers, and that helped lift his mood.

Yep, still got it.

He moved into position for an explosive start and then took off down the ice and pivoted fast, his signature move against guys who figured Mason was too big to skate with any speed or agility. One of the little figure skaters whooped and shouted, "Swing that mace!" and he lifted a hand to a round of cheers.

Yep, definitely still got it.

"Mason!" This voice came from his side of the rink. He looked to see one of the staff gesticulating wildly.

"Your phone's ringing!" the guy shouted. "You left it over here!"

"Yeah," Mason snapped as he skated closer. "You know why I left it over there? Because it rings."

The young man colored and stammered, "I-it keeps ringing. It might be urgent."

Mason grunted and reached out a gloved hand. The guy lifted the cell phone gingerly, as if afraid of smudging the screen.

You don't want to piss me off? You let me skate in peace. That's why I pay a fortune to rent the whole ice. Because the only sound I want to hear is those kids having fun.

He answered the phone with a growled "What?" as the staff member slunk off.

"It's Terrance," said the caller.

"I know. I've got this fancy feature on my phone. Call display. Ever heard of it?"

"Have you checked social media today, Mason?"

"I never check social media. That's why I have you."

"You really are in a mood. Well, maybe this will help. You're trending."

"Yeah, that's exactly what I want to hear. I'm trending, again, because I'm the world's biggest asshole, who let a kid get put in the hospital. And if you say all publicity is good publicity, I will—"

"It's not about Denny."

Mason went still. "What'd I do now?"

"It's about your appearance on *Van This Morning*. People loved it. You and the writer were adorable. That Ashley is a world-class bitch, and you deflected her like a pro. Better yet, you did it in defense of a lady."

"Yeah, yeah. I just didn't like seeing her do that to Gem."

"*Gem*, is it? So you do know her."

"It's been a while, but yeah, I know her. She's good people."

"Better and better. You like her?"

Mason's hand tightened on the phone. "What's this about?"

"Do you like her well enough to go out with her? On a date? With some specially chosen media there to snap pics? People loved seeing that side of you, Mason, and they loved the idea of a classmate basing her romance hero on you. They're hoping this is the start of something. So…maybe it could be? On paper?"

"You want me to go out with Gemma as a promo op? To polish my rep at her expense?"

"She's a brand-new author with a brand-new book. She'll appreciate the buzz."

"So I'd come clean with her. Tell her it's for publicity."

"Uh…" Terrance cleared his throat. "I don't think that's necessary."

"Yeah, it is. Like I said, Gemma's good people. I'm not doing anything that might hurt or embarrass her." *Been there, done that.* "I know her. We were friends." *Bit of a stretch…* "I'll put it to her straight up. She'll see how it benefits her."

"If that's what you think is best."

"It is. I just need her number. Get it for me."

Mason hung up without waiting for an answer. Then he smiled to himself. Part of his bad mood had been about Gemma turning him down for coffee. He hadn't known how to ask again without sounding creepy. Now he did.

CHAPTER FOUR

GEMMA

Gemma stared at the blinking cursor and wasn't sure whether she wanted to weep in frustration or pummel the laptop into submission.

More like pummel her muse into submission.

She'd blown her deadline, something she'd never even done with a school essay. She couldn't blame work, because she was on a term-long leave to write her second book, even though the advance didn't come close to covering her salary.

When she'd warned her editor about the delay, she'd blamed her endless and excruciating divorce. She hadn't expected it to be so bad, which was laughable. Alan wasn't an asshole—he was an absolute bastard. Had she really thought he'd let her off easy?

It *should* have been easy. After all, he was the one who walked away. She hadn't even asked for alimony, despite having earned it, having given up her dreams of a doctorate to get him through business school.

As soon as I'm done, it's your turn, babe.

It'd never been her turn. There'd always been something more important, even though he'd made it clear she wasn't measuring up as a corporate wife. Not pretty enough. Not charming enough. Definitely not polished enough.

So he found someone who better suited his needs. His goddamned PA, which would be hilarious in its utter mundanity if the woman hadn't been everything Alan wanted Gemma to be—charming and polished and gorgeous. Also ten years younger.

It couldn't get more humiliating than that, right? Of course it could. At the very first divorce meeting, he'd shown up with his girlfriend and their eleven-month-old son...after walking out on Gemma sixteen months earlier.

Gemma might not have been a math major, but she could do simple addition and subtraction.

The worst part wasn't even that he'd cheated on her. It was throwing that baby in her face. She'd had three miscarriages during their marriage. Three babies she'd desperately wanted, and when she broached the subject of adoption, Alan had refused. He wanted his own child. It wasn't his fault she couldn't carry to term.

Couldn't even do that right, could you, Gem?

Yes, Alan was a bastard, and the divorce had been hell, which was a fine excuse for blowing her deadline. It was also a lie.

Why wasn't the book done? Because Gemma hated her characters. She hadn't *minded* Edin and Tavish from *A Highland Fling*. She hadn't loved them the way she'd loved the ones in her unpublished romance. She'd dreamed of those characters. *Highland* had been more work, but she'd finished it. This one, though? The woman was a doormat, and the guy was an even bigger dick than Laird Tavish Argyle.

If you hate them, how do you expect readers to like them?

She pushed aside the voice, which sounded suspiciously like her sister-in-law Daphne's. She just had to get this one done, and then, if *Highland* sold decently, she could suggest a change of direction for a new contract, with characters more to her—

Someone rapped on her door, a friendly staccato knock.

Gemma frowned as she peered toward the front hall. The building might be crap, but it had controlled entry, so it couldn't be a visitor. She didn't know her neighbors yet, even though it'd been a year and she had no excuse. She always used to know her neighbors. Just like she always used to have a wide circle of friends. Then she met Alan.

Another rap, with slightly more force.

Maybe it was a service call, and she'd missed the notice. God knows, her place needed repairs. Vancouver was the most expensive city in Canada and—

The third knock fairly rang with impatience.

"Get your head out of the clouds," Alan would snap. "You're always daydreaming."

It's called escape, my dear. Mental escape from life with you.

Before she could think to check the peephole, Gemma yanked open the door and—

"Mason?"

Mason Moretti stood on her doorstep, complete with his ridiculous grin and two steaming cups of coffee.

"I brought the java to you," he said, with a little bow.

"How'd you get past the front door?"

His brows shot up. "Really? That's your question?"

"Oh, I have more."

"I tried calling," he said as he shifted his hip against the door frame. Like earlier, he was in a T-shirt. Did the man not own a jacket? Or sleeves? It was November. Except…let's be honest. If you have biceps like Mason Moretti, wearing short sleeves could be considered a public service.

Damn it. He hadn't had those arms in high school. He'd been fit, of course, but now he was just…

Fine. So fine. Hot as hell, with the kind of body that made her remember how long it'd been since she had sex. And how long it'd been since she had *good* sex.

In that regard, Mason Moretti would probably be horrible. Even more selfish than Alan.

But the Mason she remembered had been surprisingly considerate when it was just the two of them. And that kiss…definitely not selfish.

Sex with Mason Moretti would be—

What the hell? Stop. Reverse.

What had he been saying? She had no fucking idea, because Mason was standing outside her apartment, looking steamier than that coffee.

"You weren't answering," he said when she didn't respond.

Right. He said he'd called. She'd ignored three calls from a number she didn't recognize.

Her eyes narrowed. "How did you get my number? And my home address?"

"May I come in?" he asked. "I brought coffee."

His dark brown eyes twinkled. He held out one of the cups, and she hesitated, but ignoring it felt petty, so she took it with a grudging grunt of thanks.

"And I have come with something else as well." He put on a terrible Italian American accent. "An offer you can't refuse."

She met his eyes. "Wanna bet?"

He laughed. It was his real laugh, but deeper and sexier than she remembered. Because of course it was. *He* was sexier than she remembered. But not deeper. Mason Moretti was all surface and always had been, and just when you thought you were getting a rare peek at the guy behind the hockey mask, you realized you were gazing into a shallow pool, at a reflection of what you wanted to see.

Even as Gemma thought that, part of her squirmed, as if she was being unfair.

Too bad. She wanted to be unfair. Whatever it took to get this ridiculously sexy—and completely unsuitable—guy off her doorstep.

"Whatever the offer is, Mason, the answer is no. If you need to speak to me again, I have voicemail."

"So you'd rather I called?"

"Yes."

He took out his phone and hit a button. A moment later, hers vibrated on the hall table. When she glared at him, he only pointed toward her phone. She picked it up and pressed Decline.

"Fine," she said. "Spit it out."

He leaned against the doorway again, making his muscles flex. That was no accident. He knew exactly what he was doing. Damn him. And damn her, because it worked, her gaze following that flex before she remembered to look away.

"I feel bad about Ashley's stunt this morning," he said. "It was shitty, and I wanted to set things straight. I didn't know it was supposed to be a secret, that I was the model for your hero."

Gemma sighed. "About that...Just to be clear, I didn't purposely base the guy on you. Writers have lots of sources of inspiration, and you must have been one. Unintentionally."

He grinned. "It wouldn't be the first time I was the basis for a"— he winked—"bit of fantasy sports casting."

"No." Were her cheeks heating? Shit. "That's not—"

"I'm teasing. I know that's not you, Gem." He leaned forward, going serious. "But I am flattered, and I want to help."

"Help...?"

"Sell your book. Like I said, I feel bad for letting Ashley pull me into that bullshit, and I am going to make it up to you. By promoting your book."

"Nope." She stepped back, hand gripping the door. "Nope, nope, nope—"

He waggled his phone. "We're already trending on social media."

Gemma froze. "What?"

"We're trending. You and me. People loved our interview."

She stiffened. "You mean they thought it was hilarious. The romance author who based her character on an actual sports star."

"What? No. They like it. They think it's cute."

Huh. Well, that *would* explain the other calls she'd been dodging— the ones from her publicist. She'd been terrified to answer, certain it was some release-day disaster, like *your entire first printing was destroyed in a warehouse fire and we aren't going to run off any more.*

Mason continued, "They want it to be real."

"Want *what* to be real?"

"Us. Like how cool it'd be if we really did start dating." His eyes glittered, as if she'd called his bluff and he'd slapped down a royal flush. "So how about dinner?"

"Dinner?"

"You and me. A nice restaurant. A tip-off to the media…"

"You want us to…fake date?"

"I don't expect you to lie or anything. We'd just be seen together. Let people draw their own conclusions."

For three endless seconds, Gemma felt the pull of that possibility, like a tide slipping around her ankles.

The water's fine. Come on in.

Except it wasn't fine. She'd learned her lesson there. Mason's gentle persuasion and sweet smiles masked a riptide that would drag her under and leave her sputtering and gasping…and not in a good way.

"What's in it for you?" she asked.

His eyes widened, and maybe he was trying for innocence, but he looked like a five-year-old gulping down pilfered cookies.

"Me?" he said. "Nothing. What happened to you today was shitty, and I just want to help."

"Uh-huh." *Don't say it. Just don't—* "You want to fix what happened to me *today*. Only today."

"Sure. Like I said, it was shitty."

"What about what happened before we graduated high school, Mason. What you did *then*."

A slow flush crawled under his five-o'clock shadow. So he hadn't forgotten. He just hoped she had.

"Yeah." He leaned harder into the door frame. "About that…" He cleared his throat. "You got over it, right? You based a character—"

"No, Mason. I did not 'get over it.' Back then, you didn't seem to understand what you'd done wrong. Dare I hope you get it now?"

"Uh…'

"You kissed me. *You* initiated it. Right?"

He ducked his head, looking sheepish, and maybe that was supposed to make her feel bad for him, but it threw a match on very old and dry tinder.

She continued, "But when someone snapped a photo, you let your friends tell everyone you kissed me on a dare."

"I didn't *let* them, Gem. I told you that I denied it."

"To who?"

"Uh…" He looked confused.

"To your friends. You told your friends it wasn't a dare. And what about everyone else? Everyone your friends told? At what point did you publicly come out and say they'd gotten the story wrong? At what point did you stop them from continuing to spread the lie?"

"I…"

"You didn't. Your buddies decided to save your reputation and make sure no one thought you'd actually—willingly—made out with Gemma Stanton. And you let them."

She waited, just in case he had an excuse. He didn't. She knew that.

"You let me be humiliated, Mason," she said. "You made out with me and then said you'd see me the next day, and when the shit hit the fan, all I got was a sixty-second conversation in which you made sure I knew it wasn't a dare. Otherwise, you never said another word to me. Ever."

He straightened again. "I made a mistake, and I want to make up for it."

"After nearly twenty—" She bit that off, shook her head, and smoothed her tone. "I'm not going to slam this door in your face.

I'm just going to close it. Then you are going to go away and lose my number."

She backed inside. He made no move to stop her. Just stood there as she shut the door. Then she leaned against it, feeling the old shame and humiliation surge before giving herself a shake and trudging back to stare at her blank screen.

CHAPTER FIVE

MASON

Mason was spending the evening with Jesse Parnell, his best friend and former Growlers teammate. They were at their favorite pub while Mason drowned his discomfort in very expensive whiskey.

Okay, maybe he should be drowning his *sorrows* or drowning his *pain*. "Discomfort" didn't seem like the right word. But it really was. He couldn't stop thinking of what Gemma said and it made him feel…

Uncomfortable. Which felt worse than sorrow or pain. Mason was never uncomfortable. He knew where he belonged and where he didn't. He knew what he was and what he wasn't. He knew what he could accomplish and what he could not. The trick in life was to live within your boundaries. Find that sweet spot, where you can be fully confident and certain of your abilities and your right to be exactly where you are.

Knowing your place kept life smooth. It kept you from feeling stuff like pain or sadness or anger. Yeah, he knew the irony of that. He was an NHL enforcer who hated real-life conflict. Jesse teased him about it all the time. But to Mason, it made sense. Compartmentalization, Dr. Colbourne would say. If Mason had to fight on the rink, when he wasn't really an angry guy, then it made sense that he wouldn't like to fight off it.

Okay, so the doc didn't say it made sense. *She* always wanted to talk about it, but she respected that Mason didn't see the point. Or, at least, she respected it when pushing made him decide he was too busy for their monthly check-ins. Same thing, really.

What happened with Gemma twenty years ago had not been smooth and easy. It'd been... His gut twisted.

Don't think about that. Focus on what happened with Gemma today.

Shit. That wasn't much better, and a cowardly little part of him wanted to run away.

Like you did twenty years ago?

It hadn't been like that. She'd said it was fine. Said it was just a kiss, no big deal, and if that had made him feel worse, feel like...

He stopped again. Changed direction.

He wasn't running away from this. As uncomfortable as it was, being with Gemma otherwise made him feel the opposite of uncomfortable. It reminded him what it was like to be with someone who didn't need life to be smooth, who came out swinging and was always her authentic self. Someone who'd always made him feel like he could be more, could be better, that anyone who expected less didn't really know him.

Gemma had never expected anything of him but honesty. To be his real self. None of his bullshit.

And what she'd gotten, in the end, was his bullshit.

So he was drinking away his discomfort while confessing to Jesse. Mason and Jesse had met in the juniors, before both were drafted to the Growlers at eighteen. Back then, they'd had little contact.

Between the endless work and the endless competition, there'd been no room for friendship.

Even after they were drafted to the same team, that sense of competition had lingered. Soon Mason's left defense position had begun drifting into enforcer territory. Mason had seized the role with gusto. He liked mixing it up on the ice, and he liked it even better when he could mix it up in defense of his teammates.

That's how Mason and Jesse ended up behind the arena, trying to beat the shit out of each other.

Jesse was a skilled forward with a wicked slap shot. He was the kind of player who focused on his own performance and stayed out of the brawls and the backbiting and the grudge matches. The problem was that some people weren't content to let him do that. Jesse was Indigenous, grew up in the islands off the coast of British Columbia as part of the Haida Nation. There weren't many Indigenous players in the NHL, and before Jesse, there'd been none on the Growlers, and some assholes had liked it that way. Mason couldn't do anything about the fans, but he could take care of the opposing players. That was his job, after all.

Jesse had told Mason to back off and let him handle it. Mason figured Jesse was just saying that. Turned out, Jesse was *not* just saying that, and he finally decided to communicate in a language he presumed Mason understood better: talking with his fists.

In the end, Mason understood that having a white guy come to Jesse's rescue didn't help. So they compromised. Mason would signal when he sensed trouble, and Jesse needed to look up from the puck enough to catch those signals. If one guy went after Jesse, Mason would skate closer—so it didn't look as if he was making

Jesse fend for himself—but he wouldn't get involved unless the attack came from multiple sources.

With that misunderstanding out of the way, the two had become friends. They were both fully committed to the Growlers. That'd been their home team growing up, and they'd spent their careers turning down offers from other teams…while praying they weren't traded.

Part of not being traded was to make themselves irreplaceable—mostly with the fans. Because being good on the ice was one thing; putting butts in seats was another. They'd partnered in achieving that. Then Jesse suffered a concussion playing off-season overseas, followed by a second one shortly after his return. Three years ago, Jesse decided he was done. He'd made his money and invested it well, and he wanted to preserve his health and expand his work supporting Indigenous youth in hockey.

Jesse was happy, and Mason was happy for him. Some guys blossomed after retirement, while others just dried up and…

Mason shook it off. That wasn't anything he needed to worry about yet. For now, he was talking about a much happier subject: Gemma.

He had explained the romance-novel thing and how he knew Gemma and then confessed to what he'd done to her in high school.

When he finished, Jesse stared across the table at him. "You let your friends tell everyone you only kissed her on a dare?"

"I didn't *let* them."

A hard look from Jesse. "You know what I mean. You didn't undo the damage."

Mason slumped. "I know."

Jesse shook his head. "You have done some spectacularly shitty things in your life, Mace, but…" He reached out to clap Mason on the shoulder. "You've outdone yourself. Congratulations."

Mason took a hit of whiskey, noted that the glass was down to the dregs, and considered ordering a second. He wouldn't, but tonight he seriously considered it.

"I talked to her afterward, and she said it wasn't a big deal."

"Of course she did, and I'm going to bet, even then, you realized she was just trying to save face, pretend it didn't hurt like hell."

Mason lifted the glass and drained the last dribble. "But it couldn't have been too bad, right? She based her romance hero on me."

"And serious congrats on that, Mace. It really is awesome, and I can't think of a guy who deserves it more, except me…and maybe ninety percent of the male population."

Mason lifted his middle finger.

Jesse met his gaze. "If you're looking for someone to say that what you did wasn't so bad, you came to the wrong person."

Mason slumped and pushed away his empty glass. "I know. So how do I make it up to her?"

Jesse sipped his own drink, his gaze going distant. Then he mused, "This fake dating thing might work, as long as she knows it's fake."

"She does."

"And as long as you really are trying to help her career and not *just* fix your own. It's fine if it also benefits you, but it needs to be mutually advantageous."

"It will be."

"Then offer something she can't resist. Not just a date but an *experience*."

The corners of Mason's mouth twitched.

Jesse shook his head. "Not *that*. How about dinner at Nonna Jean's?"

"Take her to my own restaurant? That's a cheap-ass move."

Growing up, Mason's paternal grandmother had lived in the next apartment complex, and that's where he'd taken shelter, in the kitchen where she ran her catering service.

Mason had always sworn he'd use his first NHL paycheck to buy Nonna Jean her own restaurant. She hadn't mocked him, like his dad would have. She hadn't cried, like his mom would have. Nonna Jean just kissed him on the forehead and said nothing.

As Mason would discover, NHL starting paychecks didn't cover a restaurant purchase. But he'd saved up, and that *was* the first thing he bought: a little café where his grandmother could cook the Jewish Italian cuisine from her childhood, from before his great-grandfather decided being an Italian Jew in the forties was a damn fine reason to immigrate to Canada.

Nonna Jean was now eighty-two and, while she still kept a firm grip on the business, she'd ceded the cooking to others, though she still commandeered the kitchen now and again.

He was there himself a few times a week. When he had the time and needed to relax, he came in and cooked. That part was a secret. Patrons didn't come for Mason Moretti's cooking. They came for the food and NHL memorabilia and, maybe, to catch a glimpse of "the Mace" himself.

As proud as Mason was of Nonna Jean's, it wasn't fancy. Mason didn't even know if Gemma liked that sort of food. The last two times he'd mentioned it on dates, the women had looked at him with horror, as if he'd suggested they dine on baby seals. Italian food? All those carbs? Absolutely not.

Jesse's voice pulled Mason back. "Do it on a Monday, when the restaurant is closed. A special opening just for her. Invite media to take shots as you arrive, but then have a private meal. Show her what you've built there. Talk about your grandmother. Cook for her—"

"No."

"Why not? You're a good cook."

"I'm a *decent* cook. Not good. Decent."

"She won't care. It's not about the food, Mace, it's about—"

"Gemma deserves better. I should take her to Maize."

Maize was the hottest place in town, with a wait list so long you couldn't even *join* it . . . unless you were Mason Moretti.

"Mmm. Maize is fine," Jesse said. "But I think Nonna—"

"I'll go all out." Mason reached for the peanuts and cracked one open. "Give her an experience, like you said. A dream date with everything she could want. And me."

Jesse clapped Mason's shoulder. "Make it memorable enough, and she'll overlook that part."

Mason flicked a peanut at him.

"All jokes aside," Jesse said. "You gotta promise me something, buddy." He leaned over the table, his expression somber. "If she says she doesn't want to go out with you, you need to stop asking."

Mason cracked open another peanut.

"Mace . . . I also know you've never met a challenge you can't barrel through headfirst. But this isn't like that. She's said no already. More than once."

"I know. I'll take one last shot. Then I need to take no for an answer."

"You really do."

GEMMA

Gemma walked into the restaurant and immediately spotted her brother and sister-in-law. They were at the bar waiting for a celebratory cocktail with her before the rest of the family joined for her release-day dinner.

Chris and Daphne were deep in conversation, untouched drinks forgotten as they leaned together and talked. Gemma smiled at the sight, even if she also felt a pang suspiciously close to envy. Wasn't this what she'd always envisioned in a marriage? Two people, partners in life and best friends, endlessly lost in one another.

She could be envious, but more than that, she was happy for her little brother. There was a reason Gemma gravitated to nice guys in romance. Because all the men in her family were ridiculously nice and had made ridiculously happy marriages.

In Daphne, Gemma had also found a friend…and a writing mentor. Daphne was a Mason Moretti–level author, the sort whose debut novel sold for mid–six figures and then went on to outperform even those high expectations. Despite that fame, Daphne was as down-to-earth as Chris, generous, and, yes, nice, if in a reserved way that could come across as intimidating, especially when she was nearly six feet tall and built like an Amazon warrior.

Daphne was laughing at something Chris said when he spotted Gemma. His eyes narrowed, and her steps slowed.

"Mason Moretti?" Chris said. "*Mason Moretti?*"

Gemma sighed and pushed onto a bar stool so she could be at eye level with them. After the Mason high school incident, Chris had devised an adorable plan to waylay Mason after hockey and call him out on his bad behavior. That might have worked these days, but at twelve, Chris had been so skinny that Mason probably would have walked past without seeing him.

"Seriously, Gem? Mason Moretti?"

"I needed to write an asshole lead character, so I chose the one I knew best."

Chris eyed her. Then he took a gulp of his beer. "At least it wasn't Alan."

"Gemma's waiting until she writes a murder mystery for that," Daphne said. "Or horror."

Gemma grinned. "Definitely horror."

"He'll be that corporate guy who strides around giving orders, until he's attacked by the monsters and ripped into tiny pieces as everyone cheers."

Chris picked up his beer. "I...think I'll go drink over there."

"I write about zombies," Daphne said. "You know I can do gruesome." She looked at Gemma. "You ever want Alan to play a cameo, just let me know."

"And Mason Moretti?" Chris's voice dropped, going serious. "He hurt you, Gem."

"Okay," Daphne said carefully. "I have to ask. When Chris says this guy hurt you...I know he plays an enforcer..."

"The only thing Mason hurt was my feelings," Gemma said. "We kissed behind the school. His friends said he did it on a dare, and he corrected them, but not enough to stop the story."

"See?" Chris said. "Asshole."

"Was it a good kiss?" Daphne asked.

Gemma leaned in. "Amazing."

Chris threw up his hands.

"Hey," Gemma said. "A guy can be an asshole and a good kisser. That's what makes him romance-hero material." She glanced at Daphne. "And don't give me that look."

"What look?"

"You wanted me to be patient and not change what I write to suit the market."

"You did what was right for you, Gem. And it worked." Daphne lifted her glass. "You are officially a published author. Now, let's forget Mason Moretti and get you a drink."

CHAPTER SIX

GEMMA

Hours later, Gemma stumbled back to her apartment, a little tipsy from a dinner that may have involved more drinks than she'd had since celebrating her divorce.

Gemma had won the lottery with her family—close-knit, caring, and endlessly supportive. Oh, they weren't perfect. Chris had gone from annoying little brother to the guy who had all his shit together when Gemma absolutely did not. Dad worried about Gemma too much, and Mom was prone to musing about all the ways she'd like to make her former son-in-law pay for hurting her daughter. Grandpa Thomas always had to take Gemma aside for a pep talk about how Alan had never been good enough for her. Then there was Grandma Dot, who always had photos of eligible single men— grandsons and grandnephews of her wide social circle.

So, yep, every member of her family could be a pain in the ass, in their own unique ways, but so could Gemma, so she fit right in.

She got home just before midnight, flying so high that when her phone rang, she thought it was Mason and answered, an impulse she was too drunk to analyze.

Instead, an even more familiar male voice said, "You're dating *Mason Moretti?*"

She blinked, some of the champagne-induced euphoria fading. "Alan?"

"You went to high school with the Mace? And you never told me?"

There was genuine hurt in his voice. Was it the champagne that made a little giggle tickle up her throat? Her bastard of an ex had just discovered that she knew his favorite hockey player and never told him? Clearly a betrayal on the same level as screwing around with his PA and getting her pregnant.

Alan didn't wait for an answer. "I saw the interview. *Everyone* is sending it to me. What the hell did you do to him?"

"What?"

"He was *nice*. To you. The Mace can be a decent enough guy, but he was actually *nice*."

Huh, must be that blow job I gave him before the interview.

"Mason was nice because we've known each other since kindergarten." And then, because she was tipsy, she couldn't help rubbing it in. "You should have seen him back then, always toting around his skates. The janitor used to make a rink out back, just for Mason. It was so annoying."

"How?"

"Because Mason kept bugging me to bring my skates and join him at recess."

Dead silence. Then: "That's a joke, right?"

Gemma collapsed backward onto the love seat. "I wish. *So* annoying."

"Mason Moretti wanted you to skate with him, and you said *no*?"

"I don't like skating. You know that."

While Mason *had* asked a few times, he hadn't persisted after two—three?—refusals. Yet if Alan envisioned little Mace Moretti with a schoolyard crush on his ex-wife...

Hey, it wasn't as evil as most of her mother's revenge plans.

"So you two grew up together?" Alan said.

That suggested they'd been close, which was an exaggeration, so Gemma gave a noncommittal "Sure."

"And you were just friends."

"Hmm?"

"You weren't ever more than friends, right."

It was the "right" that pushed her over the edge. That "right" didn't ask a question. It made a statement. And she was not letting that statement pass.

Gemma stretched out on the love seat, her feet dangling. "Mostly. I mean, there was that one kiss. He wanted to tell me something in private, and the next thing you know...it was high school. These things happen."

"You...kissed Mace Moretti?"

"More like made out with him. Behind the school. I couldn't help myself. He's such a good kisser. Like, *amazingly* good." She sighed, deeply.

She was going to hell.

Alan seemed to hang there, suspended in shock.

Gemma continued, "Sadly, I didn't see a future in it. I mean, good kissing isn't everything. We both had dreams. Big dreams that would take us in separate directions. Two ships passing in the night. Well, more like two ships colliding. That kiss...wow."

She was *so* going to hell.

"So you *are* seeing him?"

"You're my *ex*, Alan. It's none of your business who I spend my days with…" She waited a beat. "Or who I spend my nights with."

She continued, "Thanks for your concern, though. I gotta say that, as hard as our divorce was, you did the right thing walking out. You freed us both to find the right person, you with Melinda, and me with…whoever."

Yep, she was going straight to hell, and as she hung up, she couldn't stop smiling.

Damn it, Gemma was never going to get this book written if her phone didn't stop ringing. Okay, fine, she knew there was a Do Not Disturb setting, and if she wasn't setting it, was that because she was hoping to hear from someone else? Someone with the initials MM?

She'd told Mason not to call. So why hadn't she blocked his number? Why was she jumping every time her phone rang?

This was so high school. Worse, even in high school she wasn't like this.

She'd said no, and she had meant it. So why was she watching her phone?

Gemma hadn't been playing hard to get. Her parents had taught her better than that. If you make a guy chase until your no turns to a yes, what have you taught him? That "no" really means "try harder."

What she wanted from Mason was…

She swallowed.

On the simplest level, she wanted an apology. She'd been honest with him about what he did and how it hurt, and then she'd closed the door because she hadn't wanted some knee-jerk insincere apology. Even more, she hadn't wanted to take the chance he'd slough it off. Make excuses. Tell her she was overreacting.

That he'd be a jerk.

That he'd be like Alan.

Except Mason wasn't Alan, was he? Mason was the anti-Alan.

No, Gemma was going to be honest. Alan had been the anti-Mason.

Not that she'd fallen in love with Mason in high school. She'd never be so foolish. Girls like her only ended up with guys like Mason in those teen movies—the star jock and the valedictorian, together forever. Forever? Hardly. In reality, smart girls don't fall for guys like Mason, because they know they'll get their hearts broken.

So she hadn't fallen for him. She'd just...stumbled. Took a chance on an unattainable guy and got her heart— No, *not* her heart. Got her ego broken. Her pride broken.

In the aftermath, she'd steered away from any guy who reminded her of Mason Moretti. And then along came Alan—Mason's polar opposite.

Which worked out *so* well.

While she wanted an apology from Mason, more than that, she'd wanted him to acknowledge he'd made a mistake. Which he did. Because he wasn't like Alan. Except he had hurt her. But also...

But also she wanted him to call.

She pressed her fingers to her temples.

Her phone rang again. And again, it wasn't Mason. It was a New York number that almost certainly belonged to the publicist whose calls she'd been dodging since the interview.

Damn it.

Gemma needed to write, which was a fine excuse, except she wasn't writing, was she? She was lost in thoughts of Mason Moretti, like she was seventeen, sitting in the newspaper office after he'd stopped by—again—with some question about his article that ended up with him hanging around for an hour, talking, until she finally kicked his ass out, reminding him he had practice, and then she'd sit there, wishing…

Wishing she hadn't reminded him. Wishing he was still there, still talking, still making her laugh and—

Damn it, she did not have time for this.

Her phone was still ringing. She leaned back in her desk chair, pushed away her laptop, and answered with the chirpiest "Hello" her non-chirpy vocal cords could manage.

"Gemma! It's Ava, your publicist. Sorry for calling without setting up a time first, but that interview yesterday was amazing, and I think we need to strike while the iron is hot."

"Uh, yeah. So, about that, I didn't actually base my character on a hockey player." *Liar.* "There are just resemblances. But I couldn't exactly say that on live TV, not with Mason right there."

"Mason, huh? You two are on a first name basis already?"

"It's not like—"

"People love this story. And you two are so cute together. That's what really sells it. All those photos of you two on the sofa, the big hockey player leaning to defend you from the evil host. That's what he does, right? On the ice? He's a defender."

"It's usually called an enforcer but—"

"Even better. 'Enforcer' is a hot word. People are loving those photos, turning them into the most adorable memes. I'll send you some."

"That isn't necess—"

"And you knew each other in high school. That's amazing. Everyone loves a second-chance romance."

"It wasn't really a romance. There was just the one kiss—" She stopped short and squeezed her eyes shut. Why did she say that?

"Even *better*!" Ava's voice vibrated with excitement. "They met as teens and shared a single kiss, but circumstances intervened."

Those circumstances being that Mason let the entire school think he'd kissed her only on a dare? Terribly romantic.

"Any chance of a reunion?" Ava said.

Gemma wanted to say no. She planned to say no. Instead, she heard herself saying, "Well, he did suggest we should pretend to go on a date. To promote my book."

A long pause. Then: "Please tell me you're serious. The hockey star you kissed in high school is now suggesting *fake dating*? After a meet-cute reunion on live TV? Can I book you guys a hotel room with only one bed?"

Gemma had to laugh at that. "Sure. All the tropes. But no, I'm not fake dating Mason Moretti to help sell my book."

"Would you fake date him just for fun?"

An image flashed. Mason, outside her apartment, leaning against the wall, looking hot as hell. Would she fake date him for fun? Depended on whether that fun included—

No. Stop.

Gemma forced a laugh. "Nice try, but no. I'm glad the interview brought some attention to the book. I'm happy to spur that along by doing anything...except fake date Mason Moretti."

* * *

It was just past ten that morning when the rap came at Gemma's door. She looked out the peephole this time before swinging it open to see, once again, Mason Moretti on her doorstep with coffees.

"Someone let you in *again?*" she said.

"I'm Mason Moretti."

"No, you're a damn bullheaded jock who thinks any wall will crumble if he just keeps charging it."

That cocky grin faltered, and she cursed inwardly. She *should* feel a thrill of victory at getting a jab to actually pierce his thick hide. Instead, it always left her feeling as if she'd punched a puppy.

His face went serious as he said, "This is the last time, Gem. I promise. One last offer, and if you say no, I'll be gone."

Damn it. What was worse than an unreasonable Mason Moretti? A reasonable one.

She sighed. "Fine, come in. But if I ask you to leave, you will, right?"

"I will."

CHAPTER SEVEN

GEMMA

One date.

That was Mason's offer.

One blowout date with all the frills. And not a date in the sense that he'd put his arm around her or fake a kiss for the cameras, because there *would* be cameras, that being the point of the exercise. This would be a celebration of her book release. Two old classmates reconnecting, one treating the other to a proper celebration. If people took it as proof of a romance, that was on them.

"One perfect night out," he said. "No expense spared. This is all about you and your book."

"Okay…" She eyed him, waiting for the punch line.

He leaned in, and she caught the faint smell of orange and cloves. He was perched on her armchair while she sat on the love seat. He seemed to dwarf the chair. He wasn't a massive guy. A bit taller than average. A bit—okay, a *lot*—better built than average, with broad shoulders and narrow hips and muscular thighs.

Thighs? Really.

Gemma had a thing for thighs. Also hands. While she wasn't into big guys—the logistics were tricky for a small woman, no matter what romance novels would have you believe—she was inordinately fond of big hands, which unfortunately were usually attached to big guys. Mason had the right kind of hands, big and rough and square. Strong hands that could lift her against a wall and…

Stop.

Was it a coincidence that Mason had exactly the kind of hands she liked? Or did she like that kind of hands because he had them?

Shit. Mason was talking. Better pay attention. To his words. Not his thighs or his hands.

"You know Maize?" he said. "The restaurant?"

"Sure. Never been there, obviously. What's the wait list up to? A year?"

He smiled. "I can get us in."

"Let me guess. Because you're Mason Moretti."

That grin grew.

She shook her head. "I don't need a fancy—"

"Too bad. That's what's on the table. Dinner for two at Maize."

Didn't he just say this was about her? Whatever *she* wanted?

"I'm pulling out all the stops," he said. "Dinner at the best place in town. Drinks and dancing afterward."

She opened her mouth to say she wasn't all that keen on dancing. But he was still talking.

"We'll go to Borealis," he said. "No line for us."

Gemma tried not to wince. Borealis was exactly the kind of see-and-be-seen club she hated.

What would be *her* idea of a perfect night? Maybe taking out her family's boat with dinner from Mason's restaurant. She loved Nonna Jean's, though she only ever did delivery and only using her married name, even as she'd rolled her eyes at the precautions.

You think Mason's going to remember you?

Yet the point of this date was to get publicity for her, which they couldn't do on a private tête-à-tête. A fake one required real onlookers, which meant, yes, the hottest restaurant and club in town.

Wait. Was she actually considering saying yes?

A posh dinner *would* be nice. What was it like to go to the hottest restaurant and hottest club? Places Gemma would never see on her own.

"Okay," she said finally, pushing the word out before she lost her nerve.

He grinned. "Excellent. You won't regret this. It'll be *perfect*. I know what I'm doing."

"Because you're Mason Moretti."

His grin widened. "I am."

MASON

Mason was pleased with himself. Very pleased. Okay, he could hear Jesse saying that being pleased with himself was hardly a new experience for Mason, and yeah, maybe he was being a little smug about the whole thing, but he knew his strengths, and planning dates was one of them.

The trick to a successful date? Have a lot of fucking money.

Fine, that wasn't a trick so much as an inside advantage. Some might call it an *unfair* advantage, but Mason had earned every penny.

Mason hadn't dated in high school. He'd been too busy with hockey, and his sports psychologist had warned against him getting too involved with a girl. Which did not mean he'd graduated a virgin, just that all his experience came from hookups that had never required actual dating.

After he got drafted into the Growlers, he'd dived eagerly into the experience of dating. He'd take women to the movies. To a quiet dinner. Out for a picnic. Rent a canoe and paddle down the river. Stuff that seemed romantic to him. The women had disagreed. Strongly disagreed.

That's when Mason discovered the secret ingredient to a perfect date. Money.

Dial it up to eleven and treat them like a princess. Take them to the *best* restaurants and clubs. Send them a whole whack of gift cards. Dress shop. Lingerie shop. Salon. Spa. Give them an experience.

He pulled up his contact list and started a text to his date-planning service. Because of course he used a service. That was just efficient.

Mason: I need the standard package for a lady friend

Mason: Skip dinner reservations. I've got it covered. Maize at eight

Mason: Oh, and skip the lingerie gift card too

He stared at that last one, his finger over the Send button. Maybe . . . ? Just as a little something extra. A thoughtful gift. Not that he was expecting to *see* whatever she bought with it.

No, Gemma would think it meant he expected to see it, and there would be no date. Possibly also a string of furious profanity and a warning of what she'd do if he ever contacted her again.

He edited that last line, just to make it clearer.

Mason: NO lingerie gift card

He popped off Gemma's contact info and eased back in his chair with a smile.

There. A job well done.

GEMMA

Gemma sat staring down at the fistful of gift cards fanned out like a poker hand. A card for a dress shop and four from the same spa complex, for hair, a facial, a manicure, and…a massage?

Okay, the massage was tempting. She might keep that one. But otherwise?

What the hell was this? Did Mason expect her prom-ready for their date?

There *would* be cameras. She *should* spend a little extra time on her appearance.

And she would, but she could do it without all this. She'd been to the salon and gotten a manicure just last week in preparation for the morning-show interview.

Did Mason presume she wouldn't have a dress worthy of Maize? It was dinner, not the Oscars. She turned the card over to see the amount. Holy shit, she'd barely spent that on her off-the-rack wedding gown.

She'd keep the massage card and donate the rest. She supported a women's shelter that would hold their holiday auction soon.

Gemma picked up the handwritten note that came with the cards.

Gemma,

Just a little something to help make our night magical.

Mace

Mace? That sounded like the cards came from Mace the hockey star, not Mason the guy she'd known since kindergarten.

She was reading too much into it. People had always called him Mace. Even she used to sometimes. Maybe he preferred Mace these days.

And yet…something about the note was odd. She lifted it for a closer look.

While it was handwritten, only the signature looked like his, and that seemed pixelated.

As if he'd had someone print off a standard note that he sent to all his—

No, now she was getting paranoid. Even Mason wouldn't do that.

She set the cards aside and went into her bedroom to pick out a dress and make sure she had the proper footwear to wear it in winter.

The rain was holding off. That was all Gemma could think as she left her apartment that Friday evening. With November in Vancouver, rain was pretty much a given, and it wasn't the sweet spring rain that exploded the city into a riot of cherry blossoms. November rain was cold and bitter, in a way that seeped into your bones and didn't leave until you could soak in a steaming hot bath.

It'd rained earlier in the day, and she just hoped the lingering humidity didn't turn her curls into a poodle do. Those were her choices this time of year. Poodle or drowned rat.

Mason had been texting to be sure she had everything. Did she need a driver to take her to the spa? He could do that. Lunch delivered to the spa? He could do that, too. It was only after she said no to both that she started to worry he really did expect her to be at the spa and might send over lunch anyway.

She'd explain later. She'd committed to this date, and she didn't want to risk any temptation to cancel, which might happen if she said she didn't need the spa visit and he suggested she did.

She looked fine. Her makeup was on point. Her hair was tamed and semi-sophisticated. Her dress was a designer piece she'd bought off the sale rack for a pre-wedding "girls' night out" with Daphne. Her shoes were a few years out of style, but she didn't expect the photographers to get full-length shots.

Mason said that his publicist had tipped off the media and confirmed there'd be cameras but only outside the restaurant and the club. No interior shots, meaning she could eat and dance without fear of cameras. Without fear of *professional* cameras, that is. He pointed that out, too. Expect some candid shots from other diners and club goers that'd be posted on social media.

She stepped onto her apartment building's front porch. Mason said he'd pick her up at seven thirty. Her apartment was on the edge of the city, and it'd take about twenty minutes to get to the restaurant.

She should have asked what he drove. Probably not a compact car or a family SUV. A sports car? A luxury pickup? Two words that should never go together: "luxury" and "pickup." You didn't actually see a lot of them in Vancouver. The city was too eco-conscious for that. Also space-conscious, the disadvantage to settling a major urban center on a peninsula.

Pickup and sports car were her guesses, so when a luxury sedan pulled to the curb, she almost ignored it. Then the driver's window rolled down.

"Ms. Stanton?" said a middle-aged guy with a hired driver's cap.

"Yes…" she said cautiously.

The man leapt from the car and opened the back door. "Mr. Moretti is waiting."

Ah, Mason had hired a driver for them. Good idea. It solved the parking problem.

She climbed in to find the back seat empty. A moment of panic flared, images of being kidnapped by some obsessed hockey fan who'd tracked her down from the TV interview.

Then she mentally replayed Mason's text.

Pickup at 7:30. Right outside your building front door.

He didn't say *he* was picking her up.

He'd sent someone to fetch her. That was… She stifled a prickle of disappointment. This wasn't a date. It was a business arrangement.

No, it was a celebration. That's what he'd said. Celebrating her book and helping promote it. *He* wasn't getting any business consideration out of it.

He wasn't, right?

Not that she'd have objected to that. She'd have preferred a fair exchange. But he'd said it was all about her, and she believed him.

What could a hockey star get from fake dating a college instructor turned romance novelist? It would be like Daphne asking for an endorsement from Gemma.

There was no reason Mason would need a publicity boost. Gemma had avoided hockey news since Alan left, but she'd checked the Growlers' stats to help with tonight's dinner conversation, and the team was doing well. Ten games into the season with seven wins, two ties, and one loss. They'd won last night.

Shit. Should she have watched last night's game? She should have at least skimmed a playthrough. She knew Mason had scored a goal, which was unusual, his role being more support, with mostly assists.

She should have watched. Maybe she still had time.

CHAPTER EIGHT

MASON

Mason stood on the sidewalk and blew into his hands, fending off the chill. When a silver sedan pulled up, he could just make out Gemma through the smoked glass. With a grin, he threw open the door and hopped in as she quickly stopped a video on her phone. Then she peered up and down the street in confusion.

"We're picking you up here?" she said. "Aren't we only a block from the restaurant?"

"I thought we should arrive together. For the cameras."

"To make people think we actually drove in together?"

There was something in her tone that gave him pause, but only for a second. Then he got a look at her. She'd made good use of those gift cards. Not that she'd needed the help. Gemma always looked good, and if he was being honest, he preferred her usual casual style. But this was for the cameras, and it worked. *Damn* it worked.

"You look good," he said. "Really good."

She muttered something like "I clean up well?" and he wasn't sure how to answer, so he went with "Did you like the spa?"

She started to reply, and the driver said, "We're here, sir."

He opened his door, only to realize he was curbside.

"Hold on," he said, and strode around to open her door, ignoring the honks of traffic.

When she reached to take her umbrella, he caught it and set it back on the seat.

"You don't need that," he said. "I'll make sure you get it later." He ushered her onto the sidewalk. "The restaurant is just around the corner."

"Should we start laughing and talking as if we actually drove here together?" she said.

"Good idea." He glanced over at her. "Do you want to take off your coat, too? It'll look better for the photos."

She hesitated, but then removed the coat and draped it over her arm. He glanced at her dress, which was...wow. He was really glad he'd sent the gift card.

The dress was two layers, the bottom one gold silk and the top one black lace. The silk left little to the imagination, but the lace obscured it just enough that he felt like a preteen boy catching a glimpse of a half-naked woman through curtain sheers. The neckline was a modest scoop, which only accentuated small, firm breasts under the clingy silk. That silk clung the whole way down, over her stomach and tight ass, and then the black lace draped lower to swish around her thighs.

Damn. He could feel himself hardening as he watched her walk in that dress.

He adjusted his sport jacket and told himself not to look at Gemma again. At least, not until after the photos.

He put his hand against her back as they approached the corner. She tensed, and he started to pull his hand away, but then she murmured, as if to herself, "Cameras," and edged closer, letting his hand rest more firmly there. It was the perfect posture. Nothing too possessive. Nothing that screamed they were a couple. They *could* just be friends. But if you wanted to read more into it...

He smiled as he turned that corner. At the last second, he realized he shouldn't look as if he was smiling for the cameras. He needed to be smiling for her, which he actually was. Or smiling because of her. Because Gemma Stanton was walking beside him, wearing a sexy dress—

At a twitch in his trousers, he changed mental tracks fast and leaned down, still smiling, to whisper, "That dress looks amazing on you."

Cameras flashed when he leaned down, and then more as she touched her head to his arm. "Thank you. I really should have gone for wool, though. Or sleeves. Yep, definitely should have worn something with sleeves."

He paused. And then he realized what she meant. That she was wearing a thin dress, outdoors, in November. Because some asshole told her to take off her coat...while he was snug in his sports jacket.

He should say something.

No, dumbass, you should offer her your coat.

But they were already at the door. Mason swallowed hard. It was a stumble. That was all. He had this. They'd have an amazing dinner, and then, afterward, he'd ensure she was wearing her coat when they left. His, too, if that helped.

This was going to be fine.

Better than fine.

It was going to be fucking perfect from this moment on. He'd make sure of it.

GEMMA

As they settled into their seats, the blood flow slowly returned to Gemma's arms, and she resisted the urge to rub down the goose bumps. Holy shit, it'd been cold out there.

Mason was going out of his way to be a gentleman. Opening the front door and then taking the coat from her arm and then pulling out her chair. She'd never pretend she didn't find gallantry charming, but it was so obviously a show that it kinda defeated the purpose.

They'd barely opened their menus when the drink server appeared. Gemma reached for the cocktail menu...and Mason ordered wine. For both of them.

Pre-Alan Gemma would have said, *Uh, I guess you're drinking that whole bottle then, because I'm having a gin fizz.*

She didn't have a problem saying that to Mason. That was the beauty of being with someone you'd known since childhood. But this was a performance, and she wouldn't do anything to spoil it, which meant she'd taken off her coat in near-freezing temperatures and now she was apparently drinking wine.

"I've heard the salmon is excellent," he said. "The crab salad is apparently also very good."

"What do you have?" she asked.

"Usually the rib eye. Sometimes the short ribs." He smiled. "Gotta keep up my protein."

She could point out that the salmon had just as much protein. But she was also thinking of how long it'd been since she had a decent steak. Alan hadn't eaten red meat in years, one of his endless health kicks. She'd thought they were a cute quirk until she realized he was only keeping in shape so he'd be ready when it was time to trade her in for a younger model.

"Rib eye sounds good," she said and braced for a comment, but he only smiled.

"Good choice," he said. "I'd suggest the scallops for an appetizer, but the tartare is good, too. Whatever you want."

She relaxed a little. "The scallops look good."

He grinned, as if she'd just gushed over his amazing taste in appetizers. She wanted to inwardly roll her eyes, but he was so damned charming in his braggadocio. As if he was still that little kid with the skates, talking about how many goals he'd scored, so self-assured that it didn't seem like boasting.

And that was how you fell for guys like Mason Moretti. You were charmed in spite of yourself. You cut them slack because they'd earned their right to boast, and if that arrogance bled into narcissism, you decided they'd earned that, too. You drank the wine they ordered and carried your coat in near-freezing temperatures when they asked. You basked in the warmth of their blaze and tried to forget that you were soaking up the rays from a sun that didn't give a damn whether it warmed *you* or not.

The trick was to figure that out. Then you didn't run the risk of getting burned again.

Gemma was here for the promo op and for the food, and if she enjoyed the company, that was a bonus.

Two ships, passing in the night.

"Share?" Mason said.

She looked up. "Hmm?"

"You were smiling. Share?"

She waved a hand. "Just thinking that I haven't had steak in a while. Not good steak anyway. I'm looking forward to it. I—"

She stopped as she saw their server heading over. The young man smiled, his gaze fixed on her. Then he saw Mason and slowed. His mouth set, and his eyes narrowed. Mason glanced over, following her gaze. The young man's mouth opened, as if to snap something. Then he spun on his heel and stalked off.

"Uh...?" Gemma said. "Did I fail to meet the dress code?"

Mason shifted uncomfortably but plastered on a smile. "I'm sure that was about me. It happens. You get a lot of other hockey fans in Vancouver. The Flames, the Leafs, everyone has a favorite, and it's not always the hometown team."

Another server approached, this one a young woman.

"Everything okay?" Gemma asked carefully, looking to where the other server had vanished.

"Yes, of course," the woman said, a little too cheerfully. "Good to see you, Mr. Moretti. The rib eye or the short ribs?"

He waved for her to take Gemma's order first. Then he snuck a glance toward where the other server had stalked off. It was obvious that the original one had refused to serve Mason. That was awkward, but it was also a dick move that had Gemma bristling in Mason's defense.

At least the server hadn't caused an actual scene. A quick glance around assured her no one else had noticed. Good.

They placed their orders. When the wine arrived, Gemma made sure to drink some.

"I saw you scored a goal last night," she said as she set down her glass.

His eyes lit so bright that she felt guilty for not having watched it live.

"You caught the game?" he said.

She smiled and hoped it seemed genuine. "It's been a while since I saw one."

"You like hockey?"

His expression was boyishly eager, and she felt a stab of guilt. When she was young, she'd enjoyed going to Growler games with Grandma Dot. But then came the Mason incident, followed by marriage to a guy who made her feel like a poseur for watching a game when she didn't understand every last nuance.

"I can follow it," she said.

The server arrived with the appetizer. She set it in the middle, and they each took a shard of baked Parmesan topped with a scallop.

As Gemma nibbled the Parmesan, she took advantage of the opportunity to get a proper look at Mason. He'd gone with a fitted dress shirt and tie. He should look like a bouncer stuffed into an ill-fitting suit. But the suit was not ill fitting.

The shirt, like his jacket, was obviously tailored, and the style chosen to suit his rough looks, smoothing them over. It was a linen shirt, rich plum, which she wouldn't have picked as his color, but it brought out the depths in his brown eyes.

A recent shave showed off his full lips and the faint cleft in his chin. His black hair was sleek, curling slightly across his forehead, and when he bent to catch a falling scrap of Parmesan, she noticed the silver threads in his hair. Even that suited him. Damn it, every-thing suited him.

No one was ever going to call Mason Moretti handsome, but he was sexy as hell, and she couldn't help being glad he was right across the table so she had an excuse for staring. Just paying attention to her dinner partner, that was all.

When they'd finished the scallops, Mason resumed the conver-sation with "Yep, I scored a goal last night, which doesn't happen a whole lot." A self-deprecating smile that sent a pang through her, reminding her of the old Mason, the one who'd appear in the news-paper office when it was just the two of them. "If they paid me by the goals, I wouldn't be able to afford dinner here."

"Because that's not your job. You get a decent number of assists, but mostly, you're clearing the way for other players to score."

His face brightened in a smile so genuine it made her heart twist. "That's right. People don't always see that, and they go on about how low my scoring is and why don't the Growlers trade me."

"You've *never* been traded. That's quite the achievement for a career as long as yours."

That smile sparked again. "I—"

"Mace Moretti," a voice said, so saccharine sweet that Gemma's hackles rose.

Gemma looked up—way up—to see a tall woman with a willowy build and razor cheekbones.

Earlier, Gemma had applauded herself for applying makeup that didn't make her look like a ten-year-old playing with her mother's stash. This woman's makeup was so perfect you could believe she was just naturally flawless. Maybe she was.

"Mason," she purred, setting long fingernails on his upper arm. "Is hockey season over already?"

"Hey…Camille."

Gemma didn't fail to notice that pause as if he'd had to search for the woman's name.

"The season *must* be over," she said. "Because you told me, very clearly, that we couldn't see each other again because you don't date during the season."

"I'm a friend," Gemma said quickly. "From high school."

"Of course you are." The woman didn't even look Gemma's way. "And how about Heidi? Is she a friend, too? Because she told me you took her out a few weeks ago, *after* the season started. But that can't be right, can it?"

"Uh…"

"Don't strain yourself looking for an excuse, Mace. One and done, that's your motto. If only you'd show us the respect of sticking to that and not promising to call. But you like to keep us dangling, just in case you ever want to reel us in again. Why? Because you're…" She leaned over Mason. "An asshole."

Camille's hand reached for Mason's wineglass, Gemma saw what was coming and opened her mouth to warn him, but it was too late.

Camille dumped the wine down the front of Mason's shirt. As he bit off a yelp, she turned to Gemma. Gemma's hand shot out to steady her own wineglass, but Camille didn't reach for it.

"Sorry to end your date this way, hon," she said. "If anything, consider it an act of sisterly kindness. Best leave this fish in the sea, swimming with the rest of the sharks."

Camille nodded a goodbye to Gemma and then strode off, chin high, and as Gemma watched her go, she barely suppressed the urge to applaud. You had to give the woman credit for calling a guy out for that shit. It was, however, far more awkward when the "guy" was sitting across the table, dripping wet and looking…

Looking mortified.

Gemma quickly handed Mason her napkin. "We should go."

"No, I've got this." He patted his shirt with one hand while reaching for his suit jacket with the other. "I'll just put this on."

"You're not sitting here with a wet shirt, Mason."

His jaw set. "I'll be fine. It was a misunderstanding."

Yeah, pretty sure the only misunderstanding was that she believed you when you said you'd call.

Gemma looked around. Everyone was staring at them.

"You wanted steak," Mason said, yanking on his jacket. "You're getting steak."

"Uh, Mason?" She nodded toward someone openly lifting a phone to snap a photo. "I really think we should go."

He glared toward the camera and rose, fists balling, and for a second, Gemma thought she'd need to leap up and stop a fight. But then he glanced her way and a guilty, almost sheepish, look crossed his face.

"May we leave?" she whispered. "Please?"

He nodded and put out a hand to help her from her chair.

CHAPTER NINE

MASON

Mason threw open the restaurant door and...it was pouring rain. Not the usual wintry drizzle, but full-on rain. Good thing Gemma brought her umbrella.

Uh, no. You told her to leave it in the car.

He yanked off his jacket and motioned for her to hold it over her head. She pretended not to see him before striding into the downpour.

Gemma was pissed. Because someone told her to leave her umbrella behind. And then told her to take off her coat on a November night. And that had only been the start of it.

What the hell had he been thinking, taking her to Maize? Taking her out *at all* while he was under this rain cloud of his own?

Except it wasn't really like that. He could go an entire day without anyone mentioning Denny. A day of being recognized with only smiles and waves.

That's because he'd been sticking to the safe zone. Grabbing coffee at his usual shop. Ordering takeout from his usual restaurants. Hanging out with Jesse. Spending his days at the gym or at a rink. He'd been gone all last week with back-to-back away games, and once he was out of Vancouver, no one gave a shit what he'd done to Denny. Hell, away from Vancouver, he was hardly recognized.

A little work—okay, a hell of a lot of work, dodging and ducking—and he'd been able to keep his life running smoothly despite the Denny fallout. Then he lost his mind and dragged Gemma into the eye of the storm.

Also, what just happened with Camille had nothing to do with Denny. Yeah, one-and-done was totally his dating life, and everyone knew it. But then, sometimes, when he tried to leave afterward, it...didn't go well.

"That was good, right, Mace?" she'd said.

"Sure. Yeah. It was great. Thanks for—"

"We should do it again sometime."

"Uh..." How the hell did you say no to that without sounding like a total asshole?

"How about next weekend?" she'd said.

"I..." *Fuck.* "I don't date during the season. You know how it is. I need to focus."

He'd love to say past dates had never confronted him in public, but yeah, it happened. Terrance insisted the incidents only bolstered Mason's rep.

Everyone loves a bad boy.

Except he wasn't trying to be a bad boy, and he didn't like the idea that being one meant he could get away with hurting people.

As for the kid who refused to serve him, Mason couldn't be sure that had been about Denny either. Hockey fans either loved Mason or loved to hate him.

He'd royally fucked up. He'd wanted to treat Gemma to a perfect date. He'd wanted to apologize—in his own way—for what happened in high school. And he'd wanted to impress her. That was the quiet part. He wanted to get her attention.

Well, he'd gotten it, hadn't he?

Now they were running through the rain, Mason waving for a cab, too distracted to have called the driver while they were still in the damn restaurant.

Was that a cab with its light on? Please be—

"Hey, Mace!" someone yelled.

Mason peered into the night, sluicing rain from his face. A kid, maybe twenty, was barreling down on Mason with his buddies in tow, all four teetering as if their Friday night had gotten off to a very early start.

"Mace!" the lead guy bellowed, though he was less than five feet away. "This one's for Denny."

Mason saw the guy swing and raised his arm to block it just as Gemma leapt between them. Mason yanked her out of the way, but the guy's punch still struck a glancing blow on her cheek, spinning her off her feet.

Mason caught her, sweeping her up and over his arms.

"Shit," one of the other young men said, dragging his friend back. "We're sorry, ma'am. He's had too much to drink. Are you okay?"

Gemma wriggled to get down. "I'm fine."

But she wasn't fine, was she? She'd nearly gotten clocked jumping in to defend him…against something he didn't deserve to be defended against.

Gemma obviously hadn't known about the Denny problem, and he hadn't told her. He'd pushed and pushed until she agreed to go out with him…while withholding vital information she should have had before making that decision.

He grabbed the taxi door handle, yanked it open, and bundled her inside.

"Go home, Gem," he mumbled, his cheeks heating with rising shame as he pulled bills from his wallet.

"Wait." She held the door. "You're coming with me, right?"

"I think I've done enough damage tonight."

He emptied every bill in his wallet, still mumbling—about her getting home safe, being careful, ordering in dinner, getting whatever she wanted. Then he shut the door, hunched his shoulders against the rain, and strode off into the night.

GEMMA

Gemma sat in the taxi and stared at the money strewn across her lap. She could only imagine what the taxi driver thought about this woman in his back seat wearing a clingy dress and covered in money. Well, at least it was fifties and hundreds.

Gemma wasn't sure whether she should laugh or spit nails. Neither, because it wasn't funny and it wasn't an insult. Oh, it *could* feel insulting. Mason had dumped her in a taxi and taken off, which would seem like an asshole move...if she hadn't seen his expression, his face flushed, eyes unable to meet hers.

As the taxi idled at the curb, she watched Mason through the rain-smeared window. He still had his jacket off, his wine-soaked linen shirt plastered to him as he jogged across the road and headed into what looked like a bar.

"Miss?" the driver said. "Where to?"

"Just...around the block, please."

His brows shot up, but he only shrugged. Clearly she had enough money to pay the fare. That made her the boss.

The driver pulled into traffic, heavy now as the light changed.

Gemma should go home. Mark this down in her journal as, quite possibly, her worst date ever, and use it for one of those scenes where the heroine goes out with the wrong guy and *realizes* he's the wrong guy after a disastrous evening.

Except…

Oh hell. She kept seeing Mason's face. His expression after the server refused to wait on their table. After Camille threw the wine at him. Then when the drunk frat boy took a swing, the genuine horror in Mason's eyes, as if she'd been knocked out cold.

After what happened in high school, Gemma had ruthlessly revised her memories of Mason. That guy she got to know in private, considerate and funny and even vulnerable? He didn't exist in real life. She must have constructed a silly schoolgirl fantasy of the superstar asshole jock who could be an absolute sweetheart in private, with the "right" girl. After the kiss, he'd reminded her who he really was. The kind of guy who'd make out with you behind the school, let his friends spread the rumor that he'd done it on a dare, and then ghost you after a few mumbled words that did not include "I'm sorry."

Twenty years of holding fast to that edited image of Mason Moretti, and then she met him again, and there was the boy she'd known, peeking through again. The boy who could be considerate, funny, and yes, vulnerable.

She squeezed her eyes shut, as if that could erase the images. Edit them again. Forget those bits and remember the guy who hopped into the hired car so it'd seem as if they were arriving together instead of actually picking her up. The guy who wanted her to walk in the freezing cold to look good for photos. The guy who put her umbrella back in the car—a car that was no longer around because they didn't even get to eat dinner before an angry mob came for him.

What had the drunken college kid said? Something about "Denny"? The name rang a bell, but she couldn't place it. Maybe another woman Mason had dated? The frat boy's friend or sister?

Even if the altercation *hadn't* been about a woman, there was no denying that the incident with Camille was clearly Mason's fault. So Gemma shouldn't feel bad for him.

And yet…

What would it be like to be Mason Moretti, one of the city's most recognizable faces?

Her mind slid back to high school, in the aftermath of that kiss, when one of Gemma's friends had commiserated as if Gemma had been holding a lottery ticket that was off by one number.

"Can you imagine what it would be like to actually date Mason Moretti? I should be glad he messed up, or you wouldn't have been hanging out with me anymore."

In high school, it wasn't uncommon for out-crowd kids to fantasize about being part of the in crowd. For Gemma, that was like contemplating a pretty dress that wouldn't suit her. In those brief moments when the possibility of a relationship with Mason had dangled before her, she'd considered that, too…and came to the same conclusion.

What she'd wanted was the private Mason. Her fantasy wasn't going to hockey games and having him skate past and blow her a kiss. Her fantasy was a secret relationship, one only the two of them knew about, where she greedily got private Mason entirely to herself.

Public Mason came with too many complications.

Like going out to dinner, having the server refuse to serve you, an ex dumping a drink on you, and a drunken lout throwing a punch at you.

Proof that she should return Mason Moretti to the high school memory trunk and go home.

Instead, she leaned over the seat and said, "Can you drive back and drop me off at the pub across the road?"

"The one where your date went?"

She nodded.

The driver glanced in the mirror at her. "That was the Mace, yes? From hockey?"

"Yes."

"He is a fine player. An excellent player. It seems like he is not having a very good night."

"He's not," she said softly. "He's really not."

CHAPTER TEN

MASON

Mason was doing something he really wasn't very good at. Getting drunk. Drag his sorry ass into some dingy bar, find a table in the corner, and drink until all his mistakes washed away, taking those unsettling emotions with them. Until the rough seas calmed. Until the world was steady again.

He'd managed the first part. Maize wasn't in the best part of Vancouver, so the appropriate dingy bar was right across the road. He got the second part, too. With the rain, the place was empty enough for him to park his ass at a back table, where he was immediately served by a middle-aged woman who didn't know him from Adam, which was the first break he'd caught all night.

The part he was having trouble with was the drinking. That first glass had gone down fine. No fancy scotch for him tonight. Just regular rye whiskey, neat, burning down his throat and letting him relax. He'd had the server bring him two doubles, which was a mistake. He'd downed the first fast and had only finished half of the second before the room started spinning.

A cheap date. That's what his dad always said when Mason got tipsy after two beers. It's also what his dad said—in his loud, aggressively teasing way—to women who stopped after one drink.

It'd been years, too many years really, before Mason understood what his father meant.

Mason shuddered to think how many times he'd used that phrase on women before Jesse told him "a cheap date" meant a woman who'd drop her panties after just one drink, meaning you didn't need to shell out more to get laid. It also implied that you *needed* her tipsy to get laid.

When Mason's father called *him* a cheap date, it meant Mason drank like a girl, and a timid girl at that. Real men could throw back both these doubles and still drive home.

Yep, apparently real men sucked back a bottle of whiskey, screwed some chick they met at the bar, and then came home and yelled at their wives for daring to ask why they hadn't come home for dinner.

Mason had messed up so bad tonight, and as he stared into that second glass, he wanted to...

His dad would say he should want to throw it at the wall. Instead, Mason wanted to huddle over it and hide his face and...

He didn't know what he wanted.

Yeah, you do.

He did, and that was the real reason he was in this shitty bar, drinking shitty whiskey, alternating between feeling sorry for himself and cursing himself out for being a shitty person who'd taken Gemma on a shitty date.

What did he want?

The same thing he'd wanted as a teenager, when he would casually suggest Gemma drop by the rink to see him play. He wanted to impress her.

He wasn't good at writing newspaper articles. All her coaching only made him adequate. He knew what he *was* good at, and he wanted her to see him do it.

He also knew he was good at planning dates. While he honestly had wanted to help Gemma's book sales, mostly tonight had been about him. About ending the date in her apartment doorway and her gazing up at him, that look on her face saying she was hoping for a kiss.

He *wouldn't* have kissed her. Sometimes, on the ice, if you really want the goal, you can't take the first shot. You need to be patient and set it up properly. That was what he planned. The perfect date. A gentlemanly goodbye at her door, maybe a hug. Leave her wanting more. Leave her ready to say yes to a second date.

Yes to a real date, not this fake bullshit.

Now he'd tossed Gemma in a cab and thrown money on her lap like she was a paid escort he'd decided he didn't want after all.

He swore he could hear his father saying that's what Mason got for reaching too high, for not sticking to what he was good at. Know his limits and stay within them. Women like Gemma were for suave guys in suits with a string of letters behind their names. Guys who never made dumbass mistakes and then didn't know how to fix them.

Mason groaned and thumped his head onto the table. Or he tried to, but the tabletop was too low, and there wasn't enough room to slump, so he kind of hung there, bent forward.

A hand appeared from nowhere and moved the empty whiskey glass in front of him.

"You look like you're going to puke. Aim there."

He lifted his head and decided he was even drunker than he thought, hallucinating Gemma shucking off a wet jacket to show an equally wet dress underneath, the dress that had already clung so nicely now plastered to her body.

Jesus, Mace. Even in your drunken, self-pitying hallucinations, you're still checking her out.

Gemma slid into the seat across from him. "Oh, you got me a drink already. How sweet."

She sipped the whiskey and made a face. "Rye? I thought you had better taste than that." She lifted the empty glass. "You've been gone fifteen minutes, and you're already down one and working on the second? Please tell me those aren't doubles."

He tried to drop his head into his hands, but again, the table wasn't made for dramatic gestures by a guy over six feet tall. His face hung a few inches over his hands. He lifted them up to cover his face, and he was pretty sure Gemma sputtered a laugh.

"Mind if I get my own drink?" she asked.

"You should go home. You almost got knocked out for being with me."

She glanced around. "That's very gallant, Mason, but I think I can take on anyone here. Also, no one is paying any attention to you."

"Maybe we should have come *here* for dinner."

"You think they have steak?"

"Wouldn't want to eat it if they did."

She smiled and patted his arm. "Let me get a drink."

A moment later she returned with a bottled cooler. "Something told me this was safest." She uncapped it and drank straight from the bottle. "Okay, so as dates go, that one was memorable."

He snorted, and the sound turned into something between a snicker and a sob. He quickly cleared his throat and straightened.

"I messed up," he said. "You shouldn't have had to go through that. I misjudged."

"Misjudged the possibility of running into an ex who's really not happy with you?"

"No, that happens."

She sputtered a laugh. "You're a little drunk, aren't you, Mason?"

"It's the other stuff. Why that guy tried to punch me and probably why the kid refused to serve us. I realized earlier that you must not have heard what happened, and I should have told you. Warned you."

"Okay, so tell me now."

"Uh... so there's this player. On the Growlers. Denny."

Her head shot up. "Denny Fowler. Right. I knew the name sounded familiar. Top draft pick, right? My ex went on about it, how the Growlers paid too much for him, blah blah."

"Your ex-boyfriend?"

"Ex-husband."

He blinked. "You were married? You didn't tell me that."

She shook her head. "We haven't exactly been having those catch-up conversations, Mason. Yes. I was married. Nine years. Recently divorced."

"I'm sorry."

"I'm not."

Huh. Well, that was good, right? She wasn't pining over this guy, whoever he was. But still, the thought that she'd been married...? For nine years, no less. It seemed as if only a few years had passed since he last saw her.

More like two decades.

Did Mason know her ex? What did he do for a living? What did *she* do for a living?

Shit. He didn't even know that. She used to talk about getting a PhD. He'd remembered that, because it'd driven home how smart she was.

College? You can barely read.

"So Denny…" she prompted.

"He got hurt during a game. A couple of weeks ago. He had to be hospitalized."

"Damn." She sat back. Then her gaze shot to him, and when she spoke, he could tell she was picking her words with care. "Did something, uh, happen? On the ice? Between you two?"

"What? No. I didn't do it."

She frowned. "Then what does this have to do with you?"

He took a gulp of his whiskey. "I didn't protect him."

Her frown grew.

"Remember what we were talking about earlier?" he said. "It's my job to protect players from the goons."

"Goons. Right. I once made the mistake of confusing enforcers and goons, and Alan set me straight."

Alan. Her ex? Did he know any Alans from high school?

She continued, "So a goon went after Denny, and you failed to get to him in time. Tough break for the kid, but I still don't see how it's your fault if you didn't notice what was happening."

"I did notice. I always do. That's part of the job."

"Okay, but you were too far away to stop it."

He took another hit even as Gemma lifted a hand, as if to slow him down. The whiskey burned, setting his head spinning.

"I was right there." The words slurred out. "Close enough to stop it. I didn't, and now everyone thinks I did it on purpose. He's the hot young player, and I'm..." Mason shrugged. "An old-timer."

She laughed. "You're thirty-six, Mason. That is far from..." She trailed off, as if realizing something.

"It's old for hockey," he said. "There are only two players over forty in the NHL right now. Only a handful over thirty-five. Oldest guy ever was fifty-two."

"Gordie Howe," she murmured.

"Mr. Hockey himself. I'm good, but I'm no Gordie Howe. People are asking when I'll be hanging up my skates, and I can get a little... sensitive about it. So when Denny got hurt, and I just stood there?"

"It looked like you let him get hurt. Like you were being an asshole."

He waited for her to ask the next question. Because she had to ask.

Is that why you did it? Are you jealous?

"So what really happened?" she asked.

His gaze shot to hers.

She rolled her eyes. "You are your own special brand of asshole, Mason. You're never intentionally cruel, and you're definitely not vindictive."

He met her gaze, or tried to, though her eyes seemed to be rocking from side to side. "That... that means a lot."

"Saying you're not the kind of asshole who'd let a kid get clobbered on the rink because you're jealous of him? If you were that guy, I wouldn't be sitting here. I wouldn't have agreed to fake date you even if you could guarantee me a bestselling book."

"You're so nice, Gemma," he slurred. "You're always nice. Even when I don't deserve it."

She seemed to be struggling not to laugh. She reached out and patted his hand.

"You're a lot, Mason Moretti, and you probably deserved that wine shower tonight, but you don't deserve the rest."

Was he tearing up? He grabbed the glass and downed it as she said, "Wait!" and then murmured, "Too late."

"I froze," he blurted. "On the ice. I don't know why. I saw trouble coming and I just...I froze."

She gripped his hand tight, not saying anything, just holding his hand, and that might have been the nicest thing anyone had done for him in a long time.

Was he going to cry?

He pushed to his feet. "We should go. Get you home." He took one step and nearly face-planted before she steadied him.

"Easy, big guy," she said. "I think that second double was past your limit. Let's get *you* home."

CHAPTER ELEVEN

GEMMA

Gemma stared down at Mason, passed out on the sofa. At least it was *his* sofa. He'd wanted to drop her off at her apartment, but she'd been afraid he'd fall asleep in the taxi, so she'd insisted on taking him back to his condo. Then she had to help him up the stairs. Also had to help him find his key, only to discover that there was no key but a numeric keypad, to which his muddled brain couldn't remember the code.

Fortunately, Mason wasn't one for complicated codes, and with some prodding, he recalled that it was his birth year plus his jersey number. If only he could remember either...

Since they shared a birth year, that one was easy. She thought twelve was his jersey number, but double-checked online and was correct.

Get the condo door open. Help him inside. Turn on a light. Ah, a sofa. Okay, so just get him to sit for a moment and rest before she left—

The moment his ass hit the sofa, he passed out.

He wasn't lying down. Wasn't sitting either. He was slumped, head lolling forward, one leg bent, the other outstretched, his whole body canted to one side.

"That really doesn't look comfortable, Mason."

She got a snore in response. With a sigh, she took his hands.

"Come on, big guy, let's get you to bed."

Another snore.

Gemma bent and slung one of his arms over her shoulders. "Okay, on the count of three. One, two—"

His snore cut her off.

She stepped back and crossed her arms. "I have never had so much trouble getting a guy into bed. I might take this personally, you know."

His head lolled back in another, deeper snore.

"I *will* get you in bed," she said. "But first, it might help if I knew where the bedroom was."

She looked around. She'd turned on one light in the hall. There was a dark shape that looked lamp-like, and she headed for it and then stopped as she looked out the window and gave a low whistle.

"Damn, Moretti. You have a *view*."

Of the ocean, no less, his building towering over smaller ones between here and the coast. The Pacific stretched out straight ahead, with the trees of Stanley Park off to the right, and then stars and a half-moon above.

Gemma's apartment also had a view. Of the neighboring building. If she craned her neck just so, she could see the sky. No stars, though. She was too deep into the light pollution for that.

Gemma decided the lamp could stay off so she could keep the view. She opened the blinds fully, and that was enough light to let her see inside the condo. Ahead was the kitchen. To her left was a hall, which presumably led to the bedroom.

She headed that way. The first door opened into a bathroom...

with a shower room. Not a shower stall. A shower *room*. Plus a soaking tub.

"I hate you, Mason," she called over her shoulder. "Just for the record."

Her apartment bathroom had what was supposed to be a shower stall but was more like a shower booth, without enough room to even turn around. It'd been over a year since she'd had a bath.

With a sigh, she shut the door to bathing nirvana and moved to the next one, opening it into what looked like a bedroom. She flicked on a light and...

And she was staring at a motorcycle. In the middle of a room bigger than her apartment bedroom. That was the only thing in there. His damned motorcycle.

"Hate you, Mason," she called over her shoulder. "Hate. You."

One more door, which had to be the bedroom. She flicked on the light to be sure. Yep, definitely the bedroom. It was twice the size of the motorcycle room and held a bed that had to be bigger than a king. The bed was unmade, crisp white sheets folded and crumpled, as if he'd just rolled out of them.

She scowled over her shoulder in Mason's general direction. What the hell was he thinking, leaving his bed unmade like that? He could have a perfectly innocent houseguest, who'd only tried to help his drunk ass home, open this door, see that bed, and be powerless against the images rising from it, of Mason, sprawled naked—

She gave her head a quick shake.

Damn him. Someone had to teach the guy to make his bed. This just wasn't playing fair.

She was joking—kind of—but she was pretty sure most women

who saw this bed also got to see sprawled-naked Mason, so it wasn't a tease. Just a preview of things to come.

Things that were not for the likes of Gemma.

There'd been a moment tonight, walking up to the restaurant, cameras flashing, Mason's hand on her back, when she'd felt like his date. As if someone seeing those photos could believe she'd really been there with Mason Moretti, Gemma in her sexy dress and heels, her on-point makeup, and her hair just so.

Now she pictured Camille, and she could laugh at her delusion.

Her mind drifted, and the dimly lit bedroom swirled into a high school hall that smelled of Axe body spray and BO. Locker doors clanging. Someone whooping. Gemma striding to her locker, navigating upstream through the crowd.

A voice whispered as it passed, "Meet me behind the school."

She looked up sharply to see Mason still moving, turning back to say, "I've got something to show you."

She arched her brows at him, but he'd already disappeared, the flow dovetailing to carry him along, lest he strain himself with effort before the next game.

The "next game" would be field hockey finals tonight. It was only three days before exams. Only three days before high school passed into the rearview mirror of Gemma's life.

And how did she feel about that?

She wasn't one of those kids for whom high school would be the best years of her life. It hadn't been the worst years either. For Gemma, high school simply existed. Much like grade school. Bigger and better things lay ahead, and she couldn't wait to get to them, starting with her acceptance to UBC's English program.

Gemma dreamed of an MFA, but from what she knew of the

UBC program, they wouldn't exactly welcome her genre of choice. Maybe she could tough it out and write CanLit for a year to glean whatever knowledge the professors could impart. Or maybe she'd skip the MFA and stick to a master's in English, with a minor in creative writing. Then it would be on to her PhD and a career as an English prof writing romance on the side.

She swapped out her textbooks for the ones she needed to take home, and then she chatted with friends before heading to the rear doors. There was never any question of *not* meeting Mason. While she felt perfectly fine telling him no—a social transgression that would put most of her classmates into a state of cardiac arrest—if she didn't plan to meet him, she'd have said so. Gemma didn't play games, and she was past the stage of thwarting Mason for the sake of proving she wasn't one of his sycophants. He'd gotten that message months ago.

She headed out back to find him leaning against the wall, oh so casual. She rolled her eyes. Such a freaking poseur, even when she was the only one around to appreciate it.

"This is the second time a guy summoned me behind the school to show me something," she said as she walked over. "The first time was in third grade."

"Yeah, that was me, too."

She laughed and shook her head. It took a moment for him to laugh, almost as if…

Wait. That hadn't been Mason, had it?

In grade school, she'd been his reading buddy and they'd talked sometimes. A lot of times, if she thought about it, that memory faded as if by yet more edits. Yes, they'd talked quite a bit, at least until they reached the age where girls and boys started noticing

each other for different reasons. Someone—had it been Ashley?—
had snarked at Gemma for "chasing" Mason—and even though
it'd almost always been Mason seeking Gemma out, Gemma had
started avoiding him, not wanting to be one of the many girls
already fawning over him.

But back to third grade…There'd been a "kissing bug" going
around at school, where kids were asking others behind the school
and then kissing them.

A boy had asked to meet her behind the school to show her
something, and she'd figured he wanted a kiss and, well, she'd been
curious, too. But instead he showed her some kind of weird insect,
and she got the feeling he'd been planning to kiss her but chickened
out, and she hadn't been sure how she felt about that. Relieved?
Disappointed?

That *had* been Mason.

Before she could comment, he was leading her behind the high
school. Out front, the great divide was taking place, students split-
ting into dual streams—the "haves" heading for the parking lot and
the "have-nots" for the buses.

Gemma had a hand-me-down car from Grandpa Thomas, but
she never drove it to school, because if she did, she'd be expected
to stuff it full of friends, and it'd end up being a longer drive than
busing. So she pretended her parents wouldn't let her take her car.
The monsters.

Gemma's family was what Dad called "comfortably middle-class"
meaning they had a three-bedroom house with a yard and enough
money to insure that hand-me-down car for Gemma. Mason did
not have a car. His family lived in an apartment, and any extra
money went to a private hockey coach, which Gemma thought

proved how much his parents must love him…until Mason said his dad called those lessons his retirement plan. Mason was their great hope, their only child, expected to do amazing things and repay their investment.

While Mason might not have a car, that didn't mean he took the bus like a commoner. Kids vied to chauffeur him, even if it meant arriving early for his practices or staying late for his games. Being Mason Moretti meant you rose above categories like "have" and "have-not" or even "popular" and "unpopular." Mason existed in a stratosphere of his own, which was always hard to reconcile at moments like this, following him as he loped along the back of the school.

Mason found what he was looking for—a recessed pair of steel doors that provided extra privacy. There he pulled a folded white sheet from his pocket and held it out, grinning like a little kid passing her a secret note.

She unfolded it, and then she was grinning, too. "You got a B plus in English? That's amazing."

"I have a B plus going *into* the exam, but I think I can hold it at a B. And it's not even inflated for the newspaper work. I actually earned this." He waved the paper. "My last essay was an A minus and the one before that was a B plus. Thanks to you."

"I only coached you. I didn't write them."

"Which makes it even better, right? My first B in English."

He grinned, and it was his real grin, so bright she couldn't look away. She wanted to hug him. He'd worked damn hard for that grade, and he hadn't needed to. He'd been promised a passing grade for his work at the newspaper. But he'd gone further, and now he was grinning like he'd scored the Stanley Cup winning goal, and she wanted to throw her arms around his neck and—

Mason kissed her. It happened so fast she wasn't quite sure *how* it happened. It was just a quick kiss, a little awkward from his having to bend over so far, and when he pulled back, his cheeks flamed and he mumbled what sounded like an apology.

"Was that a thank-you kiss?" she said.

His cheeks burned even brighter. "No, no. I just…I…" Another kind of grin sparked, this one a little bit devilish. "I wanted to do that. Been wanting to do it for a long time."

She reached up, taking hold of the front of his shirt in both hands. "And is *that* what you had in mind? It was very…quick. Not that I'm stamina-shaming."

He let out a whoosh of a laugh. "Oh, I can go longer than that."

"Can you?"

His eyes danced. "Are you calling me out, Gemma Stanton? If you want a longer kiss, you could just ask."

She pulled herself up on her tiptoes, hands wrapping more in his shirt. "Could I?"

He nodded mutely, a strange expression in his eyes.

"Hmm. Okay." She let go of his shirt. "I'll remember that for next time."

There was a split-second pause, as if he really thought she was going to walk away. Then he caught her grin and grabbed her, and the next thing she knew, she was clear off her feet, her back against the wall, his hands on her ass boosting her as he kissed her, and holy *shit*, the boy could kiss.

Her first thought was *Damn you, Mason.*

She would admit she'd been curious about what it'd be like to kiss him. If she was being perfectly honest, she'd hoped to be disappointed. That would mean she'd never have traitorous thoughts about his lips and hands on her again.

Instead, it was like touching a flame just to see what it felt like, and being engulfed in an inferno of "holy *shit*!" Which is not what she wanted, and at the same time, it was exactly what she wanted. His lips on hers, his tongue tasting hers, the heat and fire of him devouring her. His hands on her ass, fingers digging in, but staying there, making no move to do anything else or go anywhere else and—

"Mace!"

Gemma pulled back as the voice echoed around them. Then another called, "Yo! Mace! Game time!"

"Ignore them," Mason whispered as his mouth found hers again.

"Mason!" someone shouted. "I saw you come back here!"

Mason kept kissing her, but all she could imagine was his friends stumbling on them. She reached for his hands and gently peeled them away as she whispered, "You have a game."

He glared in the direction of his friends, who were still calling him.

"Go on," Gemma said, giving him a little push. "It's the finals, and you're the star."

He made a face. Then he bent to kiss her forehead. "Tomorrow, okay? I'll see you tomorrow."

She gave him a quick hug, and when she stepped back, Mason jogged out from the recessed doors.

"What were you doing back there?" one of his friends said.

"Taking a piss."

Gemma rolled her eyes. Boys. She waited until they were gone, and then she slid out and took off before she missed the bus.

CHAPTER TWELVE

GEMMA

That had been the happy-for-now ending. The actual ending
started the next day, when Gemma arrived at school to discover that someone had snapped a photo of her and Mason making
out...and his friends were claiming he'd done it on a dare.

She'd been furious, but Mason would set them straight. She'd
been sure of that.

It took all day. Then she was in the newspaper office, clearing out
her things, when Mason came in and shut the door.

"Hey, Gem."

She'd kept emptying her desk, possibly smacking each item onto
the top a little harder than necessary.

"So, uh, you may have heard—" he began.

She looked up so sharply he inched backward. "That you kissed
me on a dare? Yes, I heard."

"I didn't. My friends are just being jerks. I told them to stop."

She looked at him. He shoved his hands into his pockets, rocked
on his heels, and shrugged. "I wanted you to know it wasn't true."

"Okay, now I know."

She waited for the apology. She waited for him to come closer, try to kiss her again, and she'd duck out, still angry, but they'd talk and work it out.

Instead, he just stood there, rocking. "No hard feelings?"

She tried not to stare, even as her heart clenched. That wasn't an apology. It wasn't the prelude to another kiss. It didn't even sound...

Oh God, it didn't even sound as if he *planned* to kiss her again. He had his gaze down, hands in his pockets, like he'd come to give her a chance to blast him and then he could flee. Take his lumps and get the hell out of her life.

"No hard feelings about the rumor?" she said. "Or the kiss?"

"Both," he mumbled, and her heart cracked, but she slammed it back together and straightened.

"It was just a kiss," she said. "No big deal."

"Yeah..." His shoulders slumped. "Just a kiss."

"I need to get my things. They want the office cleared out."

"Sure." He backed up to the door and reached behind him for the knob. "So you're okay?"

"Why wouldn't I be?"

"Yeah. Good. Um, so... I'll see you around?"

She didn't answer, just kept clearing the desk, and he left. She spotted him a few times over the last days of school, but he never spoke to her again.

She'd spent a long time being hurt. A long time feeling humiliated. A long time hating Mason Moretti. And now?

Now she didn't hate him. Didn't forgive him either, because that would take an apology, which he hadn't given. With the hindsight of nearly twenty years, she finally understood what had happened that day. He'd kissed her, and then he'd had second thoughts, and if he'd been a decent guy, he'd have said so.

Mason could be a decent guy. He could also be an asshole. And in that moment of his life, he'd been a very certain kind of asshole—a teenage boy who messed up and didn't know how to handle it, so he *didn't* handle it.

While adult Mason still hadn't apologized, he did seem to understand that he'd hurt her. He hadn't made excuses, and he'd been clear that he *hadn't* kissed her on a dare. He'd owned up to the fact that he'd done a shitty thing, and she could grumble, but she'd rather he took responsibility for the mistake than give a half-hearted apology.

Gemma shook off the memories and returned to the living room. Seeing Mason awkwardly slumped on the sofa, she sighed.

"Let's give this another go, shall we?" she said.

She took his hands and tried pulling him to his feet...and nearly ended up on his lap. She put his arm over her shoulders...and nearly ended up in a headlock. And throughout it all, he snored.

Gemma crossed her arms and gave him a very disapproving look. He continued snoring.

At the very least, she felt she should get him out of that soaking wet shirt.

Oh hell, no. You are not playing out that scene, Stanton.

She smiled to herself. True, it was a romance staple. Buff hero needs to remove his shirt—as often as possible. Caught in the rain. Wounded in a fight. Sweaty with fever. Really, the only reason for even putting a buff romance hero in a shirt was so you could take it off again at the first good—or semi-plausible—excuse.

But removing Mason's shirt was just common sense. He couldn't afford to catch a cold during hockey season.

That's not how viruses work.

Or the stain might set.

It's red wine. On a plum shirt. You can't even see it.

Didn't matter. Getting Mason out of this shirt was a necessity.

The top button was undone. She flipped the next one and then the next, slowly revealing a line of dark hair and golden skin. Also muscles. The more she undid, the more muscles there were, and she told herself that would end soon. He was thirty-six, and he might be in amazing shape, but there was no need for a hockey player to have a six-pack. God knows, when she hit thirty, that's where her extra ounces went.

And…that is not where they went on Mason. The only things marring his perfectly flat stomach were muscles. Damn him. She swallowed and resisted the urge to run her fingers down his chest, even if they were close enough to feel the heat of his skin, and that smell of orange and cloves.

If her mouth was watering, it was the smell. She'd missed dinner. Salivating had nothing to do with the delicious sight revealed, inch by inch, as she carefully peeled away his shirt, and then it was off and—

Damn it. Mason had not looked like this in high school. Oh, he'd taken off his shirt plenty back then, stripping from a sweaty jersey as girls ogled. But he'd been a teenager, lean and fit and just starting to show signs of the muscles to come.

The muscles that had arrived. The body of an NHL enforcer. Bulging biceps. Ripped pecs. Muscled abs. Perfectly toned forearms and big square hands—

He needed a blanket. She looked around the shadowy room and spotted several throws neatly stacked by the fireplace. After much effort and maybe a few unavoidable touches of that warm skin, she got him lying down on the sofa. Then she quickly pulled the blanket over him and stepped back, panting from exertion.

"You really *aren't* waking up, are you?"

Snore.

"Here's my dilemma, Mace. It's seriously awkward hanging out in your condo all night without an invitation. But if you're that deeply asleep, and you drank more than you're used to, I'm concerned about you throwing up in your sleep."

Snore.

"So I guess I'm just praying when you wake up you don't think it was weird that I stayed. You won't think it was weird, right?"

Snore.

"And if I had a bath while you slept. Would *that* be weird?"

Snore.

"You're such a good host." She patted his head, rearranging his damp hair. Then she found a paper and pen and left a note, in case he woke and heard someone in his bathroom.

That accomplished, she started the bathwater. The tub was huge, and in reaching for the taps, she hit the soap and knocked it in. As she fumbled for it, a familiar scent filled the room.

Orange and cloves.

Heat flooded through her, and an image formed in the steam. Mason, in the tub, lying back, naked—

Enough of that.

She peeled off her still-wet dress and caught a glimpse of herself in the full-length mirror.

Not bad, right? She wasn't Camille, but she looked pretty good for thirty-six. Especially through a layer of steam. She laughed softly to herself. No, she wasn't playing the age game. She looked just fine.

Fine enough to catch the eye of—

Enough.

She lifted one leg over the tub and lowered herself in, hissing with pleasure as the hot water washed over her clammy skin. She sunk down and moaned softly. This felt *so* good.

A steaming hot bath after bitter November rain. A bath that smelled of oranges and cloves. A bath that had last seen Mason Moretti, not just shirtless, but naked, sinking into this same tub.

A tub that was big enough for two. Even if one was Mason Moretti.

Enou—

She stopped mid-rebuke and tilted her head, considering. Was there anything wrong with going there? She was a romance novelist after all. Consider it research.

She smiled and, as she sunk deeper into the tub, she let her imagination run wild.

MASON

That night, Mason had the weirdest dreams. He remembered getting into the taxi—after Gemma insisted on buying a bottle of water from the bar, which she made him drink on the way to his condo. He remembered, too, that he'd tried to give the cabbie her address, but she wanted to make sure he got up to his place safely, which he certainly wasn't going to argue with.

The rest was flashes. Gemma pulling him from the cab. Him

forgetting how to get in the building front door, where the elevator was, what the code was for his condo door… There'd been a lot of forgetting, and a lot of "Come on, it's just a few more steps, you can do it," Gemma propping him up and encouraging him like a skating instructor with a toddler.

Then the world went blank, and he got the weird dreams instead. Gemma talking to him. Coaxing him. Pulling. Wheedling. And finally, undressing him, which had been sexy as hell.

He woke on the couch to find he had indeed been undressed. Well, his shirt was off, at least. He'd been covered up, which was disappointing, but also sweet and…

He stretched, rolling his back up off the sofa. His mouth felt like something died in it, but there were no signs of a hangover. That'd be why Gemma made him drink the water. At the time, he'd been too fuzzy headed to figure it out and only drank because she told him to.

He stretched again, and his hand hit a paper on the console table. He picked it up and blinked against the morning gloom as his eyes focused.

Mason,

Advance warning that I'm still here, so please don't take a swing at the stranger sleeping on your recliner. I didn't feel right leaving you alone when you were passed out. If you wake up first, just give me a kick and send me on my way.

Gem

Mason lifted his head and blinked as he saw that Gemma was indeed on his recliner. How the hell did he miss that? He grinned as he sat up and leaned forward, elbows on his knees while he considered the situation.

The situation being that Gemma Stanton was asleep in his condo. Which was absolutely not a problem, and he was absolutely *not* sending her on her way. Now, what he needed to consider was how to make sure she didn't wake up and head straight out the door.

Last night had been a disaster. He wouldn't say everything was fine now. But Gemma came back and listened to him—in the bar and in the cab—and now she'd stayed to look after him, and he was damn well not letting her slip away.

Small goals first. Get her to stay through breakfast and then figure out how to get her to spend the day with him.

For years, Mason had looked back on Gemma Stanton and declared that what he'd felt for her had been nothing more than teen angst and hormones. He hadn't *really* fallen for her. He couldn't have, right? Not if he'd been such an asshole at the end.

Having her back in his life proved it'd been a lot more than angst and hormones, because what he felt for Gemma had started before angst and hormones even hit.

There was a reason he'd spent the first half of his life trying to catch her attention. Inviting her to skate after school. Bragging in front of her whenever he made MVP. Getting her behind the school for a kiss...and then realizing that was a silly idea and showing her a bug instead, which was, yep, just as silly.

There was a reason, when he'd been struggling in English, and his teacher suggested working on the newspaper, he'd pounced. That was a *great* idea. In fact, he knew the editor from grade school. If his teacher could just ask Gemma to work with him directly, that'd be perfect.

And then he did the truly shittiest thing he'd ever done in his life, which as Jesse would say, was quite an achievement. After that, he knew he'd lost any chance with her, which had been...

Devastating.

And also... a relief?

It was complicated, and he would not analyze that. The important thing was that she'd forgiven him enough to write him as the romantic hero in her book. That didn't mean she wanted to date him. He was pretty sure she actually didn't. But it meant that door had cracked open, and he was shoving his foot in the gap as fast as he could.

Gemma Stanton was in his condo. Sleeping on his recliner, adorably curled up sideways, one bare foot sticking out. His gaze slid along that foot, up her calf to—

He'd thought she was under a blanket. Now he realized she'd fallen asleep wearing his bathrobe. She must have been freezing from that rain and taken a shower or a bath. Then she'd grabbed his bathrobe and slid into it.

Mason pushed to his feet to get a better look. She looked hot in that dress last night, but it was nothing compared to seeing her in his bathrobe.

It was like an alternate version of last night, where everything had gone perfectly, that old fire between them roaring to life, Mason bringing her home, to his bed, where he never brought anyone, but she was Gemma. The OG. The girl he'd *always* wanted in his bed. And now she was finally there, when he'd shown her why he was so much better at thirty-six than he'd have been at seventeen.

He imagined all the ways he'd shown her.

Well, that was one way to start his morning. Gemma Stanton, in his bathrobe, while he sported the raging hard-on of a horny teen.

He reminded himself none of that happened and she was only wearing his robe because she'd had a shower. Something he should probably do himself.

Take a shower...where he accidentally left the door open and she walked in to see him naked, lathered up and hard as rock. She'd stand there, watching, thinking he couldn't see her, but he could, through the mirror in the shower, and he'd watch her as his hand dropped to his cock. She'd stay in the doorway, her lips parted, breath coming faster, her excitement fueling his and—

He inhaled deeply, took one last look at her, and then headed to the shower to finish playing out that scene.

When he got out of the shower—wrapped only in a towel because she had his bathrobe—she still didn't wake. He padded into the kitchen. He'd cook breakfast. She couldn't leave if he'd done that.

He opened the fridge. He'd made blintzes yesterday: cheese with berry sauce. He could fry those up for a breakfast combo, add in some turkey sausages.

He hesitated. What if Gemma didn't like blintzes? What if she expected bacon? Or pork sausages? While his parents hadn't kept kosher, they didn't eat pork, and Mason followed suit.

He could follow a recipe and knew the techniques, but he lacked his grandmother's genius with food. Stick with what he was good at. Stay in the safe lane.

He shut the fridge door. He'd get takeout.

CHAPTER THIRTEEN

GEMMA

G emma woke, stretched...and winced as she realized she'd fallen asleep in Mason's bathrobe. She shouldn't have even put it on, but it'd looked so warm and cozy that she couldn't resist.

It'd been as warm and cozy as it looked, and it smelled *so* good— like Mason's soap.

She figured she'd wake up first and change back into her dress once it had time to dry. But now Mason's spot on the sofa was empty, and he'd left her own note turned over with one written on the back. Three words.

Don't go anywhere.

Her brows rose just before the front door swung open.

"Caffeine delivery for Ms. Stanton."

Mason walked in with a tray of four drinks, plus a takeout bag hanging off each forearm.

He set the tray down and pointed to the cups. "Pour over, cappuccino, cinnamon latte, and Earl Grey tea."

"Which one's yours?"

"Depends on which you take," he said as he tugged the bags from his forearms.

Her hand hovered over the cappuccino and then veered to the cinnamon latte.

"Good choice," he said. "I'll leave the capp as your second choice and have the pour over."

He pulled foam boxes from the bags. "Breakfast burrito, egg sandwich, quiche bites, and ham and cheese croissant. Again, ladies pick first."

"Single-handedly keeping your local café in business?"

"There are also..." He opened a box to reveal an assortment of pastries and cookies.

"Damn," she said. "Thank you." She reached in for a pain au chocolat. "I'm starving."

"Shit. That's right. You didn't get dinner last night. I should have said to help yourself to my fridge."

"You couldn't remember your birth year, Mason. If I'd been hungry enough, I *would* have helped myself, as I did to your tub and bathrobe." She made a face. "Sorry about that."

"You were wearing a cold, wet dress, which was entirely the fault of the guy who made you leave your umbrella in the car. I'm the one who's sorry. You were more than welcome to my tub and robe."

She set down the pastry. "My dress should be dry by now. I'll go put—"

"No rush. Finish your breakfast while it's warm."

Someone was feeling gallant today.

Gemma sipped her latte. "I imagine it was a little awkward to wake up to find me still here."

He grinned. "Waking up to find a woman hasn't fled in the night? That's the opposite of awkward."

She laughed. "Somehow I don't think women fleeing in the night is a problem you've ever had." She bit back the obvious segue to Camille. "It's probably more awkward when you wake up to find them still here."

"Nah. I'd need to *bring* women to my apartment for that to happen." He stopped chewing. "That was a jerk thing to say, wasn't it?"

She smiled. "But the first time you do bring one back, she sticks around, which proved your point. I'll be gone as soon as I finish this. I'm sure you have a busy day."

"Nope. Tomorrow's game day, so today is all about chilling." He stretched as if to make his point. "Might as well just get comfortable."

When she hesitated, he said, "Seriously. There's no rush. You have a lot of food to finish."

She shook her head, but she did pop the recliner back. "So now that it's light out, I can see your place properly. Quite the sweet setup."

His nose wrinkled. "It's fine."

"You've got a view of the freaking Pacific, Moretti. *And* the park. How is that just 'fine'?"

"I mean the decor, which is just…" He shrugged. "What it is." He took a bite of his breakfast sandwich and said, words muffled by food, "No books. You probably noticed that."

"Actually I didn't." She looked around. There was a built-in bookshelf, but it held trophies and photos. "I'd rather not see any bookcases than see one designed purely for show. Also…" She shrugged. "I know reading isn't easy for you."

"I do read. Just audiobooks. Which don't really count."

"They definitely count." She was about to ask what he was reading now, but just because he said he read didn't mean he always had a book on the go. She wouldn't put him on the spot like that. "What do you read?"

"Mostly fiction. Guys on the team are more into self-help books, especially those ones about getting better at what you do."

"Which you don't need."

A surprisingly soft laugh. "It just isn't my thing. I like novels." He grinned over at her. "I preordered yours."

Her heart stopped. "What?"

The grin grew. "Just waiting for it to drop. There was some delay, but it's supposed to come any moment now."

"Don't read it, Mason." She looked him in the eye. "Really."

When he only gave a half shrug, her stomach knotted. If she'd known he'd bought it, she might have used his face to unlock his phone last night and delete the order, hope he'd just keep thinking it was delayed.

She did not want Mason reading *A Highland Fling*. Maybe, in her most malicious moments, she'd fantasized about Mason Moretti finding her book and recognizing himself as her asshole male lead. But he didn't deserve that. What she'd poured into that portrayal was twenty years of hurt...and none of the decent parts she'd viciously edited out.

At least the audio was late. By the time it released, she'd have found a way to gently tell Mason that his portrayal was...less than flattering.

Or maybe she was worrying too much. Early reviewers had loved Laird Tavish Argyle. He was a buff Scot in a kilt, swinging a sword and defending his land against all comers. That was hot, right? And if he was also a narcissist who trampled everyone who got in his way? A cad who treated women like a buffet? Well, that didn't matter because he was different with Edin, the heroine. Once he got to know her, he treated her as a person.

God, Gemma hated that narrative. A guy could be an asshole to every other woman, but once he realized the heroine was special, she became the exception. The *only* exception.

The trope made her grind her teeth . . . and she'd perpetuated it in her own book.

"Gem?"

She looked over to see Mason frowning at her change of mood.

Laird Argyle wouldn't even notice a change of mood, not even with his darling Edin.

Gemma balled up her wrapper and lobbed it at Mason. "Back to your condo, I've decided I hate you. You have a bathroom nearly as big as my bedroom. You have a massive shower and a massive tub. Who needs both?"

"Mason Moretti?"

"Hate. You."

"The word is 'envy,' Gem. You're a writer. Words are important."

She flashed him the finger, making him grin.

"Also," she said, "you have a bedroom for a motorcycle. A freaking Ducati, Mace."

"It gets cold at night. I hope you tucked it in."

She threw the napkin at him next. "Hate you *so* much."

"You know motorcycles?"

She sipped her latte. "I had one in uni. Just a little Honda."

"Do you miss it?" he asked.

She considered the question. She'd given up the motorcycle because Alan said it was too dangerous, and she'd thought it was sweet that he cared about her safety, but really he'd only cared that a motorcycle-riding girlfriend didn't fit his budding corporate image.

So did she miss it now? That was one of the things about life postdivorce. It hadn't been like living in a cage, and the door opens and you fly out, shrieking, *I'm free!* She didn't think of all the things she'd given up, because for her, captivity had been such a slow process that to call it captivity seemed dramatic.

Alan hadn't physically abused her. Hadn't overtly emotionally or psychologically abused her. He'd just carved away little bits of her. Slices of her self-confidence and slices of herself, all the things that made her Gemma Stanton. Quirky, opinionated, in-your-face Gemma Stanton.

Like a sculptor with his chisel, Alan had cut off all her inconvenient edges. A motorcycle. A PhD. Friends. Writing. A deft flick of the knife, and off it went. He molded her into what he wanted, until only the bare skeleton of old Gemma remained, and then he stood back, surveyed his work, and declared his masterpiece a failure.

He'd worked so damn hard, and she was no better than when he started. A shitty hostess who couldn't tell the difference between vintage wine and cheap plonk despite flying her to California for a tasting tour. Hell, she couldn't even have kids. What good was she?

"Gem?"

"Yes," she said quickly. "I miss my bike. Maybe, once I'm settled, I'll get one again."

"You'll need to brush up on your riding." He stood. "How about starting today? Take my bike out. The forecast is clear. Ride up the coast. Give you a chance to get back on the saddle."

"It's been fifteen years. You do *not* want me driving your Ducati."

"It's insured. Come on." He grabbed her hand and pulled. "Let's have some fun."

She wanted to keep protesting. She *should* keep protesting.

Why?

Because…

Because Gemma Stanton was no longer the woman who went motorcycle riding in November? Not the sort who took day trips on a whim? Who let a hockey star refresh her riding skills on his very expensive bike?

Was she *really* not that woman anymore?

Oh hell, yes she was.

CHAPTER FOURTEEN

MASON

See? Mason still knew how to woo a woman. It was just a matter of adjusting the strategy to the lady in question, and he'd been out of practice. He had a hookup type, and that type liked his fantasy dinner date bundle. Or maybe they were his type because they liked his fantasy dinner date bundle, which kept things easy. No muss, no fuss.

Gemma was different. With her, he didn't mind a little fuss. Instead of making him uneasy, he saw it as a chance to learn everything he could about grown-up Gemma Stanton.

He'd scored twice already this morning. First, with breakfast, which she'd clearly appreciated. Then the motorcycle lesson and ride, which was a stroke of fucking genius, if he did say so himself.

He'd dug up the second helmet he'd bought shortly after getting his first bike when, in his youth and naivete, he'd been convinced that women loved riding double on motorcycles. He'd suggested it a few times and gotten looks that screamed, *Why would I ever want to do that?*

In his storage berth, he'd even found an old sherpa-lined aviator-style leather jacket to keep Gemma warm. She'd laughed at the size of it, but she'd also taken it. Score three.

He'd driven Gemma to her apartment in his pickup so she could get changed—he was damn well making sure she stayed warm today. Then back to his place, where he took the bike down the service elevator.

As they walked through the aboveground parking garage, his phone buzzed for the dozenth time in the past hour. He was about to flip it into Do Not Disturb, when he saw the first text.

Terrance: How did last night go?

Mason tensed. No, he wasn't thinking about that. He was turning off his phone without reading—

"Everything okay?" Gemma asked, and he realized she could see his phone, held awkwardly as he wheeled his bike.

"Just my publicist," he mumbled. "Asking about last night."

"Ah."

Mason started to pocket the phone.

"Should you answer him?"

When he didn't reply, she lowered her voice. "I know it's probably not good, but let's get it over with so we can move on with our day."

That wasn't how he handled bad news. But this was Gemma—tear off the bandage and deal with it. He took a deep breath and opened the text stream.

Terrance: I hear there was an altercation

You could call it that.

Terrance: Have you seen the photos?

Mason winced.

A string of photos followed. The first two were Mason and Gemma walking into the restaurant, and damn they looked good. Well, she looked good. Fucking amazing, in that dress, her curls blowing in the breeze, her chin lifted, smile radiating confidence. And he looked fine. Okay, better than fine, but mostly because of her. They made a good pair. "Striking," that was the word. They made a striking pair.

Then came the next one. Mason with wine on his shirt, Gemma looking horrified, jumping up with a napkin.

His gut plummeted at the memory.

"Mason?" Gemma murmured. "If it's bad, we'll deal with it. Or our publicists can. They signed off on the idea."

He nodded, and with great reluctance, he scrolled to the last photo. Then he stopped.

Shit.

He enlarged the photo. It'd been snapped at the moment the drunk kid took a swing. An action shot of Gemma leaping between them and Mason reaching to yank her out of the way of that punch. In this one, it was his turn to look horrified. All he could see, though, was her expression. It was *fire*. Fire in her eyes, fire in the set of her mouth and her jaw.

Goddamn. She looked magnificent.

Terrance: They love that last shot. You defended her at the interview and now she's throwing herself in front of some drunk frat boy for you? Protecting a f'ing hockey enforcer? People love it.

Those texts had all come earlier. The next few from Terrance were all knocks at his virtual door, trying to get a response. So he sent one.

Mason: This is good, right?

Terrance: This is f'ing amazing. They love it, and it
puts them on your side. No one is cheering for the
drunken frat boy, especially when he nearly KO'd a
schoolteacher

Mason looked over at Gemma and started to smile.

Her brows shot up. "Not that bad?"

"Not bad at all."

He showed her the text portions, watching her expression, savoring it.

"That's…" She blinked and then looked up at him and grinned, and he was trying to decide whether he could go for a celebratory hug when her phone chirped with a message.

She looked down at it. "Seems my publicist decided she's let me sleep late enough. She's been tracking the online coverage, too."

"Is it good?"

"Either that or the exclamation mark on her keyboard is stuck. She says— Oh, it seems we have a hashtag. 'Romancing the Mace'? Uh…"

He snorted. "Not everyone can be a writer. Are they mentioning your book? That's the main thing. Connecting us to your book."

"Well, according to her, the hashtag is trending, and *A Highland Fling* is climbing the online charts." She quickly added, "In Canada, at least, but it's starting to spread."

"That's good, right?"

She exhaled. "It's good."

He checked his phone. "Terrance wants to know what I'm up to today. Is it okay to tell him I'm with you?"

She checked her watch. "It's almost noon, but I wouldn't want it to seem...you know."

"Like you spent the night? Shit. Guess I shouldn't have sent him those pics of you in my bathrobe." When her eyes widened, he lifted a hand. "Joking. I wouldn't do that. No pics without your consent."

She exhaled. "Thank you. And I guess I'm being silly, worrying about anyone thinking I slept over. That's kind of the point. I wouldn't want any pics of me in your condo, but if we posted shots of today to our personal accounts—with mutual consent—and someone drew the conclusion that we spent the night together, that's on them."

"Yep. So can I say...?"

"We'll tell them that we're going for a motorcycle ride. Just let me see any pics before you send or post them."

"Of course."

They both tapped messages into their phones, and he rolled the bike into an empty spot in the garage.

"Full confession," Gemma said. "I've never ridden on the back of a motorcycle."

He grinned, and he was about to say something about her liking the driver's seat. Then he stopped. No double entendres. Nothing that would make her think today was about seduction.

Well, yeah, it was totally about seduction, but the sort that proved he was someone she wanted to get to know better. Get to know better in *every* way, obviously, but as a whole package. Because he *could* be the whole package. Right?

Right?

The smallest bead of sweat formed at his temple, but he swiped it away. Just warm in here when they were dressed for a November ride.

"No problem," he said. "As you may be able to tell by that shiny helmet, I've never had anyone on the back either."

She paused. "If you'd rather not, just say so."

"What? No. I meant no one wanted…"

He was about to say no one wanted a ride, but that sounded a little double entendre–y. Also, definitely not true. At least, not in the other sense.

"Women usually prefer my truck," he said instead.

She frowned. "Really? Weird."

"I thought so." He patted the motorcycle seat. "However, just in case that changed, I know the passenger basics. I'm going to get on first and let you climb up."

This was *all* going to sound double entendre–y, wasn't it?

He continued, "Now, it'll be a tight squeeze."

Two-minute penalty for misconduct. Also bragging.

"The seat," he said, motioning quickly. "There's not a lot of room between me and the back post."

"Got it. I know there are usually grip bars, but I don't see those. So where do I hang on?"

Anywhere you like.

He cleared his throat. "With the tight squeeze, you don't really need grip bars."

Was he actually discouraging her from hanging on to him? That went too far.

He continued, "But once we're on the open road, you *will* want something to hold on to," he said. "Just wrap your arms around me."

Did she blush as she nodded?

"Or you can steady yourself by holding on to my hips," he said.

Yep, she was definitely blushing.

"You can also hook your hands around my thighs."

Now her cheeks went scarlet as she leaned over the bike, murmuring, "Mmm-hmm."

"Whatever feels..." He was about to say "best" but switched to "safest." Then he touched her hand, making her jump.

"Hey," he said, meeting her eyes. "I want you to be safe, but I also want you to be comfortable. No matter where you put your hands, I'm going to presume it's to hold on and nothing else, okay?"

Her lips twitched. "No matter where I put my hands?"

And *that* was a puck pass. Just not enough of one for him to reply that she could grip on to anything she wanted.

"No matter what *non-distracting* place you put your hands," he said, though he was pretty damn sure it was all going to be distracting.

She tugged on her helmet as he climbed aboard and leaned the bike her way, bracing on one leg. It took her a few tries. Then she was up and sliding down right against the small of his back, her body pressed to his, her legs wrapped around his.

Tight quarters indeed.

He grinned, pulled down his visor, and motioned for her to hold on.

CHAPTER FIFTEEN

MASON

At first, Gemma had only gripped his jacket, which was kind of disappointing, but Mason had focused on the rest—her legs, the heat of her body, the thrill of having Gemma Stanton on the back of his bike. Once they got up to speed, though, her hands moved to his hips, and when he took a tight curve, they went around his waist, nestled right under his jacket.

Yep, this had been a very fine idea indeed.

He would admit that a selfish sliver of him didn't want to pull over at the arena for a lesson. That part wanted to keep going with Gemma exactly where she was, take off up the coast and feel her pressed against him, shifting closer around every corner and down every hill.

But he had promised a lesson, and so a lesson she was getting.

He took her to a suburban arena under construction, the back lot empty. Then he stopped the bike, lifted his visor, and looked over his shoulder at her.

"How you doing?" he asked. "Warm enough?"

She flipped up her visor, and her smile made his heart skip.

"Ready for a lesson?" he said.

"You really don't need to," she said. "I know you have insurance, but this is a very expensive—"

"I don't care," he said. "I care that you're having fun, okay?"

Did her cheeks redden again? She ducked his gaze, almost shy, as she nodded.

"Now hop off, and I'll set you up."

She did, and he waited until she'd stepped away before swinging off himself.

"It really has been a long time," she said.

"Do you still remember where the gas pedal is?"

She gave him a look for that. "Yes, I remember that a motorcycle has a throttle, not a pedal. I also rode dirt bikes as a kid. I know what I'm doing. I just feel the need to be very clear that it has been a long time, in case you want to change your mind about me being on your very expensive…" She turned, following as he walked behind her. "Where are you going?"

He grabbed her around the hips, making her give an adorably girlish shriek. "Helping you up. It's a big bike. Also, you seem a little gun shy."

"I am not— Put me down, Moretti."

She squirmed and laughed. A delicious bubbly laugh that made him want to keep carrying her for as long as he could get away with it.

"Shit," she said when he hoisted her onto the bike. "You aren't kidding. This is way bigger than I'm used to."

He couldn't suppress a snorted laugh.

Her cheeks reddened, and she wagged a finger at him.

He lifted his hands. "You said it, not me."

"Yeah, yeah. I just meant it's a big bike."

"I'm a big guy. Everything's gotta be proportional."

Her cheeks flamed now, but she smiled, too.

"I'm just saying that I'm accustomed to a much smaller…" She threw back her head. "Damn it. There is no way to make this any better, is there? Fine. I give up." She looked him in the eye. "I'm accustomed to riding something much smaller."

"I'm sorry to hear that."

"Yeah, yeah. It's not about the size, Moretti. It's about maneuverability. And in the case of a motorcycle, size *is* maneuverability." She waved her boots. "My feet are nowhere near the ground. That isn't safe."

"I have an idea. First, though, let me get a photo."

He shifted so he could get a shot while she was on the bike. When he showed it to her, she rolled her eyes.

"I look like a little kid trying out a big kid's bike. Do not send that one." She chewed her lip. "I'd like something where I look…I don't know."

"More like you know what you're doing?"

She exhaled, as if relieved he got it. "Yes."

He pocketed the phone. "We'll circle back to that. For the lesson, what if I get on behind you?"

"Uh…"

He put his leg up and eased on, and he really just meant to test the fit, but then he slid firmly up against her as she bent forward to reach the handlebars.

He looked down to see his crotch pressed up against Gemma's ass. His cock had already started stirring from that conversation, and now it just kept rising as it found itself in a very comfortable spot indeed.

Oh yeah. He was really glad he stopped for this lesson.

"How's this?" he said.

"Better, I think?"

She wriggled backward, and he tensed, but if she felt anything, she must have mistaken it for his jacket and kept adjusting, her ass wriggling against his crotch.

"It feels safer knowing one of us can touch the ground," she said, "but the extra weight might make me more unsteady." She turned to look at him. "I'm just really worried about laying it down, Mace."

She'd called him Mace again. He smiled.

"Mason?"

He put his hands on her hips. Respectfully on her hips.

Respectfully? You're grabbing her hips while her ass is pressed against your cock.

"Don't worry," he said. "Yeah, it's big, but just take it slow and everything will be fine. Ease into it."

She stared at him and then burst out laughing.

He replayed what he just said. "Fuck. I didn't mean it like that."

"I know, which made it so much better." She glanced back, her eyes twinkling. "You also sounded as if you've said that before."

Were *his* cheeks heating now?

"Sorry, couldn't resist," she said, and then she twisted around again, which rubbed her ass into his cock, and she leaned back against him, as if in apology for making him blush, and damn, that was nice, Gemma relaxing into his arms, nestled between his legs, her hands on his thighs.

Could he stay here? Just for a few minutes. Let her get accustomed to the size of the bike.

She slapped his thighs as she sat up. "Enough goofing around. I will indeed take it slow, and if it's too big—" She threw her head back again, helmet clinking his. "Damn it."

"If it's too big, you can just climb off," he said.

She choked on a laugh. "That's very understanding."

He opened his mouth to say he was used to it, make her laugh, but then realized he could be overselling this. Not that he had any problems in that area. He was a big guy and well proportioned. But, yeah, best not to oversell it.

She slapped his thigh lightly again and leaned forward to take the handlebars, which again lifted her ass up into a very sweet position.

"Ready?" she said.

He slid his hands onto her thighs and eased forward. For safety.

"Ready," he said.

GEMMA

They'd rounded the block twice with Mason on the back. After that, Gemma had felt confident enough for a solo ride around the arena parking lot. He asked her to lift her visor so he could get photos, and those were the ones she agreed he could send to his publicist, along with one he'd snapped of both of them, her on the front, him leaning over her shoulder to get the shot. Once Terrance posted them, Gemma shored up her nerve and reposted the one with her and Mason, adding Fifteen years since I sold my bike. I've upgraded :) ;) :)

She knew she should add the hashtag. That was Social Media 101. But the hashtag seemed to confirm she was dating Mason Moretti and…yeah, she couldn't do that. But she came up with her own. #ChauffeuringTheMace. Which made him laugh. Before she hit Post, she considered adding something about it being a Ducati motorcycle, to be clear that's what she meant by the upgrade comment…and then she decided not to. If they thought she meant Mason, let them.

Fake dating media obligations fulfilled, Mason proposed a ride up the coast, and Gemma agreed. Soon she was holding tight to his back, and all she could think was *I needed this.* She'd needed it so damn bad that she was happy for the helmet, shielding her face as they whipped along the coastal roads. Happy that the helmet was pressed to his back as he drove, so he couldn't see her eyes brimming with tears.

They were tears of joy but also tears of grief and anger for how far she'd let her life tumble. Wasn't divorce supposed to have set her free? Shouldn't she have already bought a motorcycle? Already spent countless hours zipping along the coast, stopping to walk, finding a little cove, pulling out her laptop and working by the sea? She was free of Alan, but she hadn't flown from that cage. The door was open, her captor gone, but the world beyond still seemed…

Scary?

That sounded childish. What she feared, though, was stepping out that door and discovering it changed nothing. That she was free but still grounded, forgetting how to fly.

She needed more of *this* in her life. Spontaneity. Joy. Time spent accomplishing nothing more than making herself happy.

The motorcycle lesson had been a blast. Goofing around, a little flirty, but the safe kind of flirty she needed so badly.

Just like she needed this, being pressed up against Mason, feeling the heat of him, the muscles of his thighs moving under her hands.

It took serious willpower not to slide her hands along those thighs. The sensation of a very attractive man pressed against her, when she had not so much as kissed a man since…well, she couldn't remember the last time Alan had kissed her before he walked out.

She missed physical intimacy. Oh, she missed sex, too, but she'd lacked intimacy for so much longer.

This was safe, intimate contact with a very attractive guy, and Gemma was going to enjoy every minute of it. If she had the feeling she might enjoy reliving this ride in her dreams, possibly with a few less platonic amendments, well, she couldn't control what she dreamed, right? In reality, Mason had to stay firmly on his side of that line, and he seemed okay with that, which was…

Good, she told herself firmly. It was good.

Speaking of good, the scenery was freaking amazing—endless beaches and distant islands and then zooming up along cliff edges, the ocean below wild and raw, surf crashing.

When Mason pulled off on an interior road, disappointment pinged through her. He didn't go far—just expertly wove along narrow roads until he reached a tiny cabin on a secondary highway. A coffee shop, she realized. The parking lot was empty and the patio furniture wrapped, but a light burned inside, and a neon steaming cup proclaimed it was indeed open.

Mason parked and got off the bike, popping his face shield and then rubbing his gloved hands together. "Up for a hot drink?"

"Definitely."

"We can grab sandwiches, if you're hungry."

"You can, but I've been dreaming of those pastries and cookies we packed from breakfast."

He grinned. "Works for me."

He held the shop door open for her, and a wave of delicious heat hit. The place was tiny, with only a couple of tables, but a fireplace blasted away the dampness. While that made it tempting to sink into one of the plush chairs, Gemma had a feeling the heat would be a bit much for how warmly she'd dressed, with leggings under her jeans and thick socks in her hiking boots.

There was no one at the counter until Mason stepped up. Then a barista appeared. They were in their midtwenties, with spiky platinum hair and wire-rimmed glasses. Seeing Mason, their face broke into a grin.

"It's the Mace!" they said and then waved around the shop. "For once, there's no one to hear me say that, so you can't give me shit."

The barista went still and turned, as if just noticing Gemma, who was checking out the secondhand book selection.

"She's with me," Mason said, and as she walked over, his arm went loosely around her shoulders. "Cal, this is Gemma. Gemma, Cal, brewer of the best cup of coffee for ten miles."

"The *only* cup of coffee for ten miles," Cal said with a glare at Mason. "Ignore him. He doesn't ride all the way up here for mediocre coffee."

"Nope, it's the ocean view," Mason said. "It's worth mediocre coffee."

Cal tapped gorgeously painted nails on the counter. "You know, the other day I was thinking I hadn't seen you in a while, Mason, and I felt like my days here were missing something. Now I know what it is. Your charm." They turned to Gemma. "There's a back door if you need an escape. Just blink twice."

"The coffee is excellent," Mason said to Gemma. "Cal knows I'm kidding."

"More like being an—" Cal coughed and looked at Gemma again. "Ignore us. Mason has been coming here for a very long time, and the fact he keeps coming back tells me everything I need to know about my coffee. Now, what can I get you?"

Mason started to answer but Cal lifted a hand.

"I wasn't talking to you, Hockey Guy. Ladies first. Gentlemen second. That means *you'll* be waiting awhile."

"While I'm sure the coffee is great," Gemma said, "I'd really love a hot chocolate, if that's okay."

Cal smiled. "I make an even better hot chocolate. Milk or dark?"

"Dark please."

"Same," Mason said. "In those travel cups, as usual."

Cal reached for the travel cups, which were fancy vacuum-sealed ones with the shop logo. "You could save some money by bringing back the old ones for a refill."

"Too much work. I leave them in the locker room and pretend I don't notice that someone always walks off with them. By this point, half the Growlers are drinking coffee out of cups with your logo."

Cal's smile grew. "If you really want to make up for razzing me, I'll take a social media–suitable photo of them drinking from my cups."

Cal went still, one hand on the milk aerator, and slowly turned to Gemma. "Wait. Social media. Are you the romance author?"

Gemma tried not to cringe. She knew what would come next. What would always come next. The romance author who used Mason Moretti as the model for her hero.

"Guilty," she said, trying for a smile.

"I *heard* about that. Some chick you two went to school with tried to say you wrote your book about Mason because the guy on the cover kinda looks like him." He looked at Mason. "If you squint. A lot. Also, the cover model had all his teeth."

Mason's look of outrage made Gemma bite the inside of her cheek.

"I have all my teeth," Mason said.

"Don't joke about my coffee," Cal said to Mason, "and I won't tease you about your teeth. As for that interviewer?" An eye roll. "What a witch. Was she nicer in school?"

"Not to me," Gemma said. "I made the mistake of thinking high school mean kids could grow up to be decent people."

Cal snorted. "That's like expecting hockey players to have all their own teeth. Yes, yes, Mason. You do, and you're obviously very proud of it, as you should be. It's an accomplishment."

Mason glowered, as if not sure whether to be insulted. Gemma shook her head and took her hot chocolate as Cal passed it over. The doorbell tinkled, and Cal looked up.

"Be right with you!" Cal called. They finished the second hot chocolate, passed it over, and rang it through with perfect professionalism now that someone else was in the shop.

"Thank you, sir," Cal said to Mason. "I hope to see you again sometime."

Mason grunted something, but Gemma didn't miss the twenty he slid into the tip jar before they left.

CHAPTER SIXTEEN

GEMMA

Outside the coffee shop, they snapped a couple of photos for their social media and their publicists. Then they returned to the coastal route and went maybe another five kilometers before taking what didn't look like an actual road. It led to the kind of deserted cove Gemma had been fantasizing about writing in earlier. Mason parked the bike and led her to a spot sheltered from the wind, where he spread a blanket from the saddlebags.

She opened her mug and took a long draw, closing her eyes and sighing in pleasure as the warm cocoa slid down.

"So good." She opened her eyes and looked at him. "Thank you for this. For today. I didn't realize how much I needed a break, and this one was perfect." She looked at him. "I really had fun."

"That was the plan."

"I don't get enough of that—" She cleared her throat. "Anyway, thank you."

He stretched out his legs and took a bite of his croissant. "You think you'll get a bike again?"

"I do."

"Did you give yours up when you got married? I know a couple of guys whose wives asked them to stop riding. Motorcycles *are* dangerous. Other drivers don't always see them."

"Yes, it was when I got married, and he did claim it was for safety, but…"

She gripped the mug. That was more than she intended to say.

"He made you give up the bike?"

No one makes me do anything. That's what she wanted to say. What she wanted to snap, chin lifted, eyes flashing.

"I thought he was worried, when he was just…" She shrugged. "Clipping my wings."

Mason inhaled sharply. "Fuck. Well, I'm glad you got away."

Her fingers tightened more on her mug, and before she could stop herself, she said, "I didn't. He left."

She straightened. "Look at that view. Let's enjoy that, shall we?" She reached for the pastry bag.

"Whether he left or you did, you still got away."

"Did you pack any of those jam cookies?"

"You don't like talking about it?" he said, and she could almost laugh.

Whatever gave you that idea, Mason? Why, yes, I love talking about the humiliating experience of my divorce.

"Fine," she said. "Let's do this. I married a guy who sold me a false promise, and he'd claim I did the same. He wanted a corporate wife, and he thought—with a few tweaks—I could be that. So he wooed me, won me, and then set about trying to remold me. At this point, do you know what I should say, Mason? What I would *love* to say? That he couldn't break me. That I stood up to his bullshit with both middle fingers raised. But that's not the story. The story is that I stayed in that marriage and tried to give him what he wanted, until the day he walked out. Sixteen months later, I saw him again in the initial divorce proceeding, with his girlfriend and eleven-month-old son."

She could see Mason doing that math.

"Yep," she said. "And that is the full scope of my humiliation. Thanks for asking."

He looked over, gaze meeting hers. "I'm sorry that happened to you, Gemma."

Her eyes filled, and she looked away, wanting to stay angry, needing to stay angry. Angry with Mason, for making her admit to that.

But he didn't make her, did he?

She chose to.

"I should have left," she said. "That's the worst of it. That I stayed. But it wasn't as if he changed overnight. It was like that story about putting a frog into boiling water, and it'll do anything to get out. But if you put it in normal water and slowly turn up the heat, it doesn't notice it's dying until it's too late."

Her voice caught, and she dropped her head, eyes shutting. "I'm talking too much. Can we change the subject?"

Something brushed her leg. Gemma opened her eyes to see Mason beside her. His hand hovered over her bent knee, his expression asking for permission. She nodded, and he squeezed her knee.

"My mom never left my father," he said. "Part of me used to—" He rubbed his free hand over his mouth. "I'd get frustrated. Wonder how she stayed with him. Blame her, even. Why not get out? But it was like that frog in the water. And it wasn't as if he was always awful to her. She loved him, and she clung to those moments when he was nice, and I just wanted…"

His free hand fisted. "I should have done more. I should have seen she was trapped, but instead of helping her get away, *I* got away. Left as soon as I could and then threw money at her, as if that would fix the problem, as if it was all she needed."

He looked up. "I'm not saying your marriage was like that. Hell, I don't know what I'm saying. Just that I know it's not easy to leave— or to even realize that you need to leave. By the time I figured that out, it was too late."

"Too late?"

He shrugged. "Mom passed away seven years ago."

"Oh!" She reached to lay her hand on his. "I'm sorry. I didn't know. I remember your mother, from when she'd help at school."

He quirked a smile. "She remembered you, too. Used to ask every now and then how that Gemma girl was doing. She said—" He shook it off and cleared his throat. "Anyway, however it happened, I'm glad you got away from him, and also, I would like his home address and an identifying photo. For reasons."

Gemma smiled and shook her head. "Good thing I know you're kidding."

"Kinda not, though if he's paying alimony—which he damn well better be—you might not want me paying him a visit." He paused. "Unless he forgot to switch the beneficiary on his life insurance."

"Oh, I'm sure he did that right away. As for alimony, I didn't want anything tying me to him. Also, please don't pay him a visit. It'd make him way too happy. You're his favorite player."

Mason stared.

"Not joking," she said. "He thinks you are the *bomb.*"

"Well, he's never getting an autograph now."

Gemma choked on a laugh. "That'll teach him."

"Oh, I won't stop there. I am having my lawyer draw up a cease and desist. Your ex is not allowed to call me his favorite player ever again. I am officially evicting him from the Mace Moretti fandom."

Gemma leaned against Mason, and he put his arm around her shoulders.

"I *could* deliver my cease and desist in person," he said.

She shook her head. "It's enough to imagine his face if you did. You're right. I'm glad I got away, however it happened. I'm free of any ties to him."

"Including no kids, which must help."

Gemma stiffened.

He must have caught her expression, because his eyes widened. "Just because you don't have them doesn't mean you didn't want… Fuck. I put my foot into it, didn't I?"

She squeezed his hand, still resting on her knee. "It's okay. Yes, I wanted kids. We both did. I had…a few miscarriages, and the doctor suggested we take a break and consider other solutions, which, apparently, Alan did without me."

Mason's grip tightened. "Bastard." His head leaned against hers. "My mom lost a few pregnancies. That's why I'm an only child. I remember how hard it was on her. She cried a lot, but only when she thought no one could hear. Otherwise, everyone acted like nothing happened. One day there was a baby coming and the next there wasn't, and everyone behaved as if there'd never been one in the first place."

Gemma leaned into him, letting his arm tighten around her shoulders. "We have a weird way of dealing with miscarriages, and I never realized that until it happened to me. I don't think of them as lost children. They were never born. I never held them in my arms, but…" Her voice caught. "They had names. Hopes. Plans. Even if those only existed in my head. And then they were gone, and I got a day off work to recover, as if I'd had food poisoning. My family was different—they grieved with me—but Alan? He treated it the way you said, like they'd never been there at all, and maybe that was his way of coping, but…"

She took a deep breath, her chest constricting. "I'm sorry. This is way more than a simple explanation about why I gave up motorcycles, isn't it?"

His hands went under her, and before she knew what he was doing, she was on his lap, his arms tight around her.

She tried to force a smile and gripped his lapels. "This is a very expensive jacket, and you do not want the leather ruined by salty tears."

He didn't return her smile. Didn't say a word. Just pulled her to him and patted her back, and she tried to hold out, she really did, but then the dam burst and she started to cry.

MASON

Mason could say the universe had taken pity on him for last night, but without even trying—too hard—he had made Gemma happy. She'd cried, too, but it wasn't because of anything he'd done, which was a refreshing change of pace.

She'd opened up to him, and now he understood what she'd gone through with that absolute bastard of a husband, and he could rest easy in the confidence that he could clear that low bar without even breaking a sweat.

Now they were walking along the beach, holding hands. He'd taken hers when she'd been crying, and then he just kept holding it when she said she'd like to walk. He'd waited for her to shake him loose. She hadn't. Which was a damn good omen, if you believed in shit like that. He was going to start believing in shit like that.

He liked this, walking and sipping their hot chocolate. He couldn't even remember the last time he'd held someone's hand. Grown men put their arm around a woman. But that felt like saying, *This is mine*, while holding hands felt like saying, *I'm with her.*

Sure, this technically wasn't a date—even if he'd decided it absolutely was. Picking their way along the rocky beach hand in hand felt like being a kid and holding tight so you don't get lost. So the tide doesn't sweep either of you out to sea. It was comforting and reassuring and just...nice. Really nice.

They'd navigated to a stretch of beach where pockets of sand dotted the rocky shore. The wind whistling past made his eyes sting, but he lifted his face to it and let the mist spray him as he inhaled the briny smell of the sea. They couldn't talk over the crash of waves, but that was fine. It was peaceful.

When Gemma paused to look into a tidal pool, her curls whipped in the wind. She tucked hair behind her ears and glanced over at him and smiled, and his heart did a weird squeeze.

He shoved the insulated mug into his pocket, pulled out his phone, and snapped the photo while she was looking away. Then he tugged her over and got a couple of selfies of them both before they resumed walking.

CHAPTER SEVENTEEN

MASON

Mason had dropped Gemma off at her place. He'd offered dinner, but she had work to do, so he sent steak to make up for her missing the rib eye last night.

He parked in the back lot at Nonna Jean's. His grandmother was always there on Saturdays. It let her pretend that she hung out at the restaurant to avoid cooking during Shabbat, but really she was there to putter and to terrorize.

Mason snuck in the rear door and nearly mowed down a server he didn't recognize. The young woman backed up fast with a yelped "Oh! Mr. Moretti!" He waved without looking back and continued to the kitchen, where he found his eighty-two-year-old grandmother on a stool, peering into a simmering pot.

Even this early, the kitchen was pure chaos. Or it looked that way, though Mason knew the chaos was as synchronized as a clock. Prep cooks zipped about but never got in each other's way. The two chefs guarded their stations. Pots clattered, someone shouted orders, food sizzled and popped and boiled. It smelled like Mason's childhood—olive oil and balsamic vinegar and garlic—and he could taste zucchini carbonara in the air.

He slipped past a station where a few misshapen pieces of deep-fried artichoke had been rejected. He popped one still-hot piece into his mouth and then headed for his grandmother's station. When one of the line cooks glanced over, Mason raised a finger and she quickly looked away. Then he crept up and put his cold hands over his grandmother's eyes, making her yelp.

She turned around and swatted him. "You want to give me a heart attack?"

"Testing your ticker. Seems okay."

She swatted him again, and then gestured at his boots with a string of Italian for tracking in dirt. So he removed them right there, which earned him a third swat. He grinned and went to pick up the dirty boots, but she stopped him, catching his face between her hands, turning it this way and that as if examining him for signs of illness.

"What?"

"You look happy," she said. "I should take a picture. I don't see that very often these days."

He rolled his eyes and squeezed her hands before moving his boots to the back. When he returned, he grabbed a bowl and headed for a pan of Pharaoh's Wheel, but Nonna stopped him and, out of sight of the cooks, made a face. In other words, the baked pasta dish wasn't up to her standards. That always made him laugh because if *he'd* cooked it, it wouldn't have been nearly as good, but it would still be perfect to her.

She took a plate and went around loading it up, ignoring the cooks' protests that those were guest orders. For herself, Nonna would have placed an order and waited. But her grandson shouldn't. There was no point arguing. Mason was the only son of her only son, which made him a proper little prince, even long after he'd grown up.

Once he had his plate—kosher-compliant carbonara, crusty fresh bread, and salad—and she had a bowl of soup, she waved him to her office. As they were about to step in, the manager appeared, saying, "Mr. Moretti—"

"No," Nonna lifted a wizened finger.

"I just want—"

"If you have a question, you will ask me after my grandson leaves. You will not bother him. He must eat and have quiet. There is a game tomorrow."

Again, Mason didn't interfere. He'd speak to the manager later and find out what she wanted.

Inside the tiny office, Nonna pointed at the little table and chair. "Sit."

He did, and he dove into the food while she sat across from him and watched.

"There is a girl," she said.

He arched his brows.

"Everyone is talking," she said. "You have a girl."

"I'm thirty-six, Nonna. If I have a girl, someone should be calling the cops. Yes, I spent the day with a *woman*."

"This one they are talking about? A writer?"

He nodded as he tore off a piece of bread. "We went to high school together."

"Wait. Is this...? What was her name? Jenna?"

"Gemma. Yeah, that's her."

His grandmother's stern face lit up. "No wonder you are so happy. I remember little Gemma with the curls and the saucy tongue. The girl who used to help you with your reading. You once brought home a story she wrote and read it to me. The whole thing."

His cheeks flamed. "I don't remember that."

"I do. You had such a crush. And now you have found her again." She leaned forward. "Keep her. That is an order."

He smiled and shook his head.

"I mean it," she said. "Why did you not bring her for dinner?"

"Because I don't think she's ready to have my grandmother taking her measurements for a wedding dress."

"Ha! I would only have tried to get her finger size so you can buy the ring. First things first."

"She had to work. She's on a deadline for her next book."

Nonna's grunt said this was a satisfactory answer. "Good priorities. I hope you ordered dinner for her so she does not need to cook."

"I did."

She patted his hand. "That's my boy. So you went out with her today?"

He fished out his phone and thumbed through the pictures. As he did, Nonna's hand tightened on his.

"You look so happy," she said. "I told your mother you only needed time and then you would meet someone."

Mason's chest clenched at the thought of his mother. She'd never pushed him to find a girlfriend. Never hinted about a daughter-in-law or grandchildren. But that was how she'd been. She didn't expect life to give her a damn thing she wanted, and so she never admitted to wanting anything.

His mother *had* wanted that daughter-in-law and grandkids, though, and if the end had come slower, maybe cancer instead of a heart attack, would Mason have tried to find someone, just to make her happy in the time she had left? Probably, which would have been a disaster, but he still couldn't help wishing he'd done it for her. That he'd done *something* right for her.

"She'll know," his grandmother said. "And she will be so happy for you."

"It was one date, Nonna."

"You will get more. You always get what you want, if you try hard enough. You just haven't wanted this before."

Except he *had* wanted it before. With Gemma. And the only person he had to blame for losing it was himself.

Nonna squeezed his hand. "Do you know what the trick is to winning this girl?"

"Be myself?"

Did he imagine her hesitation? Her hand patted his again. "Be your *best* self. Now eat."

He was about to set the phone aside, when it vibrated with a message. He'd had it on Do Not Disturb, where it only let in messages from his grandmother and his coach, the two people he never dared ignore. After dropping off Gemma, he'd turned on all messages again, in case she tried to get in touch. Instead, it was his publicist, and apparently far from the first message Terrance had sent that afternoon.

Mason opened the thread.

"Mason," Nonna said, clearing her throat dramatically. "Put the phone down."

"I know." He leaned over to kiss her cheek. "But I've had it off all afternoon, and someone's been trying to get in touch with me."

"Your phone should be off. It's still early. The sun hasn't set."

"Five minutes?"

She sighed and rose. "Torta margherita or torta tenerina?"

"Margherita, please." While he liked a good flourless chocolate cake, he preferred the simple sponge one.

"Finish your dinner while you play with that thing."

He scrolled down the list of texts.

Terrance: Where have you been?

Mason: With Gemma. Remember?

Terrance: Yes, and the last thing I got was two photos outside a coffee shop, with gorgeous scenery that had me sitting by my phone waiting for more. I did not get more

Mason thumbed through his photos and sent a few.

Terrance: Excellent! Is she okay with using these?

Mason: Sure

Nonna returned with their dessert, and he was about to put the phone away when he got another notification. *A Highland Fling* had just been delivered to his audio library.

He smiled, pocketed the phone, and dug into his cake. Guess he knew what he was doing this evening.

*   *   *

Mason found a pair of earbuds in his jacket, so he started listening to the audiobook as soon as he left the restaurant. Yeah, having headphones on while driving a motorcycle wasn't safe, but he couldn't help himself.

By the time he got to his condo, he was a little confused. The book was good, obviously. He knew nothing about eighteenth-century Scotland, but Gemma took him there. By the time he was a half hour into the story, he was immersed in historical Scotland while being whisked along in an action-packed story about a young woman traveling alone through the Highlands, a governess who'd been going to meet her new charge when her coach driver turned out to be a grifter who stole everything she had and left her by the roadside.

That was all good. The confusing part was that he expected he'd have met the main character by now, but there was just this young woman, crying at the roadside in her tattered gown. That was *not* Gemma. Gemma would have grabbed the reins, twisted them around the coach driver's neck, and left *him* by the roadside.

Then along came this total asshole who gave the young woman shit for flagging him down. Okay, at first, he mistook her for a thief, but even once that was cleared up, he kept going on about how he had an important meeting because he was an important guy, and sure, he eventually let her ride in his carriage, but he made a big deal out of it, like he was doing her *such* a favor.

Then it turned out that he was the guy whose children she was going to be governess-ing. Which meant she was stuck with this asshole.

Wait, this asshole's name was Laird Argyle. Wasn't that...?

Nah, couldn't be.

Still, he was confused. This wasn't the first romance he'd read, and he was pretty sure you usually met the main couple right up front. Gemma must be doing it differently.

CHAPTER EIGHTEEN

GEMMA

Gemma had written two thousand words in two hours. Was that a record? These days, she was lucky to get a quarter of that. The words were singing tonight, and she could blame a hearty dinner of rib eye steak and loaded baked potato, with crème brûlée for dessert, but she knew it wasn't about the food. It was about how the food arrived on her doorstep. About the guy who'd sent it there. The guy who'd given her such an amazing day that she wasn't even cringing remembering how she'd broken down and sobbed on his shoulder.

She'd had fun. It was such a small thing. A thing she used to have all the time. She'd grown up in a family that was always doing something, often on the spur of the moment, heading into the world in pursuit of whatever seemed new and exciting. Climb a mountain. Ride a horse. Rent a Sea-Doo. Chris had been the quiet one, happily participating, but sometimes bringing a stack of comic books. It was Gemma who'd led the charge.

In university, she'd done the same, organizing "adventure days" with friends. She remembered coming back to her dorm, sweaty and dirt-streaked, no makeup, whooping with her roommate as they stumbled up the stairs. Alan had been standing outside her door. He'd gaped and then steered her off.

"Are you drunk?" he'd hissed. "It's not even five."

She'd rolled her eyes. "The girls wanted to go horseback riding."

"Riding? You're not twelve anymore, Gemma. Did you forget we have dinner with my parents?"

"Sure, at seven. I have plenty of time—"

"And plenty of work to do." He'd shaken his head. "Horseback riding."

She told Mason that the change had been gradual, but that was a lie. She'd always seen that side of Alan. The side that wanted someone sweeter, softer, quieter. The side that made her feel immature for having fun. And she'd fallen for him anyway because part of her wanted to be that woman. To shed the loud and boisterous Gemma. To be the kind of girl a guy like Alan would want.

A guy like Alan. Refined, sophisticated, handsome, and charming.

Not rough-and-tumble Mason. Not swaggering Mason. Not the other Mason either, though. Not the sweet one, the thoughtful one, the vulnerable one.

Alan had been the anti-Mason in every way. And that's what she'd wanted.

Now, after a day with Mason, she could not imagine how she'd ever settled for Alan. How good it felt to rediscover that old part of herself—fun, spontaneous and, yes, vulnerable. What was even better? Sharing it with someone who didn't see a damn thing wrong with any of it. A guy who said he wanted her to have fun but had also pulled her onto his lap for a good cry.

Now she was writing like the wind, with fresh character nuances popping up like spring daffodils, hidden bright spots that felt as if they'd been lurking right there waiting to be uncovered.

When the phone rang, it was Mom, who answered with "I see you had a fancy date last night."

Gemma squeezed her eyes shut. She should have told her mother, who'd been patiently awaiting her daughter's return to the land of the living... and the land of the dating.

"It wasn't a date," she said.

"Looked like one to me."

Gemma tried to gauge her mother's tone. Teasing would mean Mom approved. Yet, considering who she'd been out with, she knew Mom would not approve. The fact her tone was light, if guarded, was the best Gemma could hope for.

"It was a photo op," Gemma said. "Mason felt bad about the morning-show interview, but it was getting positive social media coverage, so he suggested a celebratory dinner."

"With cameras."

Gemma sighed. "That was all preplanned, Mom. He thought it'd be good promo for my book."

A long pause. "And for what he's going through now? With his own PR problem?"

Gemma went still. Shit. Last night, Mason had confessed about Denny, and in all the tumult, she'd never stopped to consider the implications.

He'd said their fake date was all about her. She hadn't realized what was happening to him, and how a little positive PR—showing him as a decent guy—would go a long way toward repairing his reputation.

"It was mutually beneficial," Gemma said quickly. "Are the photos okay?"

"The ones before dinner are lovely. You look wonderful, dear. The one of him with wine on his shirt…perhaps a little less lovely, although at first I thought you'd thrown it at him, which would be understandable. Then I saw it came courtesy of a former lady friend."

Gemma sighed. "Bad timing."

"Something tells me when you're with Mason Moretti, that happens more often than one might expect."

"Oh, I suspect it does." Gemma turned to her laptop and searched for photos online.

"Then there's the one where you leapt in to his defense against some drunken college boy."

Gemma winced. "How bad did *that* one look?"

"Not bad at all, Gem. All the photos reflect very well on you or I would be far more concerned about what, yes, I did suspect was more PR stunt than date. I don't begrudge you that, though I may have had to stop your father from emailing the photos to Alan."

Gemma winced harder.

Mom continued, "What I'm more concerned about are the ones from today, which look…less like a PR stunt."

"Ah, you mean the ones of me getting a motorcycle lesson."

"No, those were very cute. I mean the ones taken up the coast."

"At the coffee shop?"

"No, I saw those, too, and they were lovely if obviously posed. I mean the others."

"Others?"

She barely got the word out before she saw the results of her search. The first photo filled the screen. It was her with the wind whipping her hair around, her eyes glowing, Mason pulling her close as he grinned for the selfie.

Oh.

"Was that meant to be a PR shot, Gemma?" Her mother's voice was soft.

"I..." Something suspiciously like tears prickled, but she wiped them away fast. "I didn't know that's why he was taking it, but since we wanted publicity..."

She trailed off. She wanted to say it was fine. To say she'd known the whole day had been leading up to those photos. But the only thing that came were those damn tears.

"Be careful, baby," her mom said, her voice soft.

Gemma breathed. It was all she could do. Breathe in. Breathe out.

"Those shots before dinner last night were obviously PR," Mom said. "That was a very pretty, very confident woman who looks like my Gemma but isn't quite her. The ones with the motorcycle and at the coffee shop were more you, but still posed. The ones at the beach? Those are *all* you."

Real Gemma. Unguarded Gemma.

"I'm doing it again, aren't I?" Gemma said, her voice so quiet she wasn't sure her mom would hear it. "After Alan, you think I'd learned my lesson."

"Mason Moretti isn't Alan," her mom said firmly. "I can see what Mason is. No one saw the real Alan, not even me. He was cruel and controlling. Mason is just..." Her mother inhaled. "Careless. He's careless with you and your feelings, and he always has been, and that might not seem as bad, but in some ways, baby, it scares me even more."

"Because he's the kind of guy I could fall for, seeing all the rough edges and telling myself they don't matter."

"Rough edges *don't* matter. We all have them. It's the ones that can cut that count."

Gemma's eyes prickled. "I need to stop making the same mistake. I finally got away from one guy who hurt me, and what do I do? Bounce back to the first guy who hurt me."

A moment of silence. Then: "Has he said *why* he did that in high school?"

"No."

"What *has* he said?"

Gemma sighed and switched the phone to her other ear. "He takes the blame and acknowledges I was hurt. But he hasn't apologized. He's never apologized, and that should be my signal to get out now."

Her mother exhaled. "I'm not sure it's that simple, baby. I get the feeling Mason is a lot more complicated than he seems. If he's acknowledged the harm, then that's an apology in his way. But you deserve an explanation, and I think you need to ask him for one."

"Or just never see him again. That seems like a fine option right now."

Silence.

"Mom? It's okay to agree with me. To tell me that I should walk away."

"I'm…not sure that's the answer, Gem. You might need to work through this. Get answers about Mason and how you feel about him, either way." A deep inhale. "But I'm not going to interfere any more than I already have. Just know that if you want to talk, I'm here. Whatever you decide, we'll support you, unless we see you getting hurt." Mom's voice cracked. "We already did that once. We saw you changing, slowly, and we worried, but..."

"I put up a good front, and I wasn't letting anyone past it. Even you."

"Which is no excuse. We should have pushed. That's fair warning, though, that if we see something, we *will* say something."

"Thank you, Mom. I appreciate that."

MASON

Mason was sitting on his sofa, staring into nothing as he listened to the audiobook. His motorcycle helmet lay beside him, but he hadn't taken out the earbuds since first putting them in. And he hadn't stopped the audiobook.

He didn't understand what he was listening to. Was calling it a romance one of those marketing things? Like those ads calling Mason "the player of his generation"? Hyperbole, that was the word for it.

Was that it? The publisher wanted to call it romance, so Gemma had to pretend it was?

So far, he mostly just had this governess—Edin—and her boss, Laird Argyle. The guy was some kind of Highland knight, a really good fighter...who knew exactly how good he was.

That part wasn't bad—nothing wrong with well-earned self-confidence. The problem was how he bragged and acted like it made him better than everyone. He was rude to his staff, including Edin. And he seemed to be screwing everything in a skirt. Edin had already stumbled on him with two women, one of whom she'd later found crying because Argyle had sent her on her way with a necklace, paying her off like a sex worker.

The guy was a self-absorbed braggart who went through women like tissues and…

No, this *wasn't* the hero. It wasn't the guy Gemma based on Mason. It couldn't be.

Another character had just appeared. A baron's daughter who tore Laird Argyle a new one when he flirted with her at a masquerade ball. Fuck. *This* was Gemma.

As Mason listened, he grinned, his discomfort falling away. Okay, this new woman wasn't actually Gemma—they just shared a few traits. Still, Lilias was far more his kind of character, and far more what he expected Gemma to write.

Lilias must be the main character.

So who was *her* love interest?

Could it be Laird Argyle?

No, because if her love interest was Laird Argyle, then Laird Argyle was based on him, which he could not—

Wait. What was happening?

It was still the masquerade ball scene, and Edin and Lilias were comforting a woman Laird Argyle had "cut." That meant he'd ignored her, refusing her invitation to dance, while others whispered that Laird Argyle had bedded and abandoned her.

Edin and Lilias were comforting this woman when Laird Argyle walked over, bold as brass, and asked Lilias for a dance. Right in front of the poor woman he'd ignored. Lilias ran him off with the sharp edge of her tongue, and all that wouldn't be more than extra proof—if he needed it—that Argyle was a jerk, except…

Eighth grade. The Halloween dance. Mason came dressed as a

zombie hockey player, because everyone expected him to dress as a hockey player and he hated to disappoint. Also, it was an easy costume.

He'd been circling the dance floor, working up the courage to ask Gemma. She never came to dances, but her friends must have talked her into it, and he was going to take advantage. It was just a dance. No big deal. Except it *could* be a big deal, having Mason Moretti take her onto the dance floor, and if she liked that, maybe…

Maybe what?

He wasn't sure, only that he didn't want to blow his chance. When he saw Jennifer Miller making a beeline for him, he'd tried to duck out of sight, but he was Mason Moretti—it was hard to hide.

He and Jennifer had a bit of a thing that summer, when she'd been happy to do things to him that other girls their age weren't ready for yet, and hell yeah, he'd gone for it, but then school started and she seemed to expect to be his girlfriend. Mason didn't have girlfriends.

Jennifer found him and asked him to dance. He said no. She left. Then a few minutes later, he spotted Gemma over at the side, sitting on a bench talking to a girl. Perfect.

He made his way over, determined to ask Gemma to dance. When he realized she was talking to Jennifer, that was a little awkward, but he just kept plowing forward, like skating through the defense, his eyes on the net.

"Stanton," he said, casually leaning on his stick. "You wanna dance or something?"

Gemma stared at him like he'd asked if she wanted to light herself on fire. The music *was* really loud. She must have heard wrong.

"You're asking me…to dance?" she said before he could repeat himself.

"Sure."

She shot to her feet so fast he quick-stepped backward. Then her hands went to his chest, pushing him farther from the bench.

"You're asking me…in front of Jennifer?" she hissed when they were away from the bench. "In front of the girl who's *crying* because you turned her down for a dance?"

"Uh…"

"You are *such* a fucking asshole, Moretti."

"What? No. I'm not dating Jennifer. I wouldn't ask anyone else to dance if I were. I'm not like that."

"No, you're just the kind of guy who'll mess around with a girl all summer and then refuse to be seen in public with her."

"What, no. I—"

"The kind of guy who treats a girl like she's only good for messing around with and then asks another girl to dance in *front* of her. While that girl is *comforting* her."

"I didn't know you were—"

She grabbed the front of his hockey jersey and shoved him toward the dance floor. "Go find yourself a girl who likes assholes, Mason. 'Cause that ain't me."

Mason surfaced from the memory and hit Stop on the audiobook.

Laird Argyle was him.

He was Laird Argyle.

He was the asshole.

CHAPTER NINETEEN

GEMMA

Gemma was cross-legged on the recliner where Mason had sat—was that only a few days ago?—and hatched this fake dating plan that was all about benefiting her and not at all about him. She'd stared at his hands and his thighs like a horny teenager, barely able to focus on what he was saying.

He'd lied about the PR being all for her. He'd promised her a dream date, only to arrange it without consulting her. When they'd discussed using photos from the motorcycle ride, she'd been clear that she had to approve his choices, and he'd readily agreed...only to send ones she'd never even seen.

She should give him a tongue-lashing that'd send him running for good. That was the obvious answer. That was definitely the Gemma Stanton answer.

So why was she hesitating?

Because Mason was a liar and a manipulator, but he was also...

More. He was also more, and that's what made it so damn hard to cut him loose. Even her mother knew it, hesitating when Gemma said she should never see Mason again, gently suggesting maybe Mason was a question Gemma finally needed to answer.

A question about herself. About what she needed. And that

answer might not be Mason Moretti, but if it wasn't, then "definitely not Mason Moretti" was an answer, too, one she didn't have right now.

She remembered how he'd talked about his mother earlier that day, and it spurred another memory. Seventeen-year-old Gemma sitting at her editor's desk, working on the latest issue. The door opened, and Mason slipped in. He'd only just started his mentorship and they were still dancing around each other, uncertain, feeling the tug of childhood but also acutely aware of all the years between then and now.

"Your article isn't due until tomorrow," she said. "Do you need more time?"

He shook his head and gestured at the sofa. "Mind if I crash there?"

She frowned.

"Early practice," he said, and then, as if realizing that wasn't an excuse for a guy who had early practice almost every morning, he added, "Long night. My folks were fighting. You know how it is."

No, she didn't. But she wasn't saying that.

She pushed her chair back. "Does that happen a lot?"

Mason collapsed onto the ratty sofa with a satisfied groan, as if dropping onto the finest pillow-top mattress. "Often enough. Dad comes home drunk. Mom thinks he wasn't drinking alone, which he probably wasn't." Then he muttered, almost too low to hear, "Asshole."

"I'm sorry."

He shrugged as he plumped a throw pillow under his head. "I'm used to it. Mom's used to it, too, which is the problem." He paused. "He doesn't hit her. I'd step in if he did. When I tell her she should leave, she just cries and says everything's okay and she loves him, and there's not much I can do about that, right? Can't fix her shitty taste in men."

He shut his eyes. Then they popped open. "Fuck. That was TMI, wasn't it?"

"It's fine." She wanted to say she was here if he ever needed to talk, but that sounded trite and presumptuous. "That's why the couch is here. Like being in a shrink's office. Only cheaper. Of course, since I'm not qualified to be a shrink and can offer no useful advice…" She shrugged. "You get what you paid for."

He smiled. It was his real smile, one that warmed his brown eyes, and made him look, well, *real*. Not Mason Moretti. Just a guy.

He started to close his eyes only to pop them open again. "Uh, what I said, I'd, uh, appreciate it if you didn't tell anyone."

"I might not be a shrink, but the rules of confidentiality still apply." She sobered and met his gaze. "I don't talk about anything you tell me, Mason. Anything."

He frowned, as if genuinely puzzled. "Why not?"

Now she was the one frowning. "Do you want me to?"

"No, just…people usually do, you know? Last week, I bought throat drops in the caf, and by the end of the day, ten kids had asked how my throat was feeling."

"It's nice that people care."

He gave her a sidelong look. "It was a game night, Stanton. That's why they cared."

He was partly right, of course. But they also cared because he was the school's brightest star. Information on Mason Moretti was social currency.

Knowing that his dad screwed around and came home drunk?

That was winning the gossip lottery. As much as kids loved polishing the golden boy's crown, they loved tarnishing it even more. Gemma could bump her reputation up two levels with this story.

Instead, she wondered what it would be like, knowing people were watching your every move, hanging on your every word, not because they cared, but in hopes it could be mined for social currency.

That question seeped through time, settling in her mind now. If being high school golden-boy Mason Moretti had been rough, what was it like being the adult version? The bona fide hockey god?

The thought brought a dull ache, something that felt too much like sympathy.

Sympathy for the devil.

Mason could be an asshole. The problem was, even when Mason was being an asshole, he did it in a way that wasn't cruel. It was…

Her mother called him careless, and that was it exactly. He didn't hurt others because he was an asshole. He hurt them because he was careless.

That didn't make it okay. It didn't mean his rough edges couldn't cut her. They had already. So she should run, right? Cut him loose and count herself lucky.

She looked at the pile of takeout boxes. Yes, he could be careless, but he could also be incredibly considerate.

Telling Gemma to take off her coat for photos on a freezing night…and then tripping over himself to make sure she had everything she needed to stay warm today.

As if he'd realized his mistake and made sure he never did it again. Which was better than any apology, right?

I don't know Mason, but I get the feeling he's a lot more complicated than he seems.

Gemma looked at the photo still on her laptop, the two of them at the beach, Mason smiling his real smile, Gemma smiling hers.

Cut him loose and count herself lucky?

If only it were that easy.

MASON

Mason thought he had this book figured out. Okay, yes, Laird Argyle was clearly based on him, but that was okay because it was what they called a redemption arc. Mason had read romances before, and it was one of his favorite storylines. The heroine sees past the worst in the hero and helps him become a better person, worthy of her love. Worthy of her trust, really, because that was even more important.

This meant, following the pattern, that Lilias was the heroine. You take a guy who can be a jerk, and you pair him with a woman who won't put up with that shit, a woman who doesn't gently show him the error of his ways but kicks his ass until he wakes up.

This was probably why he liked this kind of story so much. Because it reminded him of Gemma, who'd never taken his shit.

But that wasn't how this story went. Laird Argyle sniffed around Lilias, only to be firmly rebuffed. It seemed he hadn't really been all that interested in her anyway. The true object of his desire was . . . Edin?

In Edin, Argyle apparently saw a sweet innocent virgin who would . . . ? Hell if Mason knew. Clear up the venereal diseases he must have caught dipping his wick in all those women before the age of condoms?

Apparently, it was one of those stories where the love of a good woman makes a man better. Those stories were bullshit. His mom had been a good woman, and she'd loved his dad, and look where it got her. Mason's father just took advantage, walked all over his mother, and made them both miserable, dragging Mason down with them.

It seemed that Lilias's role was the voice of reason. She kept trying to tell Edin that she was making a mistake. Sure, Laird Argyle loved his children, but that wasn't enough. He could be a strong warrior and a good lord without being a complete douchebag.

Edin didn't listen. She was in love. Or at least in lust, because that's when the sex started. And, hoo boy, once it started it didn't stop.

At first, Mason had fast-forwarded. If Argyle was him and Edin *wasn't* Gemma, it felt really awkward "watching" Argyle and Edin have sex. But eventually he was able to separate himself from Argyle and enjoy really hot sex scenes that made him temporarily forget he'd been the role model for an asshole.

Even knowing that romances required a happily ever after, Mason couldn't help hoping that this happily ever after would involve Argyle's untimely demise, freeing both Edin and Lilias to make proper matches in book two. After all, Lilias was continuing her crusade to stop Edin from marrying Argyle, and it seemed to be working. Maybe—

What the fuck?

Lilias just fell off a cliff.

Mason sped up the audio. He'd already started listening at 1.5x speed, except for the sex scenes, which sounded really weird in chipmunk voices.

Lilias had definitely fallen off a cliff, which meant Edin would nurse her back to health, and in their time together—away from Argyle—Lilias would convince her—

What the *fuck?*

Lilias was presumed dead. She fell off the cliff into the ocean and *died?*

Now Mason was fast-forwarding because he couldn't believe what he was hearing. Lilias was dead, which didn't make Edin realize her friend had been right all along. It didn't even make Argyle realize he was a jerk and vow to change. Lilias's death only removed the obstacle between Edin and Argyle, which allowed them to declare their love and make plans to marry.

There was no ass kicking. Not even a gentle nudge in the right direction. The only change was that Argyle wasn't just "not an asshole" to his kids. He'd pulled Edin into that sacred sphere. She was special, and so he would no longer be an asshole to her, and what the hell was that?

Not the story he'd expected.

Not the story he'd *wanted.*

Not one little bit.

CHAPTER TWENTY

GEMMA

G emma woke to a text asking whether she was awake. She was tempted to answer no. Instead, she shook her head groggily and peered at the name—

Mason. Of course.

Gemma: It's one in the morning, Mace

Mason: I'm downstairs. Can I come up?

Now she was tempted to copy and resend her last text. She supposed she should just be happy that no one had let him through the secure entrance at this hour.

Mason: I read the book

Shit. Gemma squeezed her eyes shut.

Gemma: I asked you not to do that

Mason: I thought you were just being humble

Mason: Can I come up?

Mason: Please

It was the "please" that did it. She stumbled to the front hall and hit the button to let him in downstairs. Then she lurched back to her room and pawed through a drawer for sweats. She'd barely gotten her sweatshirt on when Mason rapped at the door.

She opened it to see him standing there, not leaning against the doorpost, not posturing and grinning. His five-o'clock shadow was two days old now, and his eyes were bleary and downcast. If it were anyone else, she'd suspect them of putting on a show of looking dejected. But Mason didn't know the meaning of humility enough to fake it.

"It's one in the morning, Mason," she repeated.

His shoulders slumped. "I know."

She could point out that she'd been sleeping, but if she expected an apology for that, they'd be standing at this door until Christmas.

"You have a game tomorrow—*tonight*."

More slumping. "I know."

Why the hell couldn't he be angry? Why didn't he come storming over to ask why she'd based such a despicable character on him?

She'd never seen that side of Mason, though. Call him out on his shit, and he was either confident that you were mistaken or he was... this. And "this" was impossible to ignore.

She waved him inside and strode to the living room without holding the door. She plunked onto the love seat and waited. She wasn't offering him a beverage. She doubted he was staying that long. He'd just come to make sure there wasn't some terrible misunderstanding, and then he'd walk away and she'd never see him again.

Rip the bandage off. Tell him the truth. If he was angry, she'd deal with it.

If he was hurt…

Shit. That was so much harder to deal with. Maybe it shouldn't be. He'd hurt her. Tit for tat. Revenge best served cold and such.

She didn't want revenge. She'd just wanted to sell a damn book and maybe exorcise an old ghost. The old ghost was *not* supposed to show up at her door in the middle of the night and haunt her with his sad-puppy eyes.

"So you read some of the book," she said as he slouched into the recliner.

"All of it," he said. "Listened to it at least." His gaze rose to hers. "Argyle is me, isn't he?"

She bit the inside of her cheek against a denial. Those puppy eyes pleaded for that, but Mason was not a stupid man. To deny it only insulted his intelligence.

Gemma exhaled and pulled her legs up, hugging them. "You were the starting point."

"Why?"

She flinched. But he had a right to that answer, and a right to the real one. "It's a bit of a story."

"Tell me."

She shifted in the seat, knowing she had no hope of getting comfortable for this conversation. "I got back into writing after the divorce. I wrote a romance, and I loved it, but no publisher expressed even marginal interest. I joined an online writers group, and they said the problem was my hero. He was too nice."

"The sort of guy *you* like."

She ignored the implied question and kept going. "They gave me a bunch of romance books to show me what was selling."

He frowned. "You didn't read romance before writing it?"

"I've read romance all my life, Mason. I just have my preferences, and these weren't the books I was reading. One thing those best-sellers had in common was that the guys were..."

"Assholes."

"Yes, and the writers in this group pressed for me to figure out what kind of alpha hero I *could* write. A guy who fit the mold but wasn't cruel or abusive. Just..."

"Me."

Gemma rubbed her hands over her face. "Yes, okay? You were the first guy who sprang to mind."

She looked at him. "You hurt me, Mason, and I'm not going to lie. Was this catharsis? Putting the worst of you on a page and pairing you up with some simpering heroine and shoving you off into the sunset? Happily ever after and out of my head forever?" She met his gaze. "Yes."

"Because Edin isn't you. You're Lilias. The friend who tried to warn her. The friend who wouldn't put up with Argyle's bullshit. The friend who had to die so they could get together."

"That's not—"

"You had her fall off a cliff, Gemma. A literal cliff."

Gemma sighed. "Lilias isn't me, but if you want to get analytical, maybe she represents the part of me that *I* had to throw off a cliff to finish the damn book. And Laird Argyle is not you, Mason. You were...like the sourdough starter."

"There's stuff in there that was definitely me. The masquerade ball and—"

She raised her hands. "Okay, I mined some of our history. I was an idiot not to realize someone like Ashley might notice. But I never intended for anyone to see you in Laird Argyle, and if anyone asks, I'm going with what Cal said at the coffee shop. That Ashley was mistaken."

"Except she wasn't."

She looked at him again. "I am honestly sorry about all this. If it's any consolation, most readers *do* see Argyle as a hero. A hot warrior alpha hero. You can read the reviews. Ashley certainly didn't see anything wrong with the portrayal. But if it embarrasses you, I am sorry."

His gaze lifted to hers. "I deserve it, though, don't I? For what I did to you back then?"

"No, Mason. That's not what I wanted."

He looked down at his hands again, folded between his knees. "Because you're a decent person who wouldn't do that, even if I deserved it."

"The portrayal was based on the you I knew as a kid, Mason, and I didn't even know you all that well then."

"Yeah," he said, his voice low. "You did, Gem. But if you're telling me I'm not like this anymore..." His gaze lifted. "I read that book, and I didn't want to see myself, but I did."

She sighed.

"I messed up our date," he said. "I didn't warn you about the problems I was having, and then I put you in a cab and sent you home. That was a dick move."

Should she let him have that? Just roll with it?

Oh hell, it was the middle of the night, and she was Gemma Stanton.

"*That* wasn't the dick move, Mason."

He hesitated, as if replaying her words, trying to make it fit a narrative where she was telling him he hadn't screwed up.

"What was the dick move then?" he said slowly, as if sure he didn't want the answer.

Okay, she was doing this. "You told me our fake date was all about helping me, and it wasn't. You were getting PR from it, too."

His mouth opened, but she barreled on.

"I wouldn't have minded that," she said. "You just needed to be honest. But you weren't. Then you promised me the date of my dreams, whatever I wanted…and arranged everything yourself. The gift cards were—sorry—insulting."

His mouth opened and shut. Then he said, voice strangled, "How?"

"Because you don't know me well enough to offer that. If we were dating, you could treat me to a new dress and a spa day. Without that connection, it felt as if you were saying I *needed* a new dress—and salon-fresh hair and a manicure—to be your date."

"What? No. I just…it's what I do."

"For every woman you go out with."

"Yeah."

"And you don't see how that makes it worse? Like Laird Argyle having a box of necklaces, pull out one for every woman?" She waved off his response. "The date and the cards are minor offenses. Making me think the PR stunt was all for me is a bigger one. And what you did today? Just as big. Maybe even bigger."

"Today?"

"I thought we were just spending some time together. Two old classmates hanging out. Yes, we discussed releasing photos, and

I was fine with that, but I asked to approve any photos you sent. Hell, before that, you literally said, 'No personal pics without your consent,' and I thanked you for it."

He went still. Very still.

"Did someone hack your phone and release those beach selfies of us, Mason?"

He hovered there. Then he sunk back down. "Shit."

"You released them."

"My publicist asked for photos, and I sent them."

"Without my approval?"

He slumped into the chair. "It wasn't like that, Gem. I swear. I took the photos for myself, and he asked for more, and you looked really good in it, so I...I forgot what we'd said earlier."

She stood. "I really need to get back to bed. And you need to go home and sleep for the game tonight."

"I can't. Not until I've fixed this."

She squeezed his shoulder. "There's nothing to fix."

"Yeah, there is. Me." He looked up. "I need your help."

"What?"

He pushed to his feet. "Like in high school, when you helped me with my writing. Only now, you'd be teaching me how not to be an asshole."

"How?"

"With lessons and stuff."

"Reform school for assholes?"

A small smile reached his eyes. "Exactly."

She shook her head. "And what would be in that for me?"

He paused, as if this hadn't occurred to him. Because of course it hadn't.

"I could pay—" he began.

She cut him off with a raised hand. "You throw money around like water. It doesn't mean anything to you. I'm not running a reform school—"

"Your new book," he blurted. "You're having trouble finishing." He started to pace, gesticulating like he was presenting a TED talk. "It'd be a reciprocal arrangement. We'll go somewhere. I have back-to-back away games, followed by three days off. We'll take a mini-holiday. Anywhere you want. Sand, snow, safari. Your dream location. Just the two of us."

"A holiday while teaching you—"

"Two hours a day for asshole-reform lessons. The rest of the time is yours to write. I can just...cheer you on."

"Cheerleaders are not conducive to the writing process, Mason."

"Then I won't be there. Except for the two hours of lessons and meals, you'll be on your own to write. Everything will be taken care of. Dinner out if you want it. Dinner in if you want it. House-keeping done. You'll only need to *think* of coffee and it'll magically appear at your elbow."

Damned if that didn't sound...

Nope. Nope, nope, nope. It did, however, did give her an easy escape hatch.

She shook her head. "I wouldn't want to be going out for dinner or having dinner dropped off. I wouldn't want maid service. Too much of a distraction. You'd need to do all that yourself. Make the beds, take out the garbage, cook the meals..."

"Done."

She blinked at him. "What?"

"Done." He smiled. "I can't guarantee it'll be *good*, but I cook for myself all the time. I take out my own trash. And I can make a bed."

"I've seen your room, Mason."

He lifted a finger. "But I *can* make it. When I billeted with families as a junior, I needed to keep my room tidy, and I always did."

She wanted to say no. She should say no. But she'd been so certain that the housekeeping and cooking would put an end to this that she'd boxed herself into a corner. She couldn't outright refuse after he agreed to her terms.

Which meant she needed new terms.

She thought. Thought some more. She had nothing on her calendar. She could lie, but that wasn't right.

"I...I don't know," she said. "It's very sudden and..."

"Think about it. That's all I ask."

She should refuse. Find some excuse. Instead, she heard herself saying, "Okay, I'll think about it."

CHAPTER TWENTY-ONE

GEMMA

Gemma woke to a text, and for a second, she thought Mason had returned. Then she noticed the time. After seven. She picked up her phone.

Mason: Just letting you know I made it to pregame practice

Already? Damn, that *was* early. He did say he had a full day. She sent back a thumbs-up and added Hope you aren't too tired.

Mason: I'm fine. I go home after lunch and nap

Mason: Just wanted to let you know, if you'd like to see the game, I can get tickets. I know a guy ;)

Mason: I realize you're writing, so no pressure

Mason: Also, not a photo op. Just an invite. You and a guest or two

Gemma bit her lip. She really did plan to write all day, but he was being considerate, which made it hard to outright refuse.

Mason: I can promise great seats and priority parking

Mason: Also watered-down hot chocolate and stale
popcorn

Gemma smiled. Her fingers hovered over the keys before she ducked both options and went down the middle again.

Gemma: When would I need to decide?

Mason: Anytime before the game. Just let me know

MASON

Game day started with a practice, which was partly about warming up and partly about providing photo ops for whichever members of the media were currently favored enough to get this "exclusive" invitation. Lately, after the practice drills, the coach had been sending Mason to skate around the far end of the rink. That provided photo opportunities but not interviews. Today, though, when Mason started for his media-doghouse end of the rink, the coach called him back.

"You can stick around if you like," he said. "Test the waters with the friendlies."

"You sure?"

The coach considered, tilting his head as he peered at Mason. "Up to you, but you don't need to take off."

Mason settled for somewhere between the two. He didn't exile himself to the far end, but he didn't hang out at the boards either. He skated fast, turning sharp, and it might look like showing off, but mostly he was just enjoying himself. He stayed close enough to the side boards that he could field questions. Once the journalists realized Mason wasn't making for deep water, it was like enjoying the harbor seals and sea lions until an orca swam past. The crowd surged his way.

"Mason!" someone called.

He lifted a hand in greeting. Friendlier than usual, but not skating over for interviews either.

"Mason!" another called. "How does it feel to be the star of a romance novel?"

Good thing he wasn't facing them. He recovered his game face fast, though, and slow-skated past them. "If Gemma was even slightly influenced by me, it's very flattering. But writers pull from a lot of sources. Mostly, I'm just glad it gave Gemma and me the chance to reconnect."

A moment of silence, as if that wasn't the answer they expected. Mason Moretti should be grabbing the credit in his teeth and shaking it for everyone to see.

Hell, yeah, I'm a romance hero. Was there ever any doubt?

He skated out and did a quick turn to power back past them.

"Have you read the book?" one called as he went past.

"Finished it last night."

"What did you think of Ms. Stanton's decision to have Laird Argyle's castle burn down?"

He stopped sharp, ice shaving up. "You read the same book I did? It was the *neighbor's* house that burned down, and the guy tried to blame Edin, who'd been with Argyle all night but they couldn't admit to that, so it was a problem."

The journalist's mouth opened and shut. Mason fixed her with a look.

"Yeah, I read books," he said. "Shocking, right?"

"Did you like it?" another called.

"How could I not?" Mason said. "It's about a guy who looks like me."

"Is Ms. Stanton coming to the game tonight?"

He was about to say he'd invited her, when he stopped. He'd promised this wouldn't be a photo op. "She's got a deadline," he said as he skated backward. "Maybe when we're in the playoffs."

That got them off and running, asking about his thoughts on their chances, and he dove into that for the rest of the session.

GEMMA

The words weren't flying as fast as they had last night, but by noon she'd written just as much. Which meant, if she kept going, she'd be tapped out by three.

Writing was like teaching that way. She couldn't stand in front of a class and talk for eight hours, no more than she could write for eight hours a day. She'd be mentally wiped out.

So she had no excuse for rejecting Mason's offer.

She remembered when he used to invite her to games. In elementary school, it'd felt like just Mason being Mason, the popular guy charitably inviting the less popular kids. Then in high school, it felt like a reward. She was helping him, and he'd repay her with first-rate seats to his games. Yeah, no thanks.

No thanks because she wasn't interested in hockey? Or because she'd tried so hard to block out *that* Mason and focus on the one she saw in private, as if the hockey-star Mason didn't exist.

When her phone rang, she tensed, hoping it wasn't Mason pestering for a response. Then she saw the number.

"Hey, Grams," she said when she answered.

"Do you have time to talk, dear? You seem very busy, getting all over the society pages with your new beau."

Gemma sighed. "Yeah, yeah. He's not my beau, Grams."

"Sure looks like it in those photos. You two are adorable."

"Are you and Mom running tag team to check on me? Making sure I don't do anything stupid with Mason Moretti?"

"Certainly not. I am on your side, dear, *cheering* for you to do something stupid with Mr. Moretti. If you do, feel free to confess to me. All the details."

Gemma could fairly hear Grandma Dot's eyebrows waggling.

Her grandmother continued, going serious now, "I'm calling in case you want to talk to someone who isn't your mother." She quickly added, "I know you have plenty of girlfriends, but it's the weekend and they might all be busy."

Gemma slumped into her chair. *Nice save, Grams.* Apparently everyone knew the sad state of her postdivorce social life.

"Tell me about Mason," Grandma Dot said. "I've heard some from your mother, and I've read plenty of chatter online, but I'd like your version, dear."

Gemma hesitated. Then she took a deep breath and told her grandmother the whole sordid tale.

"Now he's invited me to his game tonight," she said as she wrapped up. "And I don't know what to do about that either. I can't figure out why he's asking."

Silence. Then: "Because he wants you to see him play hockey, Gemma."

"Why?"

"Because he's good at it. Very good at it. And he wants you to see that."

Gemma sighed. "He wants to show off."

"Oh, I'm sure he does, but it's more than that. This is his life. His passion. The thing he excels at. He wants you to see him play. He wants to look into the stands and see you."

"So what do I do?"

"Take your old Grams to a hockey game. Consider it a good deed. Helping the elderly."

"Do you actually want to go?"

Grandma Dot huffed. "What kind of question is that? Don't you remember all the games we went to? It's your damned grandfather who insists on watching from the comfort of his living room."

Grandma Dot mimicked Grandpa Thomas. "*Arenas are cold. The seats are uncomfortable. The food is expensive. The bathrooms have a line.*" She reverted to her normal voice. "I don't know how I ended up married to such an old man."

Gemma smiled. "Good luck, I guess."

Grandma Dot snorted. "Fine. He's a perfectly decent example of the species, but I would very much like to go to a hockey game, especially if the seats are comped. Mason gets to see you in the stands. I get to see a live game without paying for it. Win-win."

"And what do I get?"

Again, Gemma swore she could hear her grandmother's reaction, this time in a knowing grin. "Oh, you'll get something from it, dear. I have no doubt about that."

MASON

After the media skate, it was time for the pregame meeting, where the team discussed strategy and watched game tapes. Mason noticed a bit of an ache in his right knee, but he blamed the rain and yesterday's motorcycle ride. He just needed stretches, an ice pack, and a hot bath, in that order. The stretches came when the coach exempted him from the press conference. Mason grabbed his skates and headed out to enjoy an empty rink.

He was goofing around, certain he was alone, when he noticed a figure near the opposition team bench. The guy raised one gloved hand in greeting, and Mason skated closer, ready to tell him this was a closed rink. Then he saw the face of the other team's enforcer.

"Hey," Mason said, raising his own glove in a high five. Yeah, Topher was technically his opposition, but he'd known the guy for years. They'd both come into the league young and stayed there, big dogs guarding their turf, now approaching their golden years together.

Topher high-fived him back. "Looking good out there, Mace. Still fast as a fucking bullet, you bastard."

"Not *just* fast." Mason sped off and shredded ice with his turn.

"Don't let them see you doing that to the ice before the game."

"Just giving the Zamboni guys something to do. You checking out the battlefield?"

"I've played here so often I know it by heart. I swung by to see if you were around." He leaned over the boards. "About what happened with that kid…"

Mason made a face. "It's fine. My rep's bouncing back."

"Of course it is. You're the Mace. They freaking love you. The problem is that when they love you, they turn on you faster than if you're just another goon in skates."

"They expect better of me."

"Fuck 'em. I just wanted to say…" Topher looked around and lowered his voice. "You did the right thing. I wasn't sure you had it in you."

Mason thumped into the boards, stopping inches from Topher. "Huh?"

"I know how you can be." Topher rolled his blue eyes. "All about the team. Loyalty is great, buddy, but you overdo it. You gotta put yourself first. The team stuff is good for the cameras—and the locker room—but in the end, it's all about you."

"Uh-huh." Mason fought the urge to skate backward and disengage from the conversation.

"You gotta do what you gotta do," Topher said. "High-sticking anyone who even *suggests* we're ready to be put out to pasture."

"Yeah, fuck that."

"Right? And sometimes…" Topher looked around again. "Sometimes you gotta let the hotshot kids get knocked down a peg or two.

Show them what real hockey is. They're too soft these days. Not like us old-timers."

"Don't pull that back-in-my-day crap," Mason said. "Back *before* our day, you and I would've been on the permanent injury list by thirty."

"But you know what I'm saying, because you've finally figured out who you need to worry about. Not your team. The guys up there." Topher jabbed a finger toward the box where the owners sat. "You need their attention, and you got it."

Mason grunted. He had no idea what Topher was saying, but he'd learned that noncommittal noises were usually enough.

Topher continued, "You showed them who's the real MVP. Not some kid barely old enough to vote. It's the guy who protects their shiny new toy from getting broken, and if you don't? The kid's on the sidelines for a few games."

Was Topher implying he'd let Denny get hurt on purpose?

"And you made your point," Topher said. "Their new toy got broke, and the game went on. You guys are still winning, and you're personally playing better than you have in years because you've got some breathing room now, not playing bodyguard to some kid who'll crumple under a hard stick."

"Hold on," Mason said. "I wouldn't—"

Topher socked him in the shoulder. "Of course you wouldn't. You're a team player." He winked at Mason. "Your secret's safe with me. I've been telling everyone it was all a mistake. I know Mace, and he wouldn't let a kid get hurt on purpose."

"Thanks..."

Topher's eyes met Mason's. "You'd do the same for me, right?"

"Mace!" someone called. "Lunch!"

Mason glanced over. His teammate tapped his watch. "Reservation at one. Unless you're planning on skating there, you'd better move."

Mason waved that he was coming. Then he looked at Topher, but the other guy was already walking away.

If Topher thought Mason could do that, how many other players were quietly thinking the same thing?

Was Denny thinking it?

CHAPTER TWENTY-TWO

GEMMA

As Gemma led Grandma Dot into the busy arena, she checked her texts. The app opened a few messages above the one she wanted.

Gemma: Yes to tonight. I'm bringing my grandma

Mason had responded with a string of thumbs-up emojis that made her feel a little guilty for her underwhelming agreement.

Mason: I could meet you there, but I know you don't want this to turn into a photo op

A pause, as if this were a question rather than the statement it seemed to be.

Gemma: Yes, please. Thank you

Mason replied with instructions, starting with where to park—a priority lot with a private entrance that meant they wouldn't take an hour getting out of the arena later. He'd told her which door to enter and then to head for the special pickup window on her left.

She walked up to the window and double-checked the next text.

"Hi," she said. "I have tickets set aside for...Edin Argyle?"

The young woman thumbed through a stack and was about to pass them over when her eyes widened.

"You're the writer." More widening as she looked around quickly and lowered her voice. "Sorry. I guess that's why it's under a fake name. But you're her, right? Mace's writer lady."

Not exactly how she'd describe herself, but Gemma found a pleasant smile.

The young woman scrambled through a pile of stuff at her elbow. Then with a crow of victory, she pulled out a copy of *A Highland Fling*.

"I just started, but it's so good." She looked at the tickets. "Oh! Edin Argyle." She grinned. "That's a spoiler, right?"

"I think it's just Mason being funny."

Grandma Dot leaned over and whispered, "Offer to sign the book."

"What?" Gemma said.

Grandma Dot rolled her eyes and pantomimed signing.

"Oh, uh..." Gemma looked at the young woman. "Would you like that signed?"

The girl's eyes lit up. "Please!"

Gemma signed it and chatted until someone else came up to fetch tickets. When they were out of earshot, Grandma Dot said, "Wasn't that exciting?"

"It would be...if Mason hadn't set it up."

Grandma Dot fixed her with a look.

"What?" Gemma said. "You think that young woman just happened to be reading my book?"

"No, I think that girl works for the arena where Mason plays, and she heard about you two and likes romance books and decided to check out yours."

"Maybe."

"I also think Mason knows he's skating on very thin ice and wouldn't risk doing something you might be embarrassed about later if you discovered he'd set it up. Also he's not going through the trouble of using a fake name if he told her who you were."

"So you think she was really reading my book?"

Grandma Dot squeezed Gemma's arm. "Yes, dear. People are really reading your book."

Gemma's smile was so big she had to cough it away before she walked through the arena grinning like a fool.

Mason had suggested they arrive at the last minute, since she didn't need to find parking or line up to collect tickets. It did mean she couldn't stop for concessions, but she wanted to be in her seat when the game started.

They found their section—a private seat grouping at rink level—and had to show their tickets *and* be checked off a list. While the arena was packed—you didn't just decide on game day that you wanted to see the Growlers play—their little area was half-empty.

"VIP seating," Grandma Dot murmured as they went in.

Gemma was still settling in when someone bustled over. It was a young man, panting as if he'd run all the way around the arena.

"Ms. . . . Argyle," he said. "M-Mr. Moretti sent me. To get your order before the game."

"Order?"

"From the bar. Anything you like. On the house."

"Oh, that's very sweet, but we can get it ourselves—"

"No!" the young man blurted, and then cleared his throat. "I mean, there's no need. I can get anything you want and bypass the lines. It's what Mr. Moretti would want."

Gemma looked at the poor kid, his eyes a little too wide, as if begging her to let him fulfill his assigned mission.

"We'd better get something," Grandma Dot whispered.

"Okay, I'll take, uh..." Gemma began.

The young man fumbled to pull out his phone. "I have the menu."

"I'll take a beer," Grandma Dot said. "One of those fancy craft brews. And, since Mr. Moretti is paying, I'll go all out and get a coffee, too."

"Would you like a shot in it?"

Grandma Dot smiled. "Oh, that is tempting, but I'd better not. Just cream please."

"I'll take a beer, too," Gemma said. "The same kind. And maybe an order of..." She skimmed the offerings. "Wings?"

The young man subtly shook his head.

"Nachos?" she said.

He lowered his voice. "That's probably the best option. Anything else? Popcorn? Hot dog? Giant pretzel?"

Gemma smiled up at him. "We wouldn't say no to giant pretzels."

He smiled, relaxing. "Got it. I'll be right back."

As soon as he left, opening music filled the arena and Gemma's head shot up, her gaze going to the Growlers' gate. A moment later, the team skated out, one at a time.

"That's him," Grandma Dot said, poking Gemma's arm. "Number twelve."

As Mason appeared, the scoreboards flashed his mace animation, and the home crowd roared. Whatever PR problems he was having, any jeers were drowned out by that roar of happy fans.

Gemma watched Mason skate to his position at left defense. Other things were happening, particularly at center ice, as the centers prepared for the puck drop, but she only saw Mason. Once he was in his spot, he looked her way. She thought he was just surveying the stands, but his eyes seemed to meet hers, and he lifted one gloved hand, smiling wide enough that she caught a flash of his mouth guard.

The young man hurried over with their food, delivering not two beers but four, along with two coffees, two orders of nachos, four pretzels, and a paper bag full of every necessary condiment and some extras—like pepper and vinegar—that he'd clearly just thrown in to cover all bases.

Gemma took the food and fished a twenty out of her pocket. "I know Mason is comping it, but this is for you."

The young man backed away, hands raised like she was offering him a used tissue.

"It's all covered," he said. "That, too. Mr. Moretti wouldn't want me taking more."

"Then I'll tell him you did an amazing job."

The young man exhaled. "Thank you."

Once the game started, Gemma forgot about the snacks. She couldn't look away. Specifically, she couldn't look away from a certain player with the number twelve on his back.

She knew Mason was good, but seeing him play live was another thing altogether. He was *on*. Really on. The guy didn't shut down even while the action was elsewhere. He had his eye on everything, it seemed, watching for trouble.

If the other team's goon even looked at Mason's players, Mason was there. It wasn't all defensive work. He also blocked one of the opposing players in a way that earned him a penalty. Gemma didn't quite understand what Mason had done, but when it finished, he was back on the ice as if nothing happened, just part of the game.

By the end of the second period, he'd assisted in one of the Growlers' two goals and kept the other team from scoring at least once.

"He's so good," Gemma said.

Grandma Dot only smiled.

"And he's *fast*. I mean, I've seen him play on TV, but, wow."

Mason skated past and did a quick turn in front of them as he had a few times, getting the crowd screaming.

"Someone is showing off," Grandma Dot murmured.

Gemma shook her head. "It's his signature move." She motioned to the scoreboard, with a familiar graphic of a swinging mace.

"Mmm, maybe, but it's odd that he's choosing to do it right in front of *us*. Like a peacock with his mating display."

"Yes, he's showing off, but he does that. The crowd loves it. Can't fault him for winding them up."

"Hmm." Grandma Dot took a drink of her beer. "He does cut a fine figure out there. Like a redwood among the spruce."

Gemma rolled her eyes so hard it hurt. "He's not that tall, Grams. Look at that guy on the other team. He's taller. Oh, and how about that guy way over there. He's on the Growlers."

"That's Mason."

Gemma squinted. "Oh, er, right. Still…"

"Mason Moretti is one fine, tall drink of water. Makes a woman think she'd like to climb him like—"

"No!" Gemma glared over. "Do not finish. I hate that phrase."

"Scale him like a sycamore? Mount him like a maple? Ascend him like an aspen?"

"Stop." Gemma dropped her head into her gloved hands. "Please."

"If I were twenty years younger, I'd give you a run for your money."

"Twenty years younger and *not* married to my grandfather?"

"Oh, that's nothing." Grandma Dot waved a hand. "Mason Moretti is on my list."

"Your what?"

"You know. A short list of celebrity figures that married people agree, if they ever got the chance to hit that, it's a freebie."

Gemma groaned and sank her head lower.

Grandma Dot patted her back. "I'm teasing, dear. I don't have a list. However, if I did, Mason Moretti would definitely—"

"Stop."

Grandma sighed. "All right. I'll refrain from giving twenty reasons why you should take Mason Moretti up on what he's very obviously offering. Changing the subject, I saw those photos from yesterday. Your mother says you went motorcycle riding with him."

Gemma relaxed. "I did. We had a good time."

"You had a motorcycle once, didn't you?"

"Pre-Alan, yes. I might get another one. Mason gave me a lesson on his yesterday."

Grandma Dot looked out at Mason. "I realize it's none of my business, but would it be such a bad thing to climb that particular tree?"

"Yes."

"Because he hurt you before."

Gemma tensed.

Grandma Dot squeezed Gemma's leg. "And that means, sadly, that you can't just take him for a spin, as pleasant as that might be."

"That's not on the table."

"Oh, it most certainly is, dear. He isn't offering to take you away for three days because he really wants to learn how to be a better person."

Gemma sighed. "He has an ulterior motive. As always."

Grandma Dot's lips pursed. "I said that wrong. I think he does want those lessons. If he hasn't made a pass at you yet, then he's not trying to trick you into a sexy getaway for two. He's just open to the possibility. A few days away to get to know him better and to see that he's capable of changing."

Gemma groaned. "Which is what Alan tried to do. Change me. I'd never do that to someone."

"But Mason's *asking*. And Alan didn't want you to be a better person. He wanted you to be a different one. Mason realizes he can be…" Grandma Dot shrugged. "Someone who scares the crap out of innocent young men he sends to fetch snacks. Fixing that isn't about changing just to please you."

Gemma took a bite of her pretzel and watched Mason fly around the ice. She didn't say anything. She didn't think anything. She just watched and felt, and that was enough.

"Ms. Stanton?" a voice said over her shoulder.

She gave a start and looked back to see the legs of a man standing in the row behind her.

"Mind if I…?" A gloved hand appeared, waving at the empty seat beside her.

She squinted up as she twisted, at first just seeing the lights, but then a face…

"Jesse Parnell," the man said, hand still extended.

Gemma scrambled up, wiping nacho chip crumbs from her jacket before shaking his hand. She didn't have a favorite Growler, but if there was a player she admired and respected for his work off the ice, it'd be this one.

"Mr. Parnell, yes, of course. Sit. Please."

"Jesse, please," he said as he swung one leg over the seat and slid into it with a soft thump. He leaned past her, extending a hand to her grandmother.

"Sorry," Gemma said. "This is Dorothy Waters. My grandmother."

"Dot," Grandma Dot said. "Pleased to meet you, sir. I read a lovely write-up on your after-school program last month."

"Thank you." He turned to Gemma. "So, Mason finally got you out to a game, huh?"

Gemma lifted her brows.

He smiled. "He may have mentioned that he's been trying since you guys were in school together. He's in fine form tonight."

"He's really good." She felt her cheeks heat. "Obviously."

Jesse laughed softly. "Just don't go telling him that. He hears it enough. But he's playing very well, which made me wonder whether he'd gotten a certain author into the stands to watch him."

Her cheeks definitely flamed, and she mumbled something unintelligible.

"Mason tells me you teach college English," he said.

"I do. I'm off this term, writing."

He leaned on one hip. "Favorite book to teach?"

She smiled. "Toni Morrison. *The Bluest Eye*."

His brows rose. "Nice one. I took an online university course last

year, and every last book on the syllabus was written by some dead
white guy."

"Which is why I like teaching at the college level. I get a lot more
leeway to pick books I think the kids will actually enjoy."

He settled into the empty seat beside her, and they spent a few
minutes talking book lists and books in general. Gemma got the
feeling it wasn't about books at all. It was about Jesse talking to her.
Vetting her?

"I should let you get back to the game," he said, unfolding himself
from the seat. "Good to meet you."

"Likewise."

He paused, not quite standing yet, and looked out at the rink as
Mason ran defense against the other team.

"He can be a real dick but..." Jesse glanced over. "That's not the
whole story. Not even more than a couple of chapters." Another
look at Mason. "Doesn't mean you need to put up with it."

"Oh, I don't."

Jesse's teeth flashed in a grin. "I figured that. Just...give him
some wiggle room. He's a good guy."

"I know," she said softly.

Jesse said his goodbyes, and after he left, Gemma turned back to
the game.

Mason *was* a good guy. And that was the problem. She couldn't
write him off, not even to protect her own heart.

And maybe that was okay.

The thought hit her with a jolt, and she wanted to fold up against
it, protect that bruised core Alan had left behind. Not let herself
get hurt again. Not take a chance.

But she wasn't going on a "sexy getaway" with Mason. She was taking time to be with him. To figure out how she felt, like her mother counseled.

Three days to risk being hurt again.

And three days to finally take a chance on a guy she'd been dodging since childhood.

She'd written an entire damn book trying to exorcise Mason Moretti, and all it did was conjure him back into her world.

Maybe this trip would exorcise him forever or . . .

Not.

She took out her phone and, while watching him on the ice, typed in the words.

CHAPTER TWENTY–THREE

MASON

Gemma had said yes.

Okay, it wasn't exactly yes. She said she'd like to "discuss parameters," which meant she'd passed the puck his way. He just needed to get it into the net.

He texted back inviting Gemma and her grandmother out for a drink. As exhausting as a game was, he was always too wired to go straight home. The Growlers had won, which meant a celebration, but with Mason being the team's old-timer, no one blinked if he bowed out.

Mason gave a few sound bites to the media and then shed his sweaty padded uniform, showered, dressed, and took the side door to where Gemma promised to wait for him. One of the rink rats would drive Gemma's car home for her, then swing by the pub and take Mason's truck to his place, leaving them to call a driver after they'd had their drinks.

Mason met Gemma's grandmother, who was adorable and would probably cut him for saying so. But then Mrs. Waters decided it was past her bedtime. Mason insisted on driving her home while bracing for Gemma to declare she'd had a long night, too. She didn't. She was quiet, though, and he wasn't sure how to read that.

They finally reached the pub, a little place where Mason could find privacy after a game. When he walked in, he got the obligatory backslaps and high fives and "Mace!" and "Good game!"

The regulars and the staff formed a shield to keep them from being harassed by other patrons. If a phone rose for a photo, someone would stick their hand in front of it. The pub wanted the cachet of having Growlers stop by postgame, so they needed to make sure it was a safe space.

When one young couple tried to sneak a photo, Mason spun on them with a growled "Hey!"

The young woman took the guy's phone so fast you'd think Mason was about to throw a punch. He snorted under his breath. He never hit anyone who didn't hit first. A growl was enough, along with the scowl he fixed on the couple, making them both shrink back.

"Sorry," the young woman mumbled. "It was for my little brother. He's a big fan."

Mason was about to keep walking. Then he saw Gemma, and her expression was impassive, no judgment, but if he said he wanted to be less of an asshole...

"Take it," he said, stepping away from Gemma.

The young woman shot the pic and then glanced at Gemma and motioned, asking her to get into the picture. So she'd recognized Gemma, and maybe she did want a shot of Mason for her little brother, but she also wanted a shot of Mason and Gemma for social media.

Mason shook his head. "She didn't sign up for this."

"It's fine," Gemma murmured.

He nodded and put his arm around her waist, tugging her in. Once the photo was snapped, he motioned that he wanted the phone. The young woman hesitated, as if seeing a vision of it being hurled across the room.

"Show me the pic," he said.

She did, and he let Gemma confirm it was fine. Then he said, "You can post it, but you can't say where we are."

The young woman nodded, and Mason and Gemma got five more steps before someone called, "Ms. G!"

Gemma glanced around, and Mason saw a young man behind the bar, slinging his towel over his shoulder as he walked to the gate.

The bartender pulled Gemma into a tight hug that made Mason's hackles rise. He took a deep breath and rolled his shoulders and told himself there'd be none of that shit. This was obviously a former student, and Gemma was going to be a popular teacher who got a lot of hugs from former students, some of them handsome young men.

Mason pasted on a smile and hoped it didn't look feral. The kid didn't notice. He was too busy talking to Gemma. Mason walked over to hear the conversation.

"Yeah, I got a job in banking," the kid said. "Entry level. Bartending is what pays the bills, though. And the student loans."

"I hear you," Gemma said. "I tended bar for three years while teaching so I could pay off my master's."

Mason mentally filed this away. Gemma had been a bartender. She had a master's degree. All added to his growing tally of data.

He also realized that his hackle-rise was only partly about a good-looking guy hugging Gemma. It was also a spark of envy for anyone who'd had Gemma for a teacher. He remembered how good she'd been coaching him with those newspaper articles, how patient and supportive.

The kid finally noticed Mason and gave a start. Then he put out a hand. "Mr. Moretti. I've seen you in here, but haven't had the pleasure. Great game."

Mason nodded and kept that hopefully nonferal smile in place.

"We should get a table," Gemma said.

"What can I make you?" the bartender called after they said goodbye.

"Something sweet and sour," she called back. "Surprise me."

"Mr. Moretti?"

"Beer. Surprise me."

Mason led Gemma to his usual booth at the back. There were three in a row with Reserved signs on them.

"All ours," he said, taking the middle one.

"Nice," she said.

He shrugged. "The perks of being..."

She smiled. "Mason Moretti?"

"Yeah." He slid out a menu. "I know you ordered nachos at the rink, but the ones here are actually good. Steak nachos?"

"Yes, please."

He leaned out and called the order. Then they discussed the game, a bit awkwardly, Gemma obviously nervous.

He waited until the drinks arrived, and then said, "Okay, you mentioned setting parameters."

She scrunched her nose. "That sounded very teacher-y, didn't it?"

"Nope. It sounded reasonable. Yeah, this is about me learning to be less of a Laird Argyle, but it's equally about you finishing your book, and I don't want that to get lost."

"Thank you. Before we begin, though..." She took a deep breath and a fortifying slurp of her blue cocktail. "I hate talking about my ex. It gives him a power I don't want him having. But in this case, it's pertinent."

She looked up at him. "Alan tried to change me. He bought a fixer-upper and got a money pit. Nothing he could do was going to turn me into the kind of wife he wanted."

"Because he's a prick who has such shitty taste that he buys an amazing house and tears it down to put up a new one."

She smiled slightly. "Thanks, but my point is that I've been the subject of an unwanted makeover, which makes me really uncomfortable with what you're asking for." She shredded a strip off her napkin. "Your personal style works for you, Mace."

"Does it, though?" He leaned forward. "When I was a young player, I was always watching others, trying to learn. Sometimes, I'd see them making mistakes and I'd think, 'Do I do that?' I saw what Argyle did in your book and realize I do the same shit. I'm not asking you to change me, Gemma. I'm asking you to help me see what makes me an asshole. Then it's up to me to decide what I want to change."

He gestured toward the front of the restaurant. "I snapped at those kids for trying to sneak a photo. Asshole or not asshole?"

"Not," she said decisively. "They were sneaking that snap because you clearly didn't want one." She paused. "But it was nice of you to let them take it, and I appreciated that you let me choose whether or not I was in it and letting me check the picture."

"See? Stuff like that. Sometimes, though, yeah, I'm going to be an asshole. I choose to be."

"You kinda have to, Mace. Refusing photos might seem an asshole move, but they disrespected your privacy."

He leaned over, touching his fingers to hers, the barest contact.

She didn't pull away, just stared down at his hand, and he carefully risked putting his fingertips over hers.

"You didn't ask me to read that book," he said. "Hell, you told me not to. You've done nothing to suggest you want me to change. But I also know that…" He shrugged. "When I make a dick move, you start thinking maybe twenty years wasn't long enough."

She gave a soft laugh. "Not that *exactly.*"

"But kinda that."

She exhaled, long and slow. It wasn't an answer, but he could see the net, the shot lined up.

"Parameters," he said. "I'll hire a vacation planner, but you're in charge of all decisions."

She nodded and sipped her drink. So far, so good.

"You choose the destination," he said. "You pick the rooms. Is a two-bedroom suite okay? Or would you prefer two suites? I want you to be comfortable."

"Two bedrooms is fine. We also need a kitchen and a living room. I'm going to want multiple writing spots, preferably a desk or table plus a recliner or sofa where I can put my feet up and work on my laptop."

"Tell the planner, and they'll get whatever you want. Now, I did promise to cook, and I won't renege on that. Just don't expect gourmet."

She smiled at that. "All I care about is that I'm not cooking."

"Okay, well, my repertoire is…" He shrugged. "Limited. I can follow a recipe, though. You could send me ones you like."

"What do you usually make?"

"My grandmother taught me to cook, so it's mostly stuff from our restaurant."

Gemma perked up. "You can make food from Nonna Jean's?"

"Uh, yeah."

"I order from there all the time." She paused, as if she'd given away something she didn't mean to, and then plowed on. "I get delivery."

"I've never seen your name."

She hesitated, as her cheeks pinked. "I, uh, use my married one. Which is silly, I know. Not like you'd have recognized mine and you're the owner—you aren't handling takeout orders."

"I've done pretty much everything from line cook to delivery. The only thing I don't do is front of house." He smiled. "I am a shitty server."

Also, he absolutely would have recognized her name, even if he'd just been flipping through orders. Now he was going to have to look it up and see what she got.

"So that's what I cook," he said. "Italian. Jewish. Jewish Italian. The restaurant is kosher. I'm not, but I usually eat turkey sausage and turkey bacon, though obviously I'll get whatever you want."

"No, that'd be fine. I wouldn't want you cooking anything you can't eat yourself."

"That's food squared away then. What else do you need?"

"I'd like at least four hours a day, in chunks—I can't write for four hours straight. During those chunks, though, I can't be interrupted. That sounds rude but…"

"It's not. I get it. I can leave the room or leave the whole suite." He took a chug of his beer. "What else?"

"That's it, I think."

"So are you ready to answer? Or do you need more time? I wouldn't push, but this is my last stretch off until the bye week in February."

"Yes," she said, blurting the word and then inhaling and saying slower, "Yes, let's do this."

Mason swung through the back door of the bar where he was meeting Jesse and a couple of the others. When he spotted his friend, he pulled Jesse aside.

"She said yes," Mason said.

Jesse one-arm embraced him, his beer held out of spilling range. "And you're asking me to be your best man? Honored, buddy. Honored."

Mason rolled his eyes. "Not that."

"Ah, she said yes to your weird getaway idea. What did you call it? Reform school for assholes?" Jesse waved his beer. "You know, if you really wanted lessons in that, you could have asked me."

Mason waved him off.

"But you didn't," Jesse said, "because I'm not the woman you've been crushing on since kindergarten. It's almost as if this getaway isn't so much about de-asshole-ifying Mason Moretti as giving him an excuse for three days alone with his crush, trapped and unable to escape."

"Of course she can escape. If she wants to."

"Which she won't because you're Mason Moretti."

"Damn straight."

Jesse shook his head. "Would you like an anti-asshole lesson right now?"

"Nope, I'd like a beer."

Mason spotted a server with a tray of them and grabbed one. She looked over, scowling, and then saw who it was and smiled.

Jesse sighed. "At least no one can claim you don't need the lessons."

"What? She smiled at me. It's fine."

"Because you're Mason Moretti." Jesse sighed. "I like Gemma. I feel bad for Gemma. The woman has her work cut out for her." He sobered and looked at Mason. "Please tell me the asshole reform school isn't purely a ruse to make her go away with you, Mace."

"Like I said, when I read her book, I saw myself and didn't like it. I legitimately want to do better."

"For her."

"Nothing wrong with that, and sure, I want the getaway, too. Impress her, let her get to know me…maybe…" He shrugged. "Whatever."

"Yeah, it's the 'whatever' that I'm worried about. If this is a scheme to seduce her, she will see through that shit—"

"It's not."

Jesse shook his head. "Would you like me to tell you all the ways this could blow up in your face?"

Mason sipped his beer. "Not really."

"All right then." He clapped Mason on the back. "Have a good trip."

"Thanks."

CHAPTER TWENTY-FOUR

GEMMA

Gemma had spent the last three days in a strange state between "hockey with Mason" and "trip with Mason." The most significant part of that was the lack of, well, Mason. He wasn't showing up on her doorstep, wasn't texting in the middle of the night, wasn't pestering her for coffee or fake dates. Instead of enjoying the reprieve, she felt this strange sense that she was marking time, waiting.

Mason did text her a few times a day, just checking in. He was obviously busy. Which was fine. Just...disappointing.

Ava had also been delighted to share Gemma's sales figures. They were "better than expected," which would mean more if their expectations had been higher.

Now she just had to finish her second book.

Gemma swung to happier thoughts. Mason would be back tomorrow, and they'd leave for their getaway. She'd decided on a ski chalet. While she wasn't sure she'd do any actual skiing, November in Vancouver always made her long for real winter, the way other Canadians might long for summer. She wanted a cozy cabin with a roaring fire and snow.

When her phone rang, she hoped it was finally the vacation

planner—she still hadn't heard from them. She rolled over in bed, saw that it was a video call, and grinned. That was even better. She hit the Accept button and…

The face filling her screen was handsome. Very handsome, she'd always had to give him that much. A chiseled jaw, perfectly shaven, light brown hair styled just so. While she couldn't see the rest of him, she knew it from memory. Average height. Expensive suit on a trim body.

"Gemma," Alan said.

She resisted the urge to run a hand through her hair and maybe hit a blurring filter. Then she realized she hadn't considered either when she presumed it was Mason. That was significant.

"Alan," she said. "To what do I owe—"

"What is this?" He waved a paper, which was presumably the reason for being on video.

"You'll need to stop waving it so I can see it," she said.

"It's a cease and desist."

Her sleepy brain still struggled to focus. Those words sounded vaguely familiar, but where…

"From Mason Moretti," he said, shoving the page into the camera. "He's ordering me to stop being his fan."

Gemma burst out laughing.

Alan glared. "Did you send this?"

"Uh, no. That's all Mason. I told him you were a big fan, and he joked about ordering you to stop. Also, you are never getting an autograph. Just so you know."

"I suppose you think this is funny."

"Ignore it," she said. "Obviously, it's not legally binding. Now I'm going to hang up—"

"What did you do to your hair?"

Gemma tensed. Alan had always considered her hair her worst feature. In the early years, she'd had it blown out at his insistence. Eventually, she said, "Screw that," and wore it natural, curly and shoulder length. Whenever they'd had a social engagement, he'd tell her to "do something with that" as if she was leaving the house with a small animal on her head.

This was how he'd take his revenge for the letter. Insult her hair. Oh, how far the mighty had fallen, reduced to snide comments about grooming.

"It looks different," he said. "It looks *good*. You've done something." There was a weird accusation in those words, as if after all those years of him wanting her to "fix" her hair, she'd finally done it after their divorce, just to spite him.

Gemma shook her head, making her curls bounce. "Nope. This is my just-woke-up look, Alan. Always has been."

"It looks good." A grudging note edged with anger, and then she got it. This had nothing to do with her hair and everything to do with Mason Moretti wanting his ex and Alan trying to figure out why.

"Goodbye, Alan. I'm going back to sleep now."

"It's eight a.m." His gaze shot to the side, as if he could see beyond her screen, and his voice dropped. "Is he there?"

She paused before realizing he was asking whether Mason was in bed with her, and that's why she was lingering past seven.

Oh, that was tempting. So damn tempting. Inch from the middle of the bed, angle the camera away, and say innocently, *What? No*, in a way that told him Mason absolutely was there.

"No, Alan, Mason had an away game last night, remember? I'm sure you saw it. Now—"

"I saw *you* at the last home game. The camera zoomed in. You never wanted to watch hockey, and now, all of a sudden, there you are, in the VIP section. With Mace showing off right in front of you."

"Goodbye, Alan."

"Wait. I . . ." His blue eyes met hers. "I'm worried about you, Gem. I know the divorce was rough, and you're probably lonely, but when it comes to women, they call him One-Swing Mace. He hits that once and moves on."

She remembered the Camille incident. "I am aware."

"I'm sure they all imagined themselves becoming Mrs. Moretti, but it's not going to happen."

"What? He isn't going to marry me? But he promised!" She rolled her eyes. "If you really think I'm hanging out with Mason Moretti in hopes of snagging myself a hot hockey player husband, you really don't know me at all."

"Hot? He's not even good-looking, Gemma."

She bit her cheek at the earnest look on Alan's face, as if his poor ex was in need of glasses. "Hot isn't the same as good-looking, Alan, and trust me, Mason Moretti is *hot*. You can run a poll on that, and I have no doubt of the answer. He's smoking."

Alan's face reddened, and his mouth worked before he settled for "I just don't want you getting hurt, Gem. I don't want you expecting more than he's offering."

"Do you know what Mason's offering? Fun. And he delivers in spades." Which was true, and if Alan took that in another way, so be it. "Now, I really—"

Her phone audibly buzzed. Seeing the caller name, she grinned before she could stop herself.

"That's him, isn't it?" Alan said, his eyes narrowing.

"Gotta run. Bye."

She flipped over to Mason before realizing it was still on video. "Hold on. I had another call. Let me shut the camera off."

His video popped on before she could. His face filled her phone screen, complete with unruly hair, unshaven face, dancing brown eyes, and a grin that made her insides flip.

"Good morning," he said. Then the smile faltered. "Shit, did I wake you up? No, wait. You were on a call. Someone else woke you up. Whew. I'm not the asshole."

She smiled. "Yep, you're not the asshole. Are you flying back today?"

"I *am* back. Surprise!" That grin again, the one that was half-genuine, half-far-too-pleased with himself, and all charming. Also hot. *Damn it! Stop that.*

"Is it too early to ask you out for coffee?" he said. "We need to discuss trip stuff, but I wasn't sure when you woke up."

She yawned. "Usually before this, but I was up late writing. Coffee would be wonderful. You want to come by?"

"Can we meet near your place? I know a spot. Good breakfast and really quiet at this hour. Bring your laptop, and you can stick around and write after."

She stifled another yawn. "I'll probably write later."

"Well, bring your laptop anyway. Just in case."

She resisted the urge to say she could decide if and when she wrote, but she knew this wasn't a control move. He was trying to be considerate, and sometimes he stumbled.

"Sure," she said. "I'll bring my laptop."

"Meet in an hour? I'll send you the address."

"I'll be there."

Gemma was out her door forty-five minutes later. She checked the address on her GPS. She thought she knew all the local cafés, but she wasn't familiar with this one. It was within easy walking distance, though, which was a bonus.

Or it *would* be within easy walking distance, if she wasn't wearing the boots she'd bought for the morning-show interview, along with the cashmere sweater and her favorite jeans, which she'd deemed too snug for TV. Not too snug for breakfast with Mason, apparently. She wasn't going to overthink it. Not today.

She'd barely reached the corner before a car pulled up at the curb. As the driver's window went down, Gemma realized it was the same guy who picked her up for her date with Mason.

"Ms. Stanton?" he asked. "Mr. Moretti asked me to give you a ride."

She opened her mouth to say she was fine, and then said, "Screw it." These boots *weren't* made for walking.

"Thank you," she said as he hopped out and opened the door.

As she climbed in, she asked the driver how he was doing, and they chatted briefly about last night's game. Then, as she settled in, she saw the two coffees and a box of pastries in the back seat and realized why she'd never noticed a café at the address Mason had given. Because there wasn't one. Meeting for breakfast had just been an excuse to get her out of the apartment, where she could be scooped up and whisked off to some new surprise.

She relaxed in the leather seats. "Are we picking Mason up?"

"Nope, meeting him there. The snacks are all yours."

She read the cups. "Do you prefer cappuccino or hot chocolate?"

He smiled at her through the mirror. "Cappuccino."

She handed it to him along with the open box for him to select a pastry. As she sipped her hot chocolate, she smiled. She'd told Alan that Mason was fun. That'd been a bit of irresistible needling but it was true, too. Even when a date with Mason went horribly awry, it was still interesting, still memorable, still—dare she say it?—fun. The impromptu motorcycle trip. The VIP hockey seats. She needed a lot more of that in her life.

She took the quiet time to answer a few emails while resisting the urge to peer out the tinted windows and guess where they were headed. When the car finally slowed, it was to pull into a small regional airport. Huh.

As they drove in, Mason appeared from the shadows, sporting a cat-with-canary grin. The man was far too pleased with himself. Luckily, *she* was far too chill today to call him out on it. It was, she hated to admit it, part of his charm. Not the showing off, per se, but the childlike delight he took in it.

He was opening her door before she could.

"Hey," she said. "This does *not* look like a coffee shop." She smiled as she spoke so he wouldn't think she was annoyed by the change in plans.

"There is coffee inside." He leaned in and lowered his voice. "But I wouldn't recommend it. Did you bring your . . . ? Oh, good. I'll take that."

"No one touches my laptop, Moretti," she said, clutching the bag with a mock glare as she got out of the car. "You can carry the pastries, though. You can even have one."

A light flashed, and she looked over just as someone ducked out of sight.

"'There's no official media," Mason said, lowering his voice, "but Terrance made sure word got out."

"Oh, uh, okay. So, are you going to tell me why I'm here?"

He spread his arms. "Welcome to your secret getaway."

"My what?"

"Our getaway." He grinned that too-pleased grin. "I know we were supposed to leave tomorrow, but I wanted to get in as much time as possible. So I caught the red-eye back after the game."

"I . . . what? Wait. We're leaving . . . now?"

He waved toward a private charter on the airfield. "As soon as we're on the plane."

"I didn't pack anything, Mason. All I have is my laptop."

"Which is why I made sure you brought it. Everything else?" He grinned. "Supplied."

"I don't even have a power cord."

"It's all packed and ready to go."

"But . . . what . . . what happened to me choosing the destination?"

His smile faltered. "Hmm?"

Someone from the hangar peeked out, camera in hand. Gemma ducked back into the car, as if she'd forgotten something. Her heart hammered, and she knew she should be furious, but all she could feel was roiling anxiety. She hadn't packed. She didn't have her things. He couldn't just expect her to up and leave.

And yet he did, and instead of being furious, she was just disappointed. In him, yes, but mostly in herself.

She knew he was careless. He kept proving it over and over. He hadn't paused to think whether she might need medication, whether she might have plans for today, whether she might just damn well want to wear her own clothing.

She could have gotten past that. Gently explained why this wasn't the grand gesture he thought it was. That was the point of this trip, right? Showing him what he did that was problematic.

What really hurt was the lie. He'd been exceptionally clear that she would choose their destination . . . and then proceeded to plan it all himself.

Surprise!

She felt so damn defeated. But he'd promised her this writing getaway, damn it, and she wasn't losing it because Mason was being Mason.

"Gemma?" he said, sounding concerned.

"All good," she said as she backed out of the car, hoisting her almost-empty cup. "Wouldn't want to forget this."

She hefted her laptop bag and smiled for any cameras and let Mason lead her to the plane.

CHAPTER TWENTY-FIVE

MASON

They were about to take off when Mason got a text from his coach, wishing him a good trip, telling him he deserved the break and to get his ass back on game day. Mason smiled at that…and then he got the next text.

It was from Dr. Colbourne, the team shrink.

> **Dr. Colbourne:** Mason, you've been dodging my requests for a session for the past month

> **Dr. Colbourne:** You know I don't like to push the matter

> **Dr. Colbourne:** But we really need to talk. Call me

He turned off his phone. He'd worry about that later. For now, he was focused on giving Gemma the vacation of her dreams.

He was resisting the urge to ask her where they were going. That would be *his* surprise. The vacation planner had teamed with a subcontractor they used to plan this sort of spontaneous trip, complete with prepacked luggage. He'd sent them his clothing sizes and photos of Gemma, and they'd packed everything needed for the trip Gemma had chosen, including coolers of the ingredients he needed to cook.

They were on the plane now. Gemma was quiet. Overwhelmed, he figured. He'd found the bag with her charger cords, to make sure they had the right ones. When he returned, she was settled in, her laptop case on the seat beside her. That was where he'd planned to sit but no worries. He'd just take the one across from her...

She had her feet on it, her laptop on her legs. Okay, well, she wanted to get some work done. That was fine. It was hard to talk on a plane anyway. He took a seat across the aisle from her.

A flight attendant from the terminal popped on then, explaining where they'd find drinks and snacks, as there wouldn't be an attendant on the small plane. She offered champagne, and Mason was about to say no—it was barely eleven in the morning—but Gemma said, "Please," and he seconded that.

The attendant filled two glasses and handed them out. As she deplaned, Mason leaned over the aisle, smiling, glass extended.

"To our little getaway," he said.

Gemma didn't even look his way. She just bottomed-up the glass, gulping half the contents. Then she set it in the holder for takeoff and returned to her work.

He blamed the engines for the fumbled toast. She hadn't heard him. That was all.

He smiled, to no one in particular, sipped his champagne, and settled in.

GEMMA

Thank God for loud plane engines. The constant roar meant Mason didn't seem to expect her to talk, and she was able to pretend she didn't hear him when he tried. That—plus the champagne—was the only way she was getting through this flight.

The farther south the plane went, the more obvious it became that they weren't going anyplace with snow. He'd assumed she wanted a beach vacation. Because that's what every woman wants in winter, isn't it? To lie on the beach, sip daiquiris, and work on her tan.

Just like every woman dreamed of exclusive restaurants and swooned over guys who sent them a handful of gift cards to "pamper" themselves.

Would Mason make the same mistake with male friends? Presume they all liked hockey, getting plastered on Saturday nights, and eating takeout because they couldn't cook? Stereotypical "guy" stuff that Mason himself matched only on the first count.

When the pilot's voice crackled on the speaker, telling them to prepare for landing, she looked down to see the distant blue of crystal clear water, the glowing white of sandy beaches, and the rich green of waving palms. She allowed herself one final exhale of disappointment before she shifted her expectations and declared that this was still better than Vancouver in November.

She'd survive. She'd write, and she'd walk in the sand and wade in the warm water, and she'd enjoy herself, damn it.

MASON

Huh. He'd figured Gemma would pick someplace more... adventurous. Skiing in the Alps. A villa in rural Italy. A penthouse in Paris. Not that there was anything wrong with beaches. This was exactly the sort of place he came on his bye week, gathering a bunch of buddies and heading south in search of the sun.

A week of forbidden excess mid-season. Eat too much. Drink too much. Fool around too much. Then get your ass back to Vancouver a couple of days early to work it all off in the gym and spa.

This wasn't about him, though. It was about Gemma, and if this was what she'd chosen, it just proved he needed to work harder on getting to know her.

When they'd gotten into the vehicle, the driver had assured them the windows were bulletproof, which Mason figured was a joke, but they'd been in the car nearly an hour and hadn't caught more than glimpses of locals, as if they were on some extended route that actively avoided them. Finally, they reached a huge gate attached to a huge fence... with armed guards.

"Why is there a fence?" Gemma asked, rolling down the divider.

"For your protection, miss," the driver said.

"The entire resort is fenced?"

"Yes, miss."

"And guarded?"

The man smiled back at her. "Yes, miss. You do not need to worry. This is safe. Very safe. Everything you need will be inside here. Your own little slice of paradise."

The car rolled through the gates, which closed behind them with a clang.

This was...

Shit. Mason hated to judge, but this made him really uncomfortable.

"No," Gemma said, her voice almost a growl. "I am not staying here."

She turned to Mason. "I am not staying in a place where rich vacationers enjoy the best beaches behind an armed fence guarding them from the *locals*."

"Agreed," Mason said.

"You...agree?"

"This is definitely not my vibe. I'm guessing the planners didn't run the venue past you." He took out his phone. "Let me make a call and see what I can do."

He was searching for the number when he noticed Gemma staring at him.

"I...didn't pick this, Mason."

"I know. That's the problem. You told them what you wanted, and they were supposed to run all the specifics past you."

"I didn't *choose* a beach vacation."

He caught her expression, and something in him chilled. "Where did you tell them you wanted to go?"

"Nowhere. They never got in touch with me."

"*What?*"

Okay, that came out a little loud, given the way she jumped.

"So they never reached out?" he said. "Ever? They just..." He looked out again as his hands fisted. "Picked this. Themselves. Without consulting you. What the fuck?"

"You were away and busy, and I didn't want to bother you. I figured they just didn't need that much lead time."

Away and busy.

He'd spent the last three days squashing the urge to text ten times a day, to call and chat for an hour...Hell, he'd even had to stifle the impulse to send last-minute plane tickets inviting her to join him.

Gemma had work to do, and he needed to stop being a selfish ass and give her space.

"So *you* didn't pick this either?" she said.

"What? No." He stared at her. "You thought I chose the destination?"

Shit. Of course she did. She figured he'd steamrolled over his promise, like he had before.

"I did not pick this," he said firmly. "I didn't know where we were headed. I was waiting for the surprise."

"Apparently, we both were." She tried for a smile, but it was strained. "Surprise!"

"I definitely told them to call you. I said you were in charge." He fumbled with his phone. "I can show you—"

"That's fine."

"No," he said, sharper than he intended. "Please. Just look." He reached out his phone for her to see the texts and held his breath until she read them and nodded her understanding.

What an absolute fuckup.

But for once, it wasn't *his* fuckup, which meant he got to redirect his panic into well-deserved fury aimed at the people responsible.

"I'll handle this," he said, reaching for the door handle.

"I'd like to get out of the car, too," she said. "If it's safe."

"Perfectly safe," he said, "as long as you're not the person on the other end of my call."

GEMMA

Gemma thought he was joking about the person at the other end of his call. She should have known better. Mason could be chill and easygoing. He could also wield his power like, well, like a mace. One swing for a TKO. He'd made a professional career of being a very scary guy. It just wasn't the whole of him.

Because Mason Moretti, as her mother said, was complicated. He wasn't one thing or another. No one really was. But wasn't that what she wanted in high school? Just the one side of him? As if the private parts she saw were real and the public parts—Mason Moretti, hockey star—were fake.

But it wasn't fake, was it? Just other parts of the whole, and she'd known that and rejected it. Rejected part of him.

Like Alan, who'd seen things in Gemma he wanted—the intellectual Gemma, the articulate Gemma, the Gemma who "cleaned up well"—and tried to excise the rest. Was that what she'd wanted from Mason as a teen? To claim the parts she was comfortable with and shave off the parts she wasn't?

Her gut wanted to reject the comparison. If they'd gotten together, she would never have tried to get him to give up hockey, to be someone different. But she *would* have chosen what parts of his life she wanted and stayed out of the rest, and that was nearly as bad, wasn't it?

Also, a little voice whispered, it would have been a damn tragedy. Because she *did* like the other parts of Mason. She found his braggadocio charming. She admired his confidence. She'd loved watching him on the ice, loved seeing his passion for the game and his fans' passion for him. And she liked this, too. Watching him wield his power on that phone call to get what she wanted, what she had been denied. That was...

Oh, fuck, it was sexy, wasn't it?

Sure, Gemma felt a little sorry for whoever was on the other end of that line, but Mason's anger wasn't an out-of-control fire. It was a surgical laser, cold and precise. The firm really had screwed up, and he was only making that clear.

Also, it was a relief to know Mason hadn't run roughshod over his promise to her. He might make mistakes—she was trying hard not to think about her lack of luggage—but the location issue was also her own fault for not checking in.

Clearing up the choice of locale might not be as easy.

Gemma looked around the resort and tried to focus on the sunshine, so bright she'd fished long-abandoned sunglasses from the bottom of her laptop bag. She'd enjoy three days of that, right?

"Gemma!" Mason bellowed.

She looked over to see him holding out the phone. A woman walking past shot her a sympathetic look that might hold a touch of Cal's "blink twice if you need help." That confused Gemma for a moment. Then she remembered that Mason wasn't a hometown hero here. He was just a big angry guy seeming to yell a summons to his poor little wife.

If Gemma had been with Alan, she'd have cringed under that woman's look and felt obligated to smile back an *everything's fine*. But with Mason, she didn't need to defend either of them. Everything *was* fine.

"You're on speaker," he said as she walked over. "Tell Gemma how you guys screwed up."

Gemma murmured that wasn't necessary, but Mason shook his head. It was necessary to him.

The woman on the other end said something about miscommunication, not her assignment, didn't know how it happened, could only presume the subcontractor looked at Mason's file and thought they knew what he wanted, based on his past trips.

"Trips with *friends*," he said, as if this was also important. "But we don't go to places like this."

"Yes," the woman said, "but this is a top-tier couples resort, known for—"

"Not the point," Mason said. "You've confirmed that this was entirely your firm's oversight."

"Yes, sir."

"Now, Gemma, where would you like to go? Name the spot. Anywhere in the world."

The woman tentatively cleared her throat. "That is, of course, your choice, sir, but your luggage has been tailored to this climate, and you do only have three days."

"Don't care. Gemma gets what she wants. That was the deal."

"I'm fine with a beach vacation," she said. "I would like to maximize our time."

Mason gave a low growl, as if she were settling, which she was, but that was also her choice, and at a hard look from her, he went quiet and nodded.

"Not here, though," she said. "If at all possible."

"Definitely possible," Mason said, in a tone that defied the planner to disagree. "Tell her what you want, and you'll have it, because I'm an important client who not only gives them lots of business but sends lots of business their way."

"Y-yes," the woman said. "We want to make this right, Ms. Stanton, and if you're fine with staying in the general area, we will accommodate any other needs. It *is* the off-season, which helps."

"What do you want?" Mason asked, his voice low, intended just for Gemma. "Name it."

She thought of her ski-vacation idea and amended the basics to match. "A private villa, if at all possible. Two bedrooms. A living space. A kitchen."

"Full kitchen," Mason said. "Not a microwave and bar fridge."

"We can certainly get you that," the woman said. "What else?"

"The living room needs a recliner or sofa so I can write. A desk is helpful, but not essential." She looked around. "Outdoor seating would be a huge plus. Patio, balcony, anyplace where we can sit and enjoy the weather."

"And a beach, I presume?"

"I don't need beachfront. But a nearby waterfront would be great. Someplace to swim."

The woman's fingers tapped over a keyboard. "Would isolation bother either of you? A private villa that isn't close to restaurants and such? I see here that you planned to make your own meals."

"Isolation is fine," Gemma said when Mason's glance lobbed this question her way. "Oh, and if the villa was owned by locals, that would be a big bonus."

"Understood. I have a few options, but I might not be able to secure one in time to get your approval before you fly out. Is that acceptable? Taking all this into consideration, may I choose a place while you're en route?"

"That's fine," Gemma said. "Thank you."

CHAPTER TWENTY-SIX

MASON

Mason was very aware of their time together ticking away. By the time they reached the new place—if they got one—it would be dark. He'd been so pleased with himself for flying back last night to squeeze an extra day into their trip, and they'd lost it to this fuckup.

There was also another problem, which had required a text to his coach.

> **Mason:** Can't make it back until game day

> **Mason:** It's a shit show here. They completely fucked up the travel arrangements

> **Mason:** I was booked to fly out for the evening before the game, but we had to stay somewhere else, and they can't fly us out until the next morning

> **Mason:** I will make the game, though. Guaranteed

When a reply didn't come, he presumed that meant it was fine. Then, as they were settling onto the charter boat, he realized he had a missed call from his coach. He motioned to Gemma that he needed to make a call inside the cabin. Only, when he got there, he saw that he'd already lost signal. He checked his messages. Nothing.

Well, if it was urgent, he'd have gotten a "Call me back now" message.

As he pocketed his phone, he looked out the cabin window. Gemma stood at the bow like one of those wooden mermaids on old ships, leaning into the wind, her hair whipping. She'd changed into an outfit from their new luggage, a tank top and denim shorts. As the boat roared along, mist had already soaked the tank, fabric clinging to her body. Water glistened on her arms. He could only see her from the back, but he knew she was smiling.

He was getting a second chance with Gemma Stanton.

That's what this trip was about. Yes, he meant it when he said he wanted those lessons, because he wanted to do better for her. And he absolutely meant it when he promised time for her to write. That was part of showing her what he could be—a partner who understood his high-flying career wasn't the only important one.

He might not have planned the trip himself, but from here on out, it was all about giving Gemma what she needed. Proving he could be the *guy* she needed.

He'd lost her once, and he wasn't doing it again.

Lost her? Or thrown her away?

He'd fumbled the puck. He'd seen it right there and, instead of gently stickhandling it to the net, he'd turned and skated away, as fast as he could.

Why? Even thinking the question made panic rise up and his defenses slam down.

Don't look over there. Look here, at everything you've accomplished. Look at your trophies. Look at your fan groups. Look at your condo and your bank portfolio. Look at Nonna Jean's and Nonna. You did good there. Made your grandmother's dream come true. Whew. Focus on that. The other stuff doesn't count.

Except it did. It really did.

Gemma turned from the bow then, and she *was* smiling, hair blowing in her face, green eyes dancing.

He tucked the doubts into his pocket. He'd figure this out. He'd figure it *all* out. He smiled back and headed to join her on the deck.

GEMMA

Their destination was indeed going to be a surprise. Such a surprise, in fact, that they weren't quite sure what it was even *after* they arrived, because it was already pitch dark. All they knew is that it was an island. They had the sole villa on a private island. Well, she had said "isolated" was fine.

They reached the dock, and the crew helped them unload and then carried their bags up to the villa. Gemma and Mason let the crew go on ahead as they enjoyed an incredible walk along a solar-lit path, hearing only the lap of water and the crunch of sand underfoot. Soon the crew was heading back to the boat. Mason tipped them as they passed, and then they were alone.

Gemma could make out a huge front deck, with multiple options for seating, including loungers and club chairs. Down on the sand was a circular canopied daybed and, as Gemma imagined curling up there with her laptop and a cold drink, she decided this would do nicely. Very nicely indeed.

Oh, who was she kidding. This was already the nicest place she'd ever stayed, and that included vacations where Alan shelled out for the sort of fancy hotels that always made her feel underdressed.

Then they stepped inside, and Gemma whistled. This wasn't fancier than those five-star hotels, but it was definitely more her style. Cozy and casual, with an emphasis on comfort. In front of her was a full kitchen with stainless steel appliances. To her right sprawled a living room with a couch, two recliners, and huge windows. There was even a fireplace, in case nights got nippy.

"Wow," she said.

"Is this okay?" Mason said, his eyes dark with genuine worry.

"Did you miss the '*wow*'?" she said.

"Yeah, but...we should have specified a living room separate from the kitchen, so you can have privacy for writing. And from here, I see what looks like three doors—two bedrooms and one bath. You probably want your own bathroom."

She smiled at him. "We've already shared a bathroom, even if I didn't ask permission first. This is fine. As for the living room, I have noise-canceling headphones."

His eyes widened. "Shit! No, you don't, because you weren't the one who packed. I didn't think of that. You can use mine."

"I actually do have my headphones. They're always in my laptop bag." She hefted it. "I'm set." She stepped forward. "Is that a bar?"

She walked over to the small bar between the kitchen and living room. Someone had left fresh fruit and bottles of liquor on the counter, and when she opened the fridge, it had mixers and ice.

She rubbed her hands. "Can I make you something?"

He smiled. "That's right. You were a bartender."

"The *best* bartender, if I do say so myself." She pulled out glasses. "I know we should be responsible and unpack first, but I'm starting with a drink on that deck. Join me?"

"Right after I get the perishables in the fridge."

Mere hours ago, Gemma had given this vacation up for lost. Now she was on a lounge chair, listening to the lapping of the ocean and the chirp of night birds as she stared into a sky full of stars. While sipping a mai tai. Did it get better than that?

The glass door whispered open behind her.

"Snacks?" Mason said as he came out.

Okay, it could get better.

Mason walked around her carrying a tray. He'd finally changed out of his travel clothes, and he was wearing shorts and a tank top, with his feet bare. The shorts afforded Gemma her first look at his thighs, which...damn, were they worth the wait. Thick and muscled and pretty much exactly as she'd imagined.

Yep, her night had definitely gotten better.

It was like one of those divorcée dreams, where you ditch the toxic hubby and have a hot guy in a tank and shorts serving you snacks on a tropical beach.

"No?" Mason said.

She gave a little jump and realized he was still holding out the tray. He'd cut up fruit and added cheese, nuts, and little spirals of what looked like thin fried dough, dusted with sugar.

"Manicotti," he said. "My grandmother insisted on sending a care package."

"Manicotti?"

He waved at the fried dough. "It's mostly for Purim, but I like it."

Gemma laughed. "Okay, now I feel clueless. I kept seeing manicotti on the dessert menu at Nonna Jean's and thinking it was someone's idea of a joke. Those look delicious." She took one and a piece of cheese. "Thank you."

He set the tray on a table between them and stretched out on the lounge chair beside hers.

When he picked up his mojito, she said, "I went light on the alcohol. I know it's not your thing, and if you ever want your drinks booze-free, just say so."

"Going light is fine. I can have a drink or two, but any more, and you'll be abandoning me on this lounge chair."

"I will, because I cannot get you to bed."

Silence. Then he burst out laughing.

She reached over to swat his biceps. "You know what I mean. You're too big."

More laughter, snorted now.

"Fuck." She rolled her eyes. "And I've only had a few sips of my drink, so I have no excuse."

"Hey, I just want credit for avoiding the very obvious response that getting me in bed isn't that tough."

"So I've heard."

"*Ouch.*"

She grinned over at him. "The real challenge, apparently, is getting you back in bed."

"Yeah, yeah."

She glanced over at him. "Don't point out my unintentional double entendres, and I won't bring up your very generous...soul."

He sputtered a laugh. "So am I *allowed* to point out your unintentional double entendres, at the risk of you mocking my generous soul?"

"As long as you accept the penalty, you can take the shot."

"Works for me. So can I get a lesson tonight?"

She sighed. "Asshole reform already?"

"Nah." He squinted up and pointed. "I want to know what that group of stars is. The constellation."

"And you think I know?"

"You're the smart one."

"I'm an English major, not an astronomer. I have no idea what that is, but I could make something up. That is what I do, after all."

He smiled over at her. "Even better. Make something up for me."

MASON

Gemma had fallen asleep, which was perfect really, after they'd joked about *him* doing that. He was totally going to razz her in the morning. For now, he made sure she really was asleep, because while it was romantic—and hot—to carry her to bed, he didn't particularly want her waking and punching him in the gut.

She was definitely asleep, so he scooped her up and carried her inside. As he shifted her in his arms, she snuggled in.

"You smell so good," she murmured.

He went still.

"I smell good?" he ventured.

"Like oranges and cloves."

Oh, that was his soap. He liked the smell, which was mostly why he bought it, even if he'd had at least one woman wrinkle her nose and say he smelled like mulled Christmas wine, which was apparently *not* a good thing.

Unfortunately, he didn't have that soap here—no, wait, he brought it. Along with most of his toiletries, because he liked his own things.

He paused as he realized what he was saying. *He liked his own things.*

And Gemma would like her own things, too.

He winced.

She snuggled into him again, which made the guilt ebb. Also made him wonder where else he could carry her, just so she could keep cuddling against him.

Sadly, if she woke to him randomly carrying her around, he'd deserve that punch in the gut.

He settled her into her bed. As he tugged up the coverlet, she caught his hand and held it.

"I like your hands," she mumbled, her eyes still closed.

"My hands?" he murmured.

"Hot," she said.

"My hands are too hot?"

"All of you. Definitely too hot." She sighed in her sleep.

He finally realized what she was saying, and a slow grin spread across his face. Okay, that was *not* what he expected. He'd made the dumbass move of looking up a photo of Gemma's ex, and since then, he'd been reminding himself that looks weren't everything and maybe she'd be up for a change of pace?

But she'd just called him hot.

Gemma Stanton thought he was hot.

Too hot.

He grinned. Oh, he could use that. He could definitely use that.

He tucked her in, and she immediately burrowed down into the bed. Then he leaned over and whispered, "You ain't seen nothing yet," before slipping from the room.

CHAPTER TWENTY-SEVEN

GEMMA

Gemma was dreaming about Mason, damn it. She'd had many such dreams in the past week. Some took place in that cove along the coast. Some were on his motorcycle. Some were in his condo, starting with that bathroom door opening. One had even been at the hockey game, in a conveniently located closet, before he'd even taken off his uniform.

Such were the perils of being a romance writer. Her imagination got creative. Very creative.

The latest variation involved that circular sofa outside, and Mason in wet swim trunks that left nothing to the imagination. Water glistened down his chest and legs as he crossed the sand to where she lounged. Then he crawled atop her, grinning down, dripping warm water as his lips came toward hers—

A noise had her half rousing from sleep, and while her brain wanted to seize on that and pull herself out, like a swimmer thrown a life buoy, the rest of her said the water was just fine and lulled her back under.

Fantasy Mason's hands slid up her bare sides and toyed with the straps of her bikini top, teasing her, the smell of him enough to drive her mad, and she arched up into him as he chuckled and whispered—

"Gem? You awake?"

She jumped, clutching the covers to her chest like a shy maiden. That's when she noticed light streaming through the window.

A tap at her door.

"Gem?" Mason whispered.

"Hmm?" she managed.

"I'm going to take a shower. I wanted to make sure you didn't need the bathroom first."

"I'm good." The words came as a squeak.

"Give me fifteen minutes, and then I'll start breakfast."

"Okay." Definitely a squeak.

As he padded away, Gemma exhaled and flopped onto the pillow. Her body still burned with that dream, as her brain whispered she should return to it…and do whatever was necessary to alleviate that particular ache. After all, Mason was in the shower for the next fifteen minutes. No chance he'd knock on the door or hear a stray gasp—

The water started up. Right beside her wall.

Mason was having a shower on the other side of her bedroom wall. Mason, presumably naked, because that's how people showered. Mason, lathering up and—

Fuck!

Oh, one bathroom is fine. It has a lock. It's not as if I'll need to listen to him shower, which leads to picturing *him showering literally two feet away.*

It's fine. It's all fine. Just ignore—

A soft groan from the other side of the wall. No, not *that* kind of groan, just the sound you make stretching out stiff muscles. Which Mason would have. Lots of muscles. Very stiff—

Stop.

Then it did stop. The water, that is. She frowned. He'd only had time to get wet and—

The sound of lathering. How the hell did you *hear* the sound of lathering? Well, she did. The swish of soapy hands over skin. The soft groan of pleasure as he stretched those stiff muscles. The slap of the washcloth, sending a tingle through her, tongue darting between her teeth as she imagined that wet washcloth slapping—

Jesus. How did a guy make showering sound dirty?

No, that was her. Mason was just innocently bathing, and she was perving on him from the next room. She didn't even need to see him to make her breath come faster. Didn't need to see him in that huge shower, big enough for two, Mason Moretti, naked and—

Gemma sat up.

She swung her legs out of bed and caught a glimpse of herself, her color high, her pupils huge, the look of a sex-starved woman with a smoking hot guy showering on the other side of the wall.

She rubbed her face and checked again. Nope, she still looked like she'd been caught watching porn.

Time to, uh, empty her luggage. That was it. She'd unpack and dress and take her time getting ready. Oh, look, her room had a balcony. She opened the door and let the cool morning breeze waft in. There, that would help.

You know what would help a lot more?

Not an option. At least, not while Mason was on the other side of that very thin wall.

Unpack her clothes, cool down, and get ready for a day of writing.

By the time Gemma left her room, Mason was in the kitchen. She considered having a shower herself, but getting naked under steaming water would only revive the problem.

Coffee now, shower later.

She walked into the kitchen and stopped. Holy shit, was he trying to kill her?

Mason worked at the counter with his back to her...while wearing only swimming trunks. His bare torso still glowed from his shower. Damp hair. A sliver of beard shadow visible when he turned to reach for the bag of coffee beans.

Something sizzled on the stove, but she made her way straight for Mason. Because he was in front of the coffee maker, that's all.

He turned to her. "Figured I'd go for a swim after breakfast, so I just pulled on my trunks. That's okay?"

Okay...She rolled the word around as she looked at him, wearing only swim trunks, completely naked except for those trunks, which were not exactly baggy, and showed off just enough definition to—

She jerked her gaze up so fast she risked whiplash.

"Is it okay?" he asked again.

She only nodded, mutely.

"Coffee coming up," he said. "As soon as I figure out how to use this thing. Mine at home is a single cup."

"A Keurig?"

He shook his head. "The kind you pour beans into and it dispenses a single cup."

"At the touch of a button? I've seen those, and it's now official. I hate you."

He lifted a finger. "Envy, Stanton. You gotta get the words right, now that you're a writer and all."

"Yeah, yeah, let me handle this."

She walked up beside him and hip checked him out of the way, realizing too late how overly familiar that was. Damn dreams. He only chuckled, though, and hip checked her back, lingering just long enough for her to catch that smell of cloves and orange before he moved away.

"I officially put you in charge of all beverages." He handed her the coffee bag. "Did you sleep okay?"

"Very soundly," she said, firmer than necessary. Then she stopped. "I don't remember going to bed. And I woke in my clothing."

"You fell asleep outside. I carried you in." He leaned down to her ear and whispered, "You *are* very easy to get in bed, Stanton."

She hit Eject on that image fast and measured coffee into the machine. "So what's for breakfast?"

She tried to lean past him to see the stove, but he moved in front of it.

"You'll find out. Settle in with your coffee and relax. It'll be ready in about fifteen minutes, but if you're hungry, I cut up fruit. Breakfast appetizers."

She noticed the plate and reached for a piece of pineapple. "You are a god."

Godsend. She'd meant to say "godsend." Damn it.

Mason only grinned. "Oh, you ain't seen nothing yet. Now take the plate to the table, and I'll pour the coffee when it's ready. That much I can do."

Breakfast had been amazing. He'd made two kinds of blintzes—one mushroom, the other cheese filling with berry sauce served alongside turkey sausage hash and fruit. She'd eaten far too much, and she didn't care.

Mason had insisted he wasn't a great cook. From anyone else, that would now seem like false modesty. But Mason Moretti didn't know the meaning of the words, and when she'd gushed, he'd looked at her sidelong, as if she might be mocking him. That wasn't the Mason she knew.

Or was it?

Because she had seen that Mason before, in the kid who'd hesitated to write his newspaper articles, who'd ducked her praise and mumbled about them being "okay" and "nothing like yours."

Of course he hadn't produced Pulitzer prose, but it had been good. And breakfast wasn't gourmet, but it'd been good.

That wasn't enough for Mason, was it?

What had he told her once, about writing and school in general?

My dad says to stick with what I'm really good at.

His father. The original asshole. No, the real asshole.

Gemma's parents had been endlessly encouraging with zero expectations. Explore life. Have fun. Learn new things. What would it be like to have the opposite—all expectations and no encouragement to move beyond them?

She'd have to remember that about Mason. For now, she was

enjoying a damn near perfect morning, starting with an incredible breakfast and then quiet hours to write while he swam.

When she reached the end of her time, she closed the laptop to see a sight that made up for a less than stellar writing session. Mason Moretti, in wet swim trunks, heading straight for her.

It was like he'd reached into her sexy dream from last night. Except better, because last night, she'd only guessed how he'd look and now she saw the reality, which was…

He really was trying to kill her, wasn't he? Death by unrequited lust. Worse, he wasn't even trying to be sexy. He was just walking…while almost naked, muscles glistening wet in the sunshine, water dripped from his hair, those soaked trunks leaving little to the imagination.

I'm a big guy. Everything's gotta be proportional.

Dear God, he really was trying to kill her. Even when she dragged her gaze from his trunks, she only found herself caught in the tractor beam of his smile.

He walked straight to her, put one knee on the circular chair, and leaned over, dripping wet, exactly like in her dream.

"Ready for a lesson?" he said.

"Y-yes?"

"Sex," he said.

She blinked. "Wh-what?"

"I want to talk about sex. Is that okay?"

Damn it, she'd fallen asleep, hadn't she? Drifted off on the chair and tumbled back into her dream

"For our asshole lesson," he said. "That's where I want to start."

"With…sex?"

A grin. "Is that a problem?" He shook his wet hair, warm water spraying. "I'm kidding. Well, kinda. After what happened last week, at the restaurant, I'd like to talk about how I'm being an asshole with women. How I can be better."

"With sex?" she said again, relaxed into a teasing tone.

"Nah." A wicked grin. "I've got that part down pat."

He lightly smacked her bare calf. "Come on, teacher. Class is officially in session."

CHAPTER TWENTY—EIGHT

GEMMA

They were walking along the shore, quiet at first, just enjoying the gorgeous scenery—endless blue sea with not a ship or shore in sight. Gemma wore denim shorts from her prepacked luggage. And they were definitely short, leaving her feeling as if she'd forgotten to put anything on over her panties. Mason seemed to appreciate them, sneaking discreet admiring glances, and she didn't mind that. Didn't mind it at all.

"So dating," she said finally. "You wanted to talk about what happened in the restaurant."

"Yeah."

"And how to avoid it, I presume?"

He nodded, though he did seem distracted, still sneaking glimpses of her legs.

"I need you to be honest with me, Mace."

That got his attention, his gaze flying to hers and locking with it. "I will be. I want that, Gem. Being honest. No more bullshit."

"Okay, well, this might get awkward then."

He seemed to straighten his shoulders. "I can take it."

"From what I understand, Camille was angry because you lied.

You guys hooked up and you said you couldn't do a repeat because you don't date during the season."

"Yeah."

She lowered her voice. "Did you suggest that more dates were coming? Beforehand?"

"What?" His eyes widened. "No. I'd never—" More shoulder straightening. "I do a lot of shitty things, Gem, but I'd never lie to get a woman in bed. I'm really clear up front that it's…"

Her lips twitched. "A onetime offer?"

"It's my thing. I don't get involved. Too busy, you know?" He shoved his hands into the pockets of his swim trunks. "I mean, it's better now that I'm older, and I…well, I'm ready for more. With the right person, you know?" He snuck her a look. "Someone I want to be with for…"

"More than a night?"

"Yeah. But with Camille, I was clear from the start. That's how I usually operate. We go out, and if we click and we're both interested, the date goes to its natural conclusion. Everyone has fun. End of story."

"So when did you lie?"

"Afterward. Sometimes, when I try to duck out, they want another date, and I can't just say no. That'd be rude."

"So you lie."

"Which is ruder, isn't it?" He exhaled a breath. "Disrespectful."

She shrugged. "You're just too good apparently. They can't get enough."

He wagged a finger at her. "You're joking, but they're not coming back for the sparkling conversation."

"I like your conversation, Mace."

"Only because you've never had—" He stopped short. "And that's a penalty shot." A grin her way. "True, though."

Heat raced through her. That grin wasn't leering or lascivious. Just so damned confident, which was sexy as hell, because it left no doubt that he wasn't bragging. What had she just thought earlier? That "good" wasn't enough for Mason. He wasn't going to take credit unless he could claim it fully.

Another rush of heat.

"So should I be a little worse?" he said. "A little less...giving?"

She swallowed.

A sidelong grin. "Like you said, I'm a generous soul." He went serious. "I wasn't always. Back in high school, you definitely wouldn't have wanted more than that kiss. I was accustomed to being on the receiving end, and I took all I could get. But then when I reached the juniors, the puck bunnies appeared, and...you know how guys joke about notching their bedposts? That's what I felt like for them. A notch on their bedpost. Like they were collecting hockey cards."

"Once they got yours, they moved on."

"Yeah. They came back for some guys, and when they didn't with me, that felt like failure. So I improved my technique. Back then, I liked having a regular hookup. But the older I got, the more 'regular hookup' seemed to mean 'possibility of a wedding ring,' and I just wasn't ready for that."

"So you switched to your one-date policy."

"And it mostly works, but the last thing I want is to hurt someone, Gem. I know I've done that, like with you, and I hate it." He met her gaze. "You get that, right?"

"I do."

"Anyway, dating was just an example, and I don't think that'll be a problem anymore. I'm ready for more." He looked at her again. "Ready to show someone what I can be and why they want to be with me. Start something real."

A strange sensation zipped through Gemma. One that felt almost like...jealousy? She had no problem talking about Mason's hookups. That was sex. Healthy and fun, as long as no one got hurt. But what he'd just said was different. Mason was looking beyond sex, looking for commitment, saying he was ready for that, and all she could think about was how lucky someone was going to be.

Someone who was not her.

Which was good, right? Of course it wouldn't be her and—

He continued, "So mostly, I want to talk about how to get out of *all* situations where I think I've been clear, but someone expects more and I feel like an asshole saying no."

"Boundaries," she said. "You're good at setting them, but maybe not so good at defending them. Okay, let's talk about that."

They ended up at the boathouse, which held a boat, not surprisingly. It was locked, and they talked about getting the key, but then the daily delivery arrived—fresh fruit and veggies—and after that, Mason ducked inside to prepare lunch while she wrote.

Lunch was meatball soup and rustic bread and a side salad of oranges and olives, with sponge cake for dessert. Gemma dug in like she hadn't just devoured a huge breakfast a few hours ago.

Then it was back to writing, and she tried not to balk at that. She wanted to explore the island more. She wanted to go swimming. She wanted to be with Mason. Most of all she wanted to be with Mason. But she was here to get the damned book done.

She glanced through the open villa door to where Mason was fixing a snack. Her gaze slid down his bare legs and then to the food he was so carefully preparing for her.

Seeing the whole of him. *Appreciating* the whole of him.

Mason silently deposited her snack on the table. Then a slushy fruit drink appeared, hovering over her, and when she turned, Mason waved at the shot of rum he'd put on the table, beside the plate of tropical fruit and ring-shaped cookies.

"Actually, I kinda need that," she said, dumping in the rum. "Thank you."

"Writing troubles?" he asked.

She shrugged and took a long drink of the cocktail, letting the frozen burn of it slide down.

"Anytime you want someone to talk to about it..." he said. "My writing experience is pretty much limited to a few school-paper articles under the tutelage of an amazing editor, but that editor was always there to talk things through if I got stuck."

When she hesitated, he settled in beside her, perched on the edge. "You said you made some changes, but it's obviously not flowing the way you expected. Do you need to change more?"

"I can't. It sold as a two-book deal, and I gave them an outline for the second book. I've already tweaked it as much as I dare. The guy needs to be a dominant alpha male hero."

"Is that industry code for assholes?" He waved off her answer. "I'm guessing Lilias is the heroine?"

"Lilias...who *died* in the first book? You did read it, right?"

"I did, and I noted that, while she fell off a cliff into the ocean, her body wasn't recovered. Which means she's actually alive. No body. No death. That's how it goes."

"Her body wasn't recovered *because* she fell into the ocean."

He tilted his head. "Wouldn't that mean she'd wash up onshore?"

Shit. "No, the tide was going out."

"And carried her still-living body with it. Fine, Lilias is not the heroine of book two. Who is?"

"Morag. She's—"

"Edin's little sister. Who is even more of a doormat than Edin. Which was kind of a feat, Gem. Do *you* read about heroines like that?"

"No, but…if you pair an asshole hero with a heroine who doesn't put up with his shit, you get a very different dynamic."

"Like ours. Which, while I may be biased, is really hot."

She sputtered a laugh. "But it changes the dynamic, and that's not what I sold."

"Okay, so if you give the publisher a different book, they could refuse to pay your contract, which means you'd be out…"

She named the figure.

His brows shot skyward.

"I'm a debut novelist, okay?" she said. "I have to start somewhere."

"I suppose it'd be wrong for me to just give you that much to write what you want."

She shook her head. "It's not about the money, which, yes, is very little. It's about launching a career."

"A career writing assholes, because if you think readers will expect that after one book, it'll be worse after two."

Here was the hard truth she'd been dodging. The truth that Daphne had gently been trying to convey. One book was a precedent. Two was a pattern.

"Let's talk about Lilias's story," he said. "Her not-dead body washed out to sea, where it was found by some guy out on a boat. He rescues her."

Gemma shook her head. "Argyle rescued Edin in *Fling*. That'd be repetitive. And I'm not sure I want to establish being rescued by a man as sexy."

"Rescues are sexy no matter who's doing the rescuing. But okay. Lilias washes up onshore, and she would have been just fine, thank you very much, but along comes this grumpy laird who insists on helping her, even when she doesn't need it and he's not exactly gracious about it. But he does because he's a genuinely good guy even when that is inconvenient."

Gemma chewed her lip as her thoughts raced, riffing on what Mason said, imagining Lilias as the heroine and a fake asshole as a hero. She liked fake assholes—grumpy guys who were all hard edges with cinnamon-roll centers.

Mason pressed. "You mentioned that your sister-in-law is a writer. Ask her. Maybe she has some insight into what would happen if you sent the publisher something else."

"I'd have to pitch it to them. And they might say no."

"But you like this idea better?"

"I do."

"Good." He rose. "Now write the outline or whatever for that. I'll be in the kitchen. Shout if you need more brainstorming. Or more rum."

"I will. Thanks."

As he padded away, she turned to admire the view, and found herself wishing, for the hundredth time this trip, that it was *only* a view. A smoking hot body attached to a guy who otherwise did nothing for her. Pure eye candy.

Mason Moretti felt like a path untaken. A moment when her life could have gone very differently.

But was that true? What would it have been like back then, to be with an up-and-coming hockey star? All focus would have been on his future, leaving her right where she'd been with Alan, except instead of being the corporate wife, she'd have been the pro athlete wife, left behind to play house while he traveled, with endless women looking to warm him up after a night on the ice.

No, what she saw wasn't a path untaken. It was the tease of a different door opening *now*, to a hockey star on the cusp of retirement, recognizing that his life is finally big enough to include someone else.

It was a tease, though, because that wasn't on offer.

She shook off the pang of something like grief and returned to her laptop. Out of habit, she opened her email for a distraction, before forgetting there was no Wi-Fi or cell service here. Yet she apparently did have a few unread messages that came in before she and Mason had arrived.

She skimmed the list. Daphne had sent a writing pep talk. An old friend had gotten in touch to say she'd read the book. Ava had gushed over the airport-departure pics. All good. None requiring a response—

Her gaze stopped on an email from Alan.

Gemma,

Saw the pics of you going on holiday with the Mace. I'm happy for you, but like I said, I'm worried about you, too. Maybe you know the real reason he whisked you off on a getaway. Maybe you're in on the PR stunt. But I don't think you are, and I can't stand to see him making a fool of you.

You know about Denny Fowler, right? If not, look it up.

Mason took you away because Denny will be back for the next game. Everyone wants to talk to the Mace, see how he feels about it. But he's not there, is he? He's on a romantic getaway with his new girlfriend, and his publicist is pumping out photos to divert attention from that.

He's using you, Gemma.

The Mace is a great hockey player. But he's a shit human being, and you deserve better.

Alan

MASON

Gemma had been tense and quiet after taking a post-writing walk alone, but once the food came and the conversation flowed, she'd seemed to unwind. He'd made all her favorites from her Nonna Jean orders—spring-pea risotto and deep-fried artichoke for appetizers and beef-stuffed cabbage rolls and a fried escarole salad for the main course—and she'd eaten with gusto. When they finished, she started gathering plates.

"Uh-uh." He plucked both wineglasses from her hands. "Go write."

She only returned to the table and started collecting the leftovers. "So, big game when you get back."

"Huh?"

"When you get back. I heard it's a big game for you."

He frowned. "Big how?"

She shrugged as she set the leftover cabbage rolls on the counter. "I don't know. Someone just said it was a big one."

"Maybe because we're playing the Flames? That's always kind of a big deal. Plenty of Flames fans in Vancouver. It'll be rowdy, that's for sure."

"So you really need to be there."

"I always need to be there." He pulled plastic wrap over the remaining dessert and then stopped to peer at her. "Are you asking whether I could skip it and extend our stay? I'd love to, but I can't."

"You'd love to miss it?"

Now he stared at her, bewildered before laughing and shaking his head. "Uh, no, I'd love to hang out in a tropical paradise with Gemma Stanton for another day. But it's not like a regular job, where you can call in fake sick." He put the dessert into the fridge. "I even had to text and let the coach know I won't be back until game day."

"Is that okay?"

He shrugged and shifted, feeling a twinge of discomfort. "It's not ideal. Apparently, he tried to call me back instead of just texting, which makes me a little nervous but…" He rolled his shoulders and tried for a smile. "I'm Mason Moretti. What's he going to do? Fire me?"

"We'll make sure you get back."

"Oh, I will. I can joke, but I don't mess around with shit like that. As soon as we're on the mainland, I'll text and let him know I'm on my way, just so he doesn't worry."

GEMMA

Mason didn't know about Denny.

She'd finally let him shoo her onto the porch to write, mostly so she could work this through.

Mason was a lot of things, but he wasn't an actor. When she called him out on his bad behavior, he admitted to it. He made mistakes, and he owned up to them, which was part honesty and part knowing he was a shitty liar.

Denny must have been declared fit to return after they left Vancouver. That was why Mason's coach called. To warn him.

Should *she* warn him?

She'd seen how Mason talked about the Denny incident. It bothered him—a lot—and he was taking a much-deserved break after weeks of dealing with the fallout. What would be the point of telling him now? He couldn't call and talk to his coach.

Was it patronizing to withhold information, deciding that was "best" for him?

She spent a long time thinking about that, long enough for the sun to disappear without her even noticing the sunset. She'd tell him as soon as they were back in the land of cell service, and he could talk to his coach.

That was her decision. She only prayed it was the right one.

CHAPTER TWENTY-NINE

GEMMA

She went back inside to find Mason chilling on the sofa, listening to an audiobook.

When he popped out his earbuds, she asked, "Is it too late for that boat ride and swim?"

He grinned. "Never. I'm all set." He waved down at his swim trunks. "Just waiting for you."

"Give me five minutes."

Four minutes later, she stood in her room, glaring at her reflection in the mirror.

This was *not* a bikini. It was three scraps of leftover fabric on strings. The top barely covered her breasts, which might be the first time she'd ever uttered those words. The bottom did not cover her ass, and clearly it wasn't supposed to.

She didn't have any hangups about her softening middle or lack of a fuller figure. But this was not a bathing suit one wore swimming with a male friend.

It might send the wrong message.

The wrong message? Or...?

Fuck it.

She grabbed a towel and headed for the door.

MASON

Holy shit. He owed a big tip to whoever had packed that bikini.

It'd have been awkward if she had a problem with it, but she obviously didn't. He had a problem with it, though. Namely that he was going to need to carry his towel in front of him until he got into the water.

Unless...he didn't.

Unless he let her see his obvious appreciation.

No, that moved too fast. *Don't be a perv. Read her signals and respond appropriately.*

He didn't need the cover-up towel just yet, but only because she was in front of him, and he was happy to let her take the lead while he fully appreciated the rear view.

When they reached the boathouse, he swung his towel over his arm, draping it just right. Gemma opened the door and reached inside to hit the light. It gave a little flicker as if it hadn't been used in a while. Then it popped on to reveal a small building that barely contained a not-so-small boat.

"Holy shit," Gemma breathed. "I expected a little motorboat."

"Is that a cabin cruiser?"

She smiled. "No cabin, so it's just a cruiser. A sport boat. A damn sight fancier than my grandparents' old cabin cruiser."

She climbed on board and started up the boat, and he expected a smooth roar. Instead, it gave a little cough before starting rough.

Gemma turned the engine off. "Sounds like it hasn't been started in a while. Let me give it a second."

He walked up behind her.

"I don't think I'm doing anything wrong," she said. "There are instructions right there, and they're very basic."

She pointed at the laminated list, which had more instructions for using the stereo than the seemingly simple act of starting the boat.

Mason put his hands on her hips to move up behind her and read the list. She was standing on a box at the controls, which meant that her ass lined up perfectly with his cock. He'd left a gap there, but she eased back, as if to let him see the list better. Then she stopped, and he waited, breath picking up speed, ready for her to pull away. She must feel his hard cock pressing into her ass. Unlike on the bike, there was no way to mistake it for anything else.

She bent to point at the control panel, which rubbed her ass firmly against his cock.

"See?" she said. "I followed the instructions perfectly."

"So you turned this..." He reached to put his hand over hers, on the ignition.

He turned the knob, and the boat started rumbling, vibrating as he pressed against her.

"Rough, right?" she said, and it took a moment for him to correctly process those words in context.

"It sounds rough to me," he said.

She sighed, turned it off, and leaned backward into him.

Well, hello.

He put his arms around her waist. "Give it another shot. Third time's the charm, right?"

She bent over the controls, her ass firmly against him. When she turned the ignition, the boat started, smoother this time, and she twisted in his arms, grinning up at him.

"Success."

"Good thing I brought the champagne."

Another grin. "Break it out and let's go."

CHAPTER THIRTY

GEMMA

Gemma should not have poured herself that second glass of champagne. It didn't help that Mason was like a shot of tequila, going straight to her head.

His gaze made her feel like the sexiest thing he'd ever seen. She reveled in that look, and in the fact that his own glass of champagne meant he didn't bother hiding his appreciation...in any way.

She'd gotten the boat far enough from shore for a swim. Then came the champagne. Now it was time for that swim, and in preparation, she bounced on the edge of the boat's swim deck, facing him and then turning around and giving him every angle. When she bounced a little too much, the top part slid up, exposing half her breasts before she yanked it down.

"Whoops," she said. "Damn wardrobe malfunctions."

Mason pushed to his feet and started toward her. "Didn't seem like a malfunction to me."

She wagged a finger. "Are you suggesting I did that on purpose?"

"No, just saying it wasn't a malfunction. Pretty sure that's how it's supposed to operate. You should bounce again, though, to be sure."

He kept coming toward her. *Stalking* toward her, slow but steady, making no effort to hide the tenting in his swim trunks as his eyes glittered.

She still put out her hand. "Back, tiger. You don't want me to fall in."

"Don't I?"

He lunged and scooped her up so fast she let out a yelp. When he made a motion to throw her overboard, she said, "Don't you dare."

"What's that? You're daring me? Okay then."

He swung her back and then tossed her over the side. She hit the warm water with a gasp, scrambled to get swimming, and glared up at him on the boat.

"*Asshole.*"

He crouched down. "Seems I need more lessons."

She tried to splash him, but he was too high up. He reached out a hand. She took it, waited until he was leaning, off balance, and then she yanked.

Mason hit the water with a gasp and a splash. She swam away as fast as she could, but when he surfaced, he was grinning.

"I deserved that," he said.

"You did."

He dove under and headed straight for her, a ploy that would work much better in water that wasn't crystal clear under the bright full moon. Gemma easily evaded him. He only surfaced with another grin before diving back under.

Mason grabbed the anchor line and hauled himself up, bare torso half above the surface, he sluiced water from his hair. Gemma watched him in the moonlight, every glistening muscle paling in comparison to his smile.

It'd been two years. Two damn years, and whatever options existed for breaking her drought, they did not get better than this.

A smoking hot guy who wouldn't expect more than a single night, because that's what he did. One chance to hit that and then they'd both move on.

Something deep in her brain tried to speak up, but her blood pounded too hard for her to hear it.

Take what he's offering, because he's sure as hell offering.

Mason dove back in. Gemma swam away, but only half-heartedly now, teasing more than fleeing. When he did get up behind her, he caught her bikini top strap and pulled.

She spun in the water. "Are you snapping my bra strap, Morelli? How old are you?"

That blazing grin again, before he dove under. She took off, but he caught up in a few strokes and twanged the strap from underwater.

"You…" she sputtered when he surfaced. "I can fix that, you know."

She reached back, undid the clasp, and pulled the top half off, waving it over her head. "There, like to see you snap it now."

His grin lit her on fire. He swam at her, and she paused just a second before diving herself. One second, the bikini top was in her hand…and the next it wasn't.

She broke through to see him holding her top over his head. She swam over and grabbed for it but couldn't reach. He swam backward, waving it.

"The perils of being short," he said. "It's even worse in the water. Nothing to climb on."

"So you say." She swam up and braced her foot on his thigh, then she grabbed his shoulders and launched herself up. At the last moment, she realized this brought her breasts out of the water...and decided she didn't care.

After a definite ogle, he whipped the bikini top backward, out of her reach, except it kept going, flying from his hand.

"Shit!" he said, eyes widening.

She dove after it at the same time he did, and they collided. By the time they untangled, laughing, the top was nowhere to be seen. They both swam, looking for it, to no avail.

"I did not mean to do that," Mason said, panting slightly as they paused the search.

"I know. Damn second glass of champagne. I shouldn't have taken that top off."

"I wouldn't go that far..."

She swatted at him. He caught her hand and pulled her to him, and she went, his arms wrapping around her, the heat of his body radiating through the cooling water. Her bare breasts pressed into his chest, and she lifted her face to his. His mouth came down on hers, hot and hungry, and she fell into that kiss, barely aware of her legs wrapping around him, his hands dropping to cup her ass.

It was only when water filled her nose that she realized there was one problem with kissing while swimming. Neither of them was actually still swimming.

She broke the kiss, laughing. Then she wriggled from his arms and swam away. He came after her, grabbed her leg, and pulled her back, flipping her over into another kiss that made her forget she didn't know how to breathe underwater.

Again, she swam away. Again, he caught up. Again, holy shit, this guy could kiss. Again, holy shit, they were drowning.

Another laugh, another escape and paddle, and the next time he caught her, she was hanging off the boat ladder. She hooked one arm through the rope for support and let herself fall back, legs around his hips, his hands behind her back, pulling her to him, his mouth on hers, driving every possible thought from her head.

Was it possible to have sex hanging off a boat ladder? Even her romance-writer imagination hadn't considered that one, but right now, she was ready to do the research. She pressed into him, making him groan, and his hands slipped up to her breasts.

They kissed for just long enough to make her wonder whether she needed to take the initiative here, show she was clearly ready for more. Then he broke the kiss, his lips sliding to her breast, the heat unbelievable on her ocean-chilled skin. She bent back into the boat and let herself fall into pure sensation, as a little voice whispered, *Foreplay. Right. There is a step between kissing and penetration.* She'd forgotten that. A low chuckle started in her chest, becoming a rough moan by the time it reached her lips.

Okay, the man had not lied. He knew what he was doing, and if he kept doing it, she was going to have to admit that something she'd thought existed only in romance novels—coming from having your breasts teased—was actually possible. Very possible. *Holy shit.*

She arched back, writhing and panting and—

And he eased away, not breaking contact, but his tongue circling wider. She whimpered and twisted, trying to get him back where he'd been, but his lips only continued downward.

Over her torso, down her stomach, his hands moving to her ass and then boosting her up higher before he ended up underwater. She chuckled at that and shifted up the ladder until her shoulders were on the deck. Then a tug, and her bikini bottoms were off, hitting the deck beside her. He lifted her higher, his tongue on her inner thighs, white hot against her chilled skin.

She whimpered again, knowing where he was heading, every fiber aching for him to get there, to hurry up, please hurry up and—

Oh *God*.

His tongue went in, and that was almost enough to send her over the edge. Too long. Too goddamn long, years where the only person who gave a damn whether she came was her, struggling to get there, desperate to achieve what had once been a given.

Tears sprang to her eyes, and she found herself struggling to hold on to this moment. To make it last. Draw out every last millisecond of pleasure—

And then she realized she didn't have to. That this wasn't one shooting star moment of opportunity she had to seize before she lost it. She trusted Mason in that. He would give her what she wanted, whatever she wanted, and she could have this. She could have it and have it again.

She reached down, hands wrapping in his hair, legs around his shoulders, and she let herself come, let the waves wash over her.

When they subsided, Mason kissed the insides of her thighs and then pulled her down into an embrace, and she clung to him, still shaking until she forced herself to pull back.

"Your turn," she said.

"Nope."

She paused, going very still. "You don't want—"

"Oh, I want whatever you're offering." A quick kiss. "But not yet. Unless you're done." He looked her in the eyes, his sparkling. "You done, Gem?"

Her eyes prickled, and she could only shake her head.

His grin grew, self-satisfied and confident and sexy as hell. "Then let's get up on deck and see what else I can do." He tilted his head. "You didn't like that fistful of gift cards, right?"

It took her a moment to segue, and she hesitated before murmuring, "Not really my thing."

"Well, this is a new bunch. On each one has something you *would* like from me. You just tell me which one you want to redeem." He bent to her ear and whispered, "And they're all infinitely redeemable."

She laughed softly.

"You like the sound of that?" he said.

"I do. On one condition."

His brows rose in near-comical surprise. "Condition?"

"That you accept the same cards from me. With the same terms."

"Tomorrow," he said, lifting her onto the deck. "I've got a whole lotta mistakes to make up for, and I'm starting now."

CHAPTER THIRTY-ONE

MASON

If Mason had known multiple orgasms would be the way to Gemma's heart, he'd have pulled that trick out of the bag long ago. He chuckled to himself as he lay in bed, arms around her, feeling her breath against his chest.

He'd done it. Gemma was his.

Okay, fine, one night didn't mean she was ready to be sized up for a diamond ring, but he had the puck, and he could see the net, and there were no obstacles in sight. He wouldn't slap shot it in. That sort of play didn't work with Gemma. Handle the puck with care as he slowly worked it down the ice, giving everything plenty of time and attention until he was perfectly lined up for that gentle nudge in.

He glanced at the bedside clock. They had one more full day on the island. Then, tomorrow morning, they'd head back to Vancouver. *Early* tomorrow, which meant they had less than twenty-four hours, but he'd make full use of every last minute.

Did Gemma like wake-up sex?

Did *he* like wake-up sex?

Dumb question. His cock was already stirring thinking about it. He'd start between Gemma's thighs. Licking her awake. Feeling her writhe against him, hearing those moans. Teasing her until she was ready to scream and then—

Whoa, boy. Don't get ahead of yourself. Step one is figuring out whether she'd be okay with waking up to your tongue in her. Because that's not a given.

He considered the matter. Not being accustomed to waking up with someone, this was uncharted ground.

The trick, he figured, was to let her know what he was about to do and give her a chance to say yes, even if it was a sleepy and half-awake yes. And then, afterward, ask whether, in future, he could just go for it.

He eased out from under Gemma. When she stirred, he kissed her shoulder. He was about to start moving down the bed, when she lifted her head.

"Whose room is this?"

He gave a soft laugh. "Yours."

"Mmm. Okay." She yawned. "So you're going back to yours?"

"Uh, no..."

Another yawn, her eyes mostly closed. "You can. That's fine. I get it."

"You get what?"

She smiled down at him, eyes barely cracked open, obviously unable to see his expression in the shadowy room. "You don't need to worry about that with me, Mason."

"Worry about what?"

A shrug as she sleepily rolled onto her back while he sat up, barely able to breathe, knowing what she was saying and trying very hard to tell himself he was wrong.

"Me expecting more," she said. "It was great. Amazing. And exactly what I needed."

"What you needed…"

She ran a hand through her hair and snarled another yawn. "Sex. Good sex. And I got better than I dared hope for, so thank you."

His gut twitched. Why did this feel like she was thanking him for dinner?

She tilted her head, as if finally seeing him. "I mean it. You don't need to worry about me pulling a Camille." She grinned. "If there's more where that came from, I'll take it, but no pressure. And once we're home…" She shrugged again, still smiling. "What happened in paradise stays in paradise."

His stomach roiled now, and he could feel the emotions rising. Hurt. Humiliation. Even a touch of anger. He wanted to shove them down, to laugh and say, *Sure, that was good. A bit of fun. Nothing wrong with that.*

But there was no way in hell he was getting those words out.

He should retreat. Get out of here before he said something—

"And if that's not what I want?" he said.

She stopped mid-yawn. "Hmm?"

Was he doing this? Fuck, yes, he was. Push past every impulse to flee. This was just a misunderstanding. She knew his usual style, and he thought he'd been clear that this was different, but obviously he hadn't been clear enough.

Time to fix that.

"I wasn't serving up dinner last night, Gem." Okay, that was a little harsh, her eyes widening. He cleared his throat. "What I mean is that it wasn't meant to be just sex. I thought that was obvious. I want more. Like I said yesterday."

"With me?"

No, with the other woman in this room.

Stop. That was anger, and anger is dangerous. Keep this smooth. Work it out.

"Yes, with you." He shifted to face her. "I know I screwed up twenty years ago. I wasn't ready. But I don't think I've ever gotten over you." He stopped. "No, scratch that. I haven't gotten over you. I've been chasing you since kindergarten, and when I finally got you, I messed up. Messed up bad. I'm not doing that again."

She stared at him. Just stared.

Okay, it was a lot. More than he meant to say. She was processing it. Any second now, she'd smile and slip into his arms—

"Me?" she said.

Annoyance flared but he tamped it down. "You, Gem. I want you."

"Like, you meant last night to be the start of something?"

"Yeah."

"Oh."

She pulled back. Pulled in on herself. He saw the moment it happened. When she withdrew, shut down.

The moment she rejected him.

"I, uh," she managed. Then she blew out a breath. "Okay, that isn't what I expected. I think you're great, Mason, but I'm not—"

He didn't hear the rest. He was already out of the room.

Out of the room, down the hall, and out the front door.

GEMMA

What the hell just happened?

You kicked Mason Moretti in the gut, that's what happened.

Gemma dropped her face into her hands and took deep breaths as her brain swirled and her stomach twisted.

She handled that badly.

Oh, you think?

Fine. She could not possibly have handled that worse.

It just ... it wasn't what she expected. She'd woken to feel Mason's warmth slipping away, and she'd been so sure she knew why, and she'd tripped over herself in her eagerness to let him know it was all right.

To let him know it was fine to leave. That last night hadn't meant anything.

But it had for him.

And for her? Gemma's stomach seized.

She needed time. Last night had been incredible, but she'd kept reminding herself it was temporary. Enjoy it while it lasted.

That had been her mantra ever since that motorcycle ride. Ever since she'd started falling for Mason Moretti again.

It's temporary. Enjoy it while it lasts. Do not fuck this up again. Do not fall for him. He's not for you.

Yesterday, he'd told her he was ready for a committed relationship, and she hadn't for one second considered he might mean her. Because of course it wasn't her. Ha! Silly thought. And if a little corner of her thought it wasn't so silly, she'd squashed it before it blossomed into anything close to an actual hope.

So *how* did she feel about Mason Moretti?

Right now? Confused.

And scared.

She had to admit to that part, too. She was scared. It was like when she'd had a dream that her book went viral and she hit

Daphne-level fame. Most of her had swooned at the thought...but a little bit said no, it would be too much, too overwhelming, too life altering.

Being with Mason Moretti would be too much. Too overwhelming. Too life altering.

What mattered at this moment wasn't how she felt. She could work that out. What mattered was that he'd just backed out of the room looking like she'd sucker punched him.

She had to fix this.

Gemma found Mason easily enough. He'd left the villa but was already coming back, wearing his swim trunks from yesterday, her bikini in one hand.

"Got this," he said, lifting the bikini. "Before the tide took it away."

"Uh, okay. So—"

"Breakfast will be a redo of yesterday. Like I warned, my repertoire is limited. Give me half an hour. You want coffee?"

"I—"

"Course you do. Silly question." He smiled then, and it was an awful smile, the fakest she'd ever seen. "Grab your laptop. I'll make coffee. And fruit?"

"Mason—"

"Sure, fruit. Maybe a smoothie."

She stepped into his path, and she swore his nostrils flared, the briefest show of anger before he reined it in.

"I'd like to talk," she said.

"No need. You made yourself very clear." He rubbed his face.

"That came out wrong. You know what I mean. Miscommunication, that's all. No harm, no foul, right?" That fake grin again, wider now.

"Mason—"

He put his hands on her shoulders, leaning down. "Seriously. It's fine. Last night was great. I took my shot. Can't blame me for that. And I can't blame you for not feeling the same way."

"Can we talk? Please?"

"Nothing to talk about. Except breakfast. Let me get going on that."

He ducked around her and headed into the villa, leaving her standing there, feeling worse than she had in a very long time.

It'd been three hours since Mason walked out of her bedroom, and it felt like thirty. Gemma had figured he just needed a little time to recover, and then they'd talk. But that wasn't happening, and the more she pushed, the more he retreated.

Everything was fine. Just fine. Sure, he didn't want to spend two minutes with her, but it was fine.

He'd made breakfast and then gone into his room "to dress," telling her he wasn't hungry, go ahead and eat. A half hour later, he came out and declared he was going for a swim. She asked to join, but nope, she was here to work, and it was work time. He'd see her at lunch.

Gemma didn't know how to deal with this. He refused to talk. He refused to acknowledge anything was wrong. He refused to *feel*. If an emotion seemed ready to surface, he tamped it down, grinned, and said, *Nothing to see here.*

That . . . oh hell. It scared her.

Her family was all about emotions, expressing them and acknowledging them, the good and the bad. Alan had hated that. It was messy and gauche.

So for all the ways that Mason was nothing like Alan, was this a thing they had in common?

They were bound to have a lot in common. Likes, dislikes, pet peeves . . . but this one was a problem, in a way that Alan's hatred of green beans had not been. She could live without green beans. Or bacon. But she could no longer live without acknowledging when she was angry, hurt, frustrated.

She'd hurt Mason, and he wasn't going to let her fix it, and if this was how they were going to spend the rest of her trip . . .

Her stomach clenched.

She checked her watch and headed inside to do the only thing she could think of.

CHAPTER THIRTY-TWO

MASON

Mason had spent the last hour wandering the island, trying to get cell signal so he could call a boat to get them out of here. Yeah, the vacation planners probably couldn't book them a charter until morning, but he didn't care how much it cost. He was cutting this vacation short.

Asshole move.

He cringed at the whispering voice. Cringed because it was right. Was he really going to drag Gemma home early because his feelings got hurt? He'd already stomped off. Wasn't that enough childish behavior for one day?

It was like when he was a kid, and his parents fought, and he'd crawl out the window. Down the fire escape. And then run. Run as fast as he could.

And what good had that running ever done?

Did it help his mom? No, it just let Mason block all his feelings, so he could go home later, when they were making up, cuddling and cooing, and tell himself that's how it was all the time.

That his dad never threw shit around their tiny apartment.

That his mom never cried quietly in the bathroom with the door locked.

That the neighbors never called the cops, and the cops came by and his mom said everything was fine, her husband never touched her, and then the cops would go away and his dad would start yelling again.

"Do you see what you did? All that crying? Don't you ever think about anyone but yourself? Mason's gonna be a star. You know that? A goddamn star. What if his coach found out the cops were coming by? You think foster parents are going to pay for private hockey lessons? Think of him. Of Mason."

Mason pressed his hands to his ears, wincing, as if he could still hear his dad shouting.

And that had nothing to do with Gemma. Nothing to do with why he was out here, sulking.

When he heard a motor, he stopped walking. He squinted and made out a small craft pulling up to the dock.

Right. The daily delivery.

He looked down at the phone in his hands. He'd been trying to get a boat, right? Surely he could offer enough to make this guy drive them to the mainland.

Was that what he wanted?

No.

He clenched his fists. He was being an asshole, hiding out here. And he'd be a bigger one if he ended Gemma's vacation early just because they'd had a misunderstanding.

That was on him. He hadn't been clear, and now he had, and she'd said no, and that was her right. No matter how much it hurt. No matter how sure he'd been that there'd been more between them.

Like he'd been sure twenty years ago.

Fuck.

His chest seized as the memories hit. How it'd felt that day, when he'd told Gemma it hadn't been a dare and she'd said it was fine. No big deal. Just a kiss.

He'd been hurt. Which was ridiculous considering what he'd let happen to her. His friends tried to protect him by hurting and humiliating Gemma, and he'd weakly protested…and then *he'd* been hurt when she said it was no big deal?

He was doing that again, wasn't he? Hadn't learned anything.

No, he had learned something. He'd learned that he'd made a mistake twenty years ago. Gemma hadn't scared him off then. He'd left. He'd hurt her and then felt hurt himself when she brushed it off.

Because he'd been a stupid kid. Confused and conflicted and scared.

Was he doing that again?

No, he was not.

Mason swung into the villa. "Gem?"

Silence.

He eased barefoot down the hall. If she was writing, he didn't want to interrupt. He'd fucked up enough today. He could wait. Take some time to collect his thoughts and decide what he wanted to say.

Unless "collecting his thoughts" really meant "losing his nerve and deciding to just let it all blow over."

He squared his shoulders. Nope, he wasn't doing that. He strode to her door…and found it open. Her room was silent, the blinds still drawn. He flipped on the light.

The room was empty.

Gemma's luggage was gone.

He raced into the bathroom, where they'd been keeping their toiletries in their little bags, one on either side of the vanity. Gemma's wasn't there.

Mason slowly remembered what he'd heard a few minutes ago. The delivery boat.

As he reached into the living room, he noticed a folded note on the counter, with *Mace* written across the back in Gemma's perfect handwriting. He didn't detour to grab it. There wasn't time. He'd fucked up, and Gemma was leaving, and he couldn't let her go. Not again.

He barreled onto the deck and squinted out at the ocean. The boat was just pulling from the dock. He buckled down and ran as fast as he could. He was going to catch up, even if it meant diving into the water and swimming with everything he had—

Someone was still on the dock. Walking his way. Pulling a suitcase. His heart stuttered. The sun was in his eyes, but he'd know that figure anywhere.

"Gem?" Her name came out as a croak, and he started to run again. Then he saw her expression and stopped short.

"Did you miss the boat?" he asked.

She continued along, pulling the bag onto the sand, where it promptly sunk. He strode over and picked it up, and she hesitated, but then let go.

"I was going to leave," she said finally.

"And you didn't get there in time?"

"No."

His heart hammered. She hadn't stopped and come back. She'd missed—

"I changed my mind," she said. "I realized if I was dealing with you running away by running away myself, we don't have a hope in hell of making this work."

"I wasn't run…" No, honesty. He took a deep breath. "Yeah, I was running away."

"And so was I. I've been running away for thirty years. Since kindergarten." She stopped and looked up at him. "You confessed how you feel this morning, and I choked, not because I don't feel anything for you, Mason, but because I feel too much and it scares the shit out of me. It always has. I've spent a lifetime denying how I feel about you."

"Because I hurt you."

"No, I was denying it long before that." She pulled off her sunglasses, eyes meeting his. "I always noticed you, Mason. Even when I tried not to. Then, in high school, I started falling for you, and I stopped. Because I wasn't going to be that girl."

"That girl?"

"The silly fool who fell for Mason Moretti. Who thought she had a chance with *the* Mason Moretti, hockey god. I didn't want to be with him. I wanted to be with you."

"But…" He shifted, his skin prickling. "That *is* me, Gemma."

"I know, but back then, I really was a silly fool. Not for falling for you, but for telling myself there were two of you. Mace, hockey god, and Mason, the sweet, fun guy I loved being with, loved getting to know better. I wanted one and not the other, and that isn't how it works."

"Okay." He tried not to shuffle his feet, struggling to figure out where this was going, his gut telling him it was goodbye, while his heart hoped it wasn't.

"You scare me, Mason."

He stepped back, blinking. "What?"

"Not like that. Sorry. *You* don't scare me. The thought of being with you scares me." She shoved one hand in her pocket and then pulled it out, like she wasn't sure what to do with it. "In high school, I had this fantasy of a secret romance with the boy no one else saw."

She looked up at him. "That wouldn't have worked, and it's not what I want now. I want all of you. Every bit. That means being with you publicly, going to your games, being Mason Moretti's girlfriend. And I'm not ready for that. I'm not ready for people to rip me apart online."

"But they love us together."

"For now. If it gets serious, that's when your fans will strike back. I've seen it. I'm sure you have, too."

His shoulders slumped. "Yeah. I have."

"I'm not a twenty-year-old fashion model, Mason."

"I don't date twenty-year-olds, and I don't only date models." He lifted his hands. "Which isn't what you mean. I know. But *I'm* not an MBA who *looks* like a model either." A sidelong glance. "I've seen your ex."

She shook her head. "For every person who negatively compares you to Alan, a hundred will say I traded up, and a thousand will say I don't deserve it. But that's not your problem, Mason. It's mine. I want to say it doesn't matter. But my confidence, my self-worth? It's in tatters. I spent nine years trying to be the wife Alan wanted, and now I'm terrified of needing to be someone else. Not the girlfriend you want—I know being Mason Moretti's girlfriend will be fucking terrifying and…"

She took a deep breath. "And I want it. I want it bad enough to face that. I just need you to know that I'm scared and why. It might seem silly to you, and it's definitely not the Gemma you remember—"

"It's how you feel now. I get that, Gem. I've seen other players and their breakups and their divorces, and I know that being with me won't be easy." He shifted. "Everyone acts like it'd be so romantic to snag a sports star. It's not. Like being a star yourself. It's amazing, but it's also…" His voice dropped. "Not perfect."

She reached and took his hand. "I can imagine, and I'm going to need to do more than imagine it. I'm going to need to understand it. Through you."

He nodded.

"There's something else that scares me, Mason," she said. "What happened in high school. I've tried so hard to get past it but…" She exhaled. "I need to know why. Why you let your friends say you kissed me on a dare, why you took all day to talk to me about it, and why you walked away after that. You led me to believe we were starting something, and then you just…left."

He stilled, his heart thumping so hard he struggled for breath.

"I made a mistake," he said finally. "A really stupid one, and I regret that I hurt you."

"Because we were teenagers, and teenagers make stupid choices."

"Yes." The word came on a flood of relief. "I've *always* regretted it, Gemma. When I heard my friends were telling people it was a dare, I felt sick. Sick and furious."

"So why didn't you fix it? You seemed to want to be with me. Why not walk up to me and *show* everyone it wasn't a dare?"

"I…" He seemed to hang there, on that single word.

She waited.

He shut his mouth and pulled back. "I regret it. I hurt you, and that was wrong, and I don't blame you for not forgiving me. But I swear I won't do that again. I mean, obviously, I wouldn't do that exact thing. But when people say stuff about us, I will stand up for you. Always. And I won't ghost you. You have my word."

"I'm not asking for promises, Mason. I'm only asking for an explanation."

Deep breaths, in and out, like Dr. Colbourne taught him.

"You didn't seem to want to be with me, Gem," he said finally. "You said it was just a kiss. No big deal."

"Because I was hurt. And, yes, young and stupid. I was protecting myself." She peered at him. "Is that it? You hurt me, and I threw up a wall, and you thought that meant it was over?"

He should jump on this excuse. That'd be the easy answer. A vicious circle of hurt and miscommunication, nothing more.

But there was *more*, and he'd vowed to be honest, and if he lied now, he'd always wonder what she might do if she found out the truth.

"Can we go inside?" he said. "Please. I'll explain in there."

She seemed to search his eyes. Then she nodded and let him lead her back to the villa.

CHAPTER THIRTY-THREE

MASON

They settled into the living room, him on the sofa, her on the recliner. The air-conditioning was on, but sweat still trickled down his cheek.

"I told you I read," he said. "A lot, actually, and in books, characters always know why they do things. Even if they act on impulse, they can look back and know why they did it. That's not me."

He ran his hand through his hair. "You never liked me saying I'm not very smart. It isn't only the dyslexia. No one expected me to be good at school. The dumb jock and all that. They definitely didn't want me to waste time studying when I could be practicing. So I won't say I'm stupid. I don't think I am. But whatever lets people understand why they do things? I don't have that."

She nodded, watching him, wary but patient.

"Sometimes," he said, "when I try to think about things, something in my head shoves back. My stomach hurts, and my brain screams to just let it go. Don't think about it. Don't analyze it. I won't be able to figure it out, so just stop."

"When you think about what sort of things?"

"Things that make me feel bad."

She didn't answer. She was waiting for more. For an example.

Was he doing this? Fuck. Fine, yes, he was doing it.

He took a deep breath, steeling himself, and then said, "Like when I was little, and my parents would fight, and my mom would cry. I hated my dad. Hated him for how he made her feel. Hated him for how he made me..."

"How he made you feel."

Mason shifted and waved that aside. "I'd be mad at him for making her cry, and then I'd get mad at her for not leaving him, and that made me feel bad, too. I just...I didn't know what..."

"What to do with how you were feeling?"

"Maybe? When I was a kid, it was easier just to ignore that. Don't think about it. Let my parents handle it. Not my problem, right?"

"It *shouldn't* have been your problem," she murmured. "You were a child."

"Then I got older, and it wasn't about my father hurting my mother's feelings. I was the one..." Mason swallowed hard, feeling his throat constrict. "I was the one hurting people's feelings, and most times, I didn't know why I did. I didn't mean to. Maybe my dad never meant to either. I don't know."

That was a lie. His dad liked hurting people. Mason had seen that malicious gleam in his eye. For his father, landing an insult was like hitting a slap shot, satisfying in a way Mason never understood.

"So you have no idea why you let your friends say it was a dare?" she said.

He squirmed. Could he say yes? Would she accept that? It'd be a lie, and hadn't he already said he wouldn't do that?

"I don't know exactly why I did it," he said. "I only know what I was feeling at the time."

"Okay."

He waited for her to tell him to go on. When she didn't, he realized Gemma wasn't going to demand he vomit out his feelings for her to dissect. Continuing had to be his decision.

"I know how I felt after the kiss," he said. "Good. Really good. Like I'd scored a championship goal, and I was flying."

She waited, still not prodding. But it wasn't enough. He had to keep going.

"That night, after I got home from the game, all these thoughts came rushing at me. What was I doing? I didn't have time for a girlfriend. You were going off to university. You wouldn't have time for me either. And how was that supposed to work, me in the juniors while you were in university? I needed…"

He bent forward, hands running through his hair. "I was seeing a sports psychologist to help me deal with the pressure. He always said that if I wanted a girlfriend, it had to be someone who supported me completely. Someone who understood that the game came first, and that if they were going to be in my life, any time they took from that, they had to give back by helping me. Making sure I ate right. Keeping my schedule. Answering my emails."

"Acting as your personal assistant."

"Everything was about getting into the NHL, and I'd never expect a girl to help me with that, so…" He shrugged. "No girlfriends. Just…you know."

"Hookups."

"I wanted more with you, but I'd never expect all the focus to be on me. You had your own goals."

"Then you found out what your friends were saying…"

"And I was furious. I told them it wasn't a dare, and they were being assholes, and stop that shit. They promised they would. But it was too late, and I knew I needed to say something. It took all day for me to work up the nerve, and when I did..."

He squeezed his eyes shut. "I don't know what I wanted from that conversation, Gem. I really don't. When you said it was no big deal...I'm not gonna lie. That hurt. But I also—" He swallowed. "I leapt on it, too. You didn't feel the same way I did, and that stung, but also...I was relieved."

There it was. The true confession. That he wasn't just an asshole. He was also a coward.

He kept going. "I knew it wouldn't work, and I didn't have the guts to say that. I wanted you, and when I realized I couldn't have you, I felt like a little kid, stamping my feet and saying it wasn't fair. I was Mason Moretti. I should get what I want. But if you didn't want me back, then that was..."

"The perfect solution," she murmured.

"I didn't really understand it all until now. I remember this jumble of feelings, and I got caught up in all that, and when it ended, you were gone, and I felt...I felt a lot of things, but mostly I felt like an asshole, and I hated that, so I told myself you were better off, and maybe you were, but that wasn't my decision to make."

Silence. Then she whispered, "It really wasn't."

He nodded, his insides clenching, as if he'd hoped for another response, one that told him he'd done the right thing. Except he hadn't.

"I..." Gemma took a deep breath. "I won't say you were wrong about us. It *wouldn't* have worked. We could have tried, and maybe that would have hurt even more, in the long run. Or you could have said you'd made a mistake, and that would also have hurt. The problem was how you did it."

"You trusted me, and I betrayed that. I didn't have the guts to say it wouldn't work. I didn't trust that you'd have seen that yourself. I just let that tide roll over us and make the decisions for me."

She pulled her legs up under her. "I appreciate that, however it came about, you didn't expect me to be that kind of girlfriend. I could say that I wouldn't have stood for it, but that'd be a lovely bit of self-delusion because I *did* stand for it, with my ex. He needed the kind of wife who put his career first and worked in service of that. The fact that you knew, even then, that that was wrong for me…" She looked up at him. "Thank you."

He let the silence fall. Then he said, "If you want to leave, I won't stop you. I'd like to go along, if that's okay."

She shook her head. "I don't want to leave." Her gaze rose to his again. "Unless you'd like me to."

He met her gaze and felt his heart clench. "I never wanted you to go, Gem. That was the problem."

She stood and walked over to him. When he hesitated, she said, "May I?" and gestured at his lap. He nodded mutely and put out his arms, and she straddled his lap, her hands lacing behind his neck. Then she kissed him.

GEMMA

As Gemma kissed Mason, her hands dropped to the hem of his tank top. She tugged the shirt over his head and dropped it to the side. Then she ran her fingers down his chest and over his abdomen as she traced the muscles there.

"I had to take off your shirt that night I stayed over," she said, her attention still on tracing those muscles. "Camille had spilled wine on it and it was drenched, and it was really wrong to make you sleep that way," she said. "I had a good reason, but it felt like an excuse. I just really wanted to take your shirt off."

He chuckled, the sound vibrating under her fingers.

"So I did take it off, as you may have noticed," she said. "Which was a mistake."

"A mistake?"

"Once I looked, I wanted to touch. I've spent the last few days wanting to touch. And you know what?" She leaned to his ear. "It was worth the wait."

She only smiled and resumed her exploration, letting her fingers run over his biceps.

"Want to hear another dirty little secret?" she said.

"Absolutely."

She leaned to his ear again. "When I had a bath in your apartment, I left the door unlocked." She pulled back to run her fingers over his chest again. "Couldn't quite bring myself to leave it open. But it was definitely unlocked. Just in case."

A wicked grin sparked. "In case I woke up and walked in on you and whoops, you didn't mean to leave that open."

"It's a sexy romance staple. Along with the hero really needing to take his shirt off. I was running through them all."

"Except in the sexy romance version, I would have woken up and stumbled into the bathroom, which I didn't do."

"Probably for the best. Those scenes work much better in books."

"True. If I really did open that door, I'd have been a gentleman and backed out fast. And probably not seen more than a bare arm."

She sighed. "Exactly."

"Well, since we're sharing, wanna know my dirtier little secret from that night?"

Her brows shot up. "Absolutely."

"Well, it started with seeing you in my bathrobe, which was incredibly hot. So hot I needed a shower. And I didn't lock the door either. Instead, I enjoyed a nice long shower, imagining you coming in there and seeing me enjoying more than a nice long shower."

She bit her lip, and his eyes sparked.

Now he was the one leaning toward her ear to whisper. "Which I did. I *thoroughly* enjoyed myself in that shower."

Her cheeks went as hot as the rest of her. "And I missed it."

"Probably for the best. Like you said, real life doesn't quite work the same."

"Me shrieking and backing out babbling apologies *isn't* sexy?"

"Not *my* kind of sexy."

"Good. Which is exactly what I would have done…and then spent the rest of the day forcing myself to wait until I was at home alone to replay the scene." She tickled kisses up the side of his neck. "Over and over again."

He groaned.

She kept kissing his neck and shoulders, until she realized she couldn't quite do that and talk. Sadly. So she settled back and ran her fingers over his nipples again, enjoying his exhale of pleasure before her fingers ran down the rest of his chest.

"I dreamed of you the other night," she said. "After I fell asleep outside. So many dreams of us. In bed. At the arena. Out on the deck furniture."

That wicked grin. "Talking, right?"

"I do not remember any talking. And then I woke up to you having a shower, right on the other side of the wall, which meant I didn't dare follow through on those sexy dreams. In case I wasn't...quite as quiet as I needed to be."

His breathing picked up.

"But then all I could do was think about you, naked on the other side of that wall." She slid from his lap, her hands running down his chest. "Which did not help at all." She eased his knees apart and knelt between them. Then her hands went to his waistband. "May I?"

When he hesitated, she looked up. "No?"

"Normally, hell yes, but if you're going to do what I think you're going to do...?" His fingers toyed with her hair. "Is it rude to ask for a rain check? 'Cause I'd kinda rather have you up here a little longer."

Her cheeks flamed, but she nodded and let him draw her up onto his lap again, straddling him.

He tugged off her shirt and then expertly flipped open the front clasp on her bra. He pushed off the bra, but his hands went instead to her sides, running up them, his thumbs grazing across her breasts without stopping.

"Tell me again how you like my hands," he said.

"Hmm?" Her eyes half closed as she fell into his touch, the slightly rough feel of his fingers on her skin.

"That night I carried you to bed. You woke up a little and said you liked my hands."

She smiled. "I do. I have a thing for guys with hands like yours." She met his gaze. "But I think that's just because I knew a guy who had hands like that. A guy in high school, who picked me up with them and kissed me like I'd never been kissed."

"Huh. I'm jealous."

She laughed softly.

"Did he do this?" His hands cupped her breasts.

"Sadly, he did not."

"This?" Those rough fingertips ran over her nipples, making her gasp, her back arching into his hands for more.

"He did not."

"Probably just as well," he mused. "As I may have mentioned, he was kinda shit at it back then."

"Maybe, but he is *outrageously* good now."

His grin lit up his whole face. "Outrageously?"

"Outrageously."

"Well, he did work on it." His hands slid under her arms and boosted her a little as his tongue went to her breasts, and after a few seconds of that, she forgot all about the conversation, startling a little when he continued. "See, there was this girl in school that he really liked, and he didn't want to disappoint her if he ever got another chance."

He looked her in the eye. "I'm crazy about you, Gem. Always have been. I'd say more, but I don't want to scare you off."

She wanted to say he couldn't scare her off, but her heartbeat picked up, just a touch of panic igniting.

He moved his lips to her ear. "I'll take it slow. I promise. I know you've been hurt. I know I've hurt you."

She bit back a denial. No more of that. No more pretending she was okay when she wasn't, that she felt less than she did, that he hadn't hurt her, couldn't hurt her again.

"I won't," he whispered, as if reading her thoughts. "But I know

I've got a long way to go proving that. So I won't tell you how I feel. But…"

He pulled back, looked her in the eye. "Last night was amazing, but it was also me showing off. Now that we know where we stand, can I do something different? Can I show you how I feel?"

Her cheeks heated, and she didn't trust herself to speak, so she just nodded, and he pulled her into a kiss.

CHAPTER THIRTY-FOUR

GEMMA

They hadn't gotten much sleep last night, which was fine, considering their very early wake-up. As they waited on the beach, Gemma snuck a look at her watch. Their pickup had been scheduled for 5:30 a.m. It was now 5:40. Mason was chill, plunked down on the sand, shoes off.

He patted the spot beside him. "Come watch the sunrise with me."

"The boat is late."

He shrugged. "We're on island time."

He was right—ten minutes wasn't a big deal.

As Gemma walked toward Mason, she surreptitiously checked her cell. No signal, of course. No way to confirm that the boat was just delayed.

She should have told him about Denny. Then he could have decided whether he wanted to leave yesterday with the delivery drop-off.

She checked her watch again as she sat down beside him.

Mason put his arm around her. "Stop worrying." He pulled her against his shoulder. "Hey, maybe we'll get an extra day."

Her stomach clenched. "You can't miss a game."

He shrugged. "They'd understand it's not my fault. I warned the coach that I'd be returning today, and I can prove I made all the arrangements to get me back in time. I might pay a penalty, but I'd survive."

Except it was also Denny's first game back, and if Mason skipped, everyone would think he did it on purpose.

"I'm not planning to miss the game," he said, turning to kiss the top of her head. "If our ride's not here in thirty minutes, I'll find another way."

He pulled out his phone. "Yep, still no signal, but worst case, we'll boat out a bit and get one. See what's—"

He stopped and started tapping his phone.

"Mace?"

"I have a partially downloaded email," he said. "It seems to have come in last night when we must have had signal for a bit. It's from the private charter that's supposed to fly us to LA and— Fuck."

He ran a hand through her hair. "Well, it looks like we're getting that extra day after all. They canceled the charter."

"What?" she said.

He held out the phone. The email warned that it had only partially downloaded, but what she could see was enough.

```
Mr. Moretti,

I just realized we're double-booked in the
morning. The other client reserved their
flight earlier, so unfortunately, they take
precedence. I've rescheduled your boat
pickup for the following morning at 5:30,
with your flight now departing
```

It ended there.

Oh no.

Gemma's gut clenched. Someone in the charter office screwed up, and their flight had been canceled with only a few hours' notice. And the charter had helpfully canceled their boat, too, meaning they couldn't get to the mainland and rebook on another plane.

Mason shrugged. "Nothing we can do." His smile was tight, but he only said, "My coach will understand. We'll drive the boat out later and find a signal, and I'll give him a heads-up. Take my licking."

When she didn't respond, he squeezed her shoulders as he stood. "It really is okay, Gem. I'll just be told I shouldn't cut it so close. Now, do you want coffee? Or a sunrise swim first?"

"Mason?"

He looked down at her. "Don't worry. Really. You might find this hard to believe, but I am Mr. Responsibility on the team. Never miss a game. Never miss a practice. Never even show up late. The coach—and the owners—know that."

"It's not…" Her stomach lurched. "Oh God, Mace. I screwed up. I really screwed up."

He frowned at her. Then his eyes widened. "Shit. Do you have someplace you need to be tomorrow? I never thought of that." He cursed under his breath. "Asshole move, right? Only thinking of myself."

"No, this time I'm the asshole. I wasn't thinking of myself—I swear I wasn't—but I made a decision for you, and that was wrong and…"

She couldn't get the rest of the words out. He was there, holding her arms as if to keep her from falling over. The beach swayed, and sweat broke out on her forehead.

"Gemma? You're kinda scaring me. What's wrong?"

She looked up into his face, dark with worry, and she tried to push the words out.

Denny's coming back. This is his first game.

When nothing came, she fumbled for her phone. "Al—my ex—emailed."

Mason exhaled, as if in relief. "Okay. So he's being a jerk." He stopped. "Or is it something else? The divorce wasn't finalized?"

She shook her head and mutely held out the email.

Mason started reading it. When he tensed, she thought he'd hit the pertinent part, but he only said, "PR stunt. Just warning you. What a—" He stopped. Then his eyes moved faster. Too fast for his dyslexia, and she cursed herself for making him read. Speaking of thoughtless...

"Sorry," she murmured. "I can read that for you."

"No, I've got this." His breath was coming quickly. "Denny. He's saying Denny will be back for this game— No." He nudged the screen away. "He's lying, Gem. Being a jerk. If Denny was coming back, my coach would've..."

"Would have called you," she murmured when he trailed off. "I am so sorry, Mason. I knew, and I...I kept it from you. I'd seen how upset you got over Denny, and there was nothing you could do—which is not an excuse. There is no excuse. I should have told you and let you decide. At the very least, I should have made sure we got off this island yesterday. I never thought of it. If I had—" She swallowed and rubbed her face. "No excuses. I screwed up. I screwed up so badly."

"It'll be okay," he said, but his voice was hollow. "This isn't your fault."

"It is. I—"

"I blew off the call. Blew off messages from the team shrink, too. She wanted to talk to me about Denny, and I ignored her. I did what I always do. Brushed it off and—"

His breathing came in quick gasps, and his hand shot to his chest. "Fuck. I can't breathe."

She grabbed his hands. "Where does it hurt?"

He motioned to his chest as he struggled for air. She helped him sit down on the sand, and he didn't resist, just kept gasping. She machine-gunned questions and got enough to know he wasn't having a heart attack.

A panic attack.

She didn't say that. She wasn't risking him arguing, and it hardly mattered what label she stuck on it, as long as she knew what it was.

She had him close his eyes and focus on breathing deep, counting to five with each inhale and exhale.

Oh God, she'd screwed up so much.

No. She could not make this about her. She'd known the thing with Denny bothered him, but his panic suggested there was more to the story.

She'd already presumed there were nuances she was missing, nuances that couldn't be understood by anyone who didn't play professional team sports.

She hadn't pushed, because it was none of her business, and Mason obviously hadn't wanted to talk about it…which should have been a clue that he *needed* to talk about it. Mason said yesterday that he didn't understand why he did things. From what he described, though, she didn't see a lack of self-awareness. She saw avoidance.

I did what I always do. Brushed it off. Touching a hot stove hurts, so I won't touch it.

He wasn't avoiding feeling guilty. He was avoiding *feeling*. Dodging strong negative emotions, particularly ones that he hadn't developed the skills to handle.

Was that shocking? Pro sports had a culture of machismo, and hockey even more so. Add to that the fact that Mason grew up with a father who'd mocked Mason's mother for her tears and unhappiness. As a boy, Mason learned not to dwell on things that upset him, and Gemma was sure part of that had been survival. His father would not have put up with a son who let himself feel any strong emotion except anger.

Internalizing those emotions could have made Mason hard. Could have made him callous. Could have transformed him into his father. Instead, in avoiding that, he'd avoided the hot stove. Something upsets you? Don't think about it.

She couldn't blame Mason for that. It was how Gemma got through the last few years of her marriage.

Once Mason's panic attack subsided, Gemma held his hands in hers and sat on the sand and gave him a moment before saying softly, "I'll fix this, Mason. I swear I will."

"There's no way. We're trapped here, and it's my fault."

"I should have told—"

"No, please," he said. "I don't want to argue. I know why you didn't tell me, and it wouldn't have mattered if you did. I wouldn't have left yesterday."

"I'll still fix this," she said firmly. "We'll head out on the boat. The guy who brought us here said we should be able to pick up a signal to the east, heading for the mainland. If we don't, we keep going."

"But the boat's running rough."

"Yes, but we took it out yesterday. While we'd need to leave it on the mainland for the owner to deal with, I presume that's better than missing the game."

He nodded silently.

"I'm going to get you to the mainland," she said firmly. "Then we'll see what our options are from there. Fly to LA or anyplace that can get us a flight up to Vancouver. Even if we can only reach Seattle, we can rent a car and cross the border. The game starts at seven thirty. You'd need to be there by seven at the absolute latest, right? As long as they know you're coming."

Another nod.

"We can do this," she said. "As soon as we have a cell signal, we start looking for options. We'll have everything arranged before we reach the marina."

It would help if she knew where the marina was, but she'd figure that out. Head due east and pull up a map as soon as she could.

The main thing was that they knew no one was coming to pick them up, so they had to leave now.

"Ready?" she said.

He took some time getting to his feet, as if still numb. Then he looked at her and caught her up in a fierce hug.

She hugged him back. "We've got this. Now let's go."

CHAPTER THIRTY-FIVE

MASON

The boat was dead. It had started up, sounding like it always did, just running rough. Gemma steered it out and headed east, and they'd left the island behind, weaving through a few others—all of them dark and seemingly empty—until they were in open water, the lights of the mainland ahead. That's when the boat died.

Gemma kept her cool. Of course she did, because she was Gemma. Before they left, she'd checked the radio, obviously, but it had only blasted static. She'd also checked the fuel, and they had plenty. There were no warning lights on the running board. It just ran rough, as it had since day one. Then it started running rougher and rougher until the engine sputtered and died.

Gemma had spent the last twenty minutes trying to get it started while Mason messed with the radio, hoping for something, anything. Although the boat captain said they could expect a cell signal "a bit east," they didn't have any.

"It's not going anywhere," Mason said finally, touching her arm as she tried again.

Her shoulders slumped. "I'm sorry. I shouldn't have risked it."

"I don't know what the alternative was," he said.

"*Not* being stranded in the ocean?"

"We can see land. We aren't stranded." He shielded his eyes against the rising sun. "How far off do you think it is?"

"Eight miles? Definitely not swimming distance." She looked around, and then tears glistened. "I'm so sorry, Mace."

He pulled her to him in a hug, and focused on breathing as his heart sped up and his lungs struggled to get enough oxygen.

Don't freak out. It's no big deal.

Except his gut said it was a big deal, a huge one, and if he missed tonight…

He couldn't even mentally finish that sentence. Thinking it sent his pulse racing, his breath coming short.

Gemma stepped back. "If you have any ideas, I'm listening."

The panic licked through him, and he could only manage a shake of his head.

"Okay, so…" She looked around. "The only thing I can suggest is that we drop anchor. Either another boat will come along, or we'll pick up a cell signal or the boat will start again after a rest. That's not exactly the foolproof plan I'd like right now, but…"

It was all they had. Waiting and hoping.

He dropped anchor while Gemma used binoculars to scan the horizon for boats. He could see dots in the distance, but they were much too far away to make contact.

She lowered the binoculars. "Let's keep our phones out, in case we pick up a signal. I'll watch for boats behind us if you watch in front."

They settled in on the bow. Gemma sat with her legs against his, and he inched closer, the contact calming him.

"Since we're stuck here," she said. "Can I…ask about Denny?"

That calm evaporated, his breath quickening. He thought he hid his reaction, but she rested her hands on his leg.

"We don't have to," she said. "But I'd really like to understand. I'm not a pro athlete. Not even much of a sports fan. So I'm missing nuances here, and I want to understand what you're going through."

He managed a shaky "Okay," even as his brain screamed it was not okay, that he didn't want to talk about this. He'd made her talk about her writing, hadn't he? He'd pushed and pushed, wanting to understand an issue with her career. He couldn't deny her the same.

She continued, "Denny got hurt because you weren't there to defend him, and that it's your job to defend him, especially because he's young and playing center. Right?"

Mason nodded.

"Some fans think you refused to help him. That you're jealous of a young player whose star is rising as..." She swallowed sharply, as if to avoid finishing that, but he knew what she'd been going to say, and his heart picked up speed again.

"But that's not true," she said firmly. "And no one wants people spreading lies that make them look bad."

Like letting his friends say he'd kissed her only on a dare.

Maybe she didn't think that. But he did.

She shifted, her hand moving to rest on his thigh. "But...you must be used to that, Mason. You've spent your career as an enforcer. To be blunt, you're a professional asshole, and you've always seemed okay with it. Fans love you for it or they love hating you for it. Am I wrong that you're okay with that?"

He relaxed. This was easy territory. "I'm fine with it. I've been dealing with the hate part since..." He shrugged. "Forever. I don't know what you remember from when we were kids. Maybe it seemed as if I was some kind of golden boy, and I was, don't get me wrong. People spoiled me, and I loved it. Still do. Can't deny that. But there have always been those who hated me. It wasn't even other kids as much as their parents."

"Parents?" Gemma bristled. Then she said, "Okay, no, that makes sense. I've had friends with kids in sports, and I know parents are the worst. I'm sorry you had to put up with that."

He shrugged again. "It came with the territory. I've always had thick skin. Coaches and my shrink told me to tune out the negativity, so I did. And then I started to embrace it. Those parents were angry because I was better than their kids. Let them be angry. It confirmed I was better. As an enforcer, I know what I'm doing: helping my team win. If I need to be an asshole, I will be an asshole, and if I'm jeered by fans, then it's because I'm a threat to *their* team's chances. As I should be. Do I get jeered by Growler fans? No, but they do grumble sometimes, if I take attention from their favorite player—like parents jeering at me for taking attention from their kids. I know what I'm doing, and I know it's for my team, not for me, so fuck them."

He glanced at her. "That's the very long way of saying I'm fine with it."

She smiled and squeezed his knee. "Good. You're right, on all of it. Your job is being an asshole on the ice."

"I just need to carry less of that off the ice."

"A little, yes." The smile faded, her brow furrowing. "But if it's not the negative press that's bothering you, what is it? Do you feel bad because the kid got hurt? That's understandable."

His gut clenched, and he scanned the horizon, reaching for the binoculars.

"Mason?" She gently pulled the binoculars from his reach. "Can you tell me how it happened?"

His heart hammered, and he shook his head.

"Is it like with what happened between us?" she said. "You don't know how it happened? Or why?"

He nodded.

She exhaled. "Okay. Can we walk through it? People think you're jealous, which you aren't—"

"Envious," he blurted. Then he pulled back, rolling his shoulders. "To me, envy means you want what someone has. Jealousy means you want what someone has *and* you don't think they should have it."

He pushed past the urge to duck and dodge. *Be honest with her.* "Do I wish I had the body of a twenty-one-year-old again? Fuck, yeah. Do I wish I had fifteen years in the NHL ahead of me? Yeah, I do, but I..." His breathing quickened. "I don't."

She slid closer, right up against him now.

He kept going, knowing if he paused, he'd stop. "I'm only thirty-six. I feel as if I've just gotten started, and now the end is right in front of me, and I...I don't...I don't know what to do with that."

She hugged him, tight and fierce.

"I'm not an old horse ready to be put out to pasture, Gem," he said. "For a player my age, I'm in really good shape. For an enforcer my age? Just still *being* an enforcer at my age is an accomplishment. I work my ass off to stay healthy. I'm careful in my fights, and I take the recovery time I need. But all that means shit, because all people see is a number. My age. My advanced fucking age at thirty-*six*."

She took his hands, holding them tight and saying nothing, just letting him talk.

"I have one physical issue right now," he said. "My knee acts up. It doesn't give out. It doesn't stop me from doing anything. It just reminds me that it's there, and I look after it."

"What does the team doctor say about it?"

"I haven't told her. At my age, if I even suggest my joints are giving me trouble, the team will start quietly making plans to replace me…if they don't already have those plans in place. So I'm stuck hiding an otherwise minor injury, like some fucking horse afraid of being put down for spraining a leg. I like Denny. I really do. And I'm glad he's on our team because he's an amazing player, but do I feel twinges of envy? *More* than twinges. I don't think it's jealousy, though."

He inhaled and forced the words out. "But what if it is? Like I said, I'm not the most self-aware guy. What if this is jealousy, and I'm kidding myself, and I really am the asshole who let him get hurt?"

"Can you walk me through that game?"

He hesitated.

"Mace?"

He forced his gaze up to hers. "There are reasons why I worry that I did it on purpose. Things that happened that night."

Her hands tightened on his. "Let me say this, right up front, Mason. If you had a spurt of jealousy and let him get hurt, I would understand that completely. I have had some…" She swallowed. "Some thoughts about my ex's new girlfriend that really do not reflect well on me. I don't know her, but I'm sure she didn't need to seduce him, and even if she did, then she set me free, and I feel bad for what's in *her* future. But I still get these moments where I think of all the nasty things I'd like to have happen to her, and then I'm ashamed."

She looked at him. "If you let Denny get hurt out of jealousy, then I know you regret it. That's not the person you want to be, which is all that matters to me."

With each word she said, the tightness in his chest eased.

What was he most afraid of?

Realizing he'd been a bitter aging athlete who vented his frustration on an innocent young player. He didn't want to be that guy. Ever. He'd seen that guy. Faced him on the team, and all he'd felt was pity. He did not want to be pitied.

But he was also afraid of Gemma thinking he'd been that guy. That she'd want nothing to do with him if he made that mistake. If that *is* what he'd done and if *she* could forgive him, maybe he could forgive himself.

"I was in a bad mood," he said. "Nothing to do with hockey. I don't...I don't talk to my dad much, and Nonna tries to run interference, and I'm torn between not wanting to deal with his bullshit and thinking I should suck it up for her. Nonna wanted me to visit him, and that put me in a bad mood. Then I get a text from the coach saying they wanted me in early for a media interview. Already being in a mood, that made me even crankier because interviews are supposed to take place early on game day so they don't cut into my pregame rest time. But I never argue. So I show up...and it's for a piece on aging players and their post-career plans."

Gemma winced.

Mason continued, "I get a lot of that these days. Like, let's just keep reminding the old guy that he's old. I don't handle it well. I get defensive. Ask them where they got the idea I was retiring, trot out my stats, how they're better than they were five years ago. I do that interview, but it puts me in a worse mood. Then it's game time. I skate out, like usual, and take my place. The fans make noise—cheering or jeering for me—and that's all good. A few moments later, Denny skates out and...I don't know whether he gets more cheering than me. Usually I try not to measure that or it'll eat me up. But that night, it's different. His applause was definitely bigger, and then I see why."

His stomach twists, and he shifts, embarrassed by this next part. "You know how when I skate out, I get an animation? On the screen?"

She smiled. "I do. It's very cute."

"It is, and I never thought much of it. No one else gets one, but I figured that's just the AV guys playing to the crowd, winding them up. It's part of the show and not really about me. That night though...Fuck, this sounds so childish." He snuck a look at her. "Denny got an animation, too."

"And you weren't warned."

Again, he wants to dodge and deny. Really? He'd been upset because another player got a silly animation on the scoreboard? How old was he? Five?

He shook his head. "No one told me, and I get that, because it's such a little thing."

"Uh, no, it's not. You were the only player introduced that way, and there already had to be some sense of competition between you and Denny, no matter how well you get along. The hotshot rookie versus the aging powerhouse. It's a classic setup, and if you ask me, giving Denny an animation was a deliberate attempt to play into that narrative. Yours is because you have a nickname and a signature move. Does Denny have that yet?"

Mason shook his head.

"So what was his animation?"

"A shooting star."

She cursed. "Does his name or nickname have *anything* to do with stars?"

"No."

"Then at best, whoever came up with that was just inconsiderate. At worst, it was deliberately provocative. Either way, you should have been warned. It must have stung."

He rolled his shoulders. "It did, and then I felt foolish for letting it sting, except that didn't stop it from stinging, and it was just this vicious circle in my head. Between the animation and the interview and the shit with my dad, I was off my game. I couldn't focus. That's not an excuse. I'm embarrassed about it because I can always focus. I'm not a good enforcer because I can fight. I'm a good enforcer because of my instincts. I can *feel* trouble brewing, and I head it off before it becomes a fight. But that night, I was off. I knew the opposition would target Denny. I even knew who'd go after him and how. But I was zoned out, and when it happened, I was caught off guard. I swung around to help Denny...and my damn knee gave out. Not completely. It never does that. It just gave a hitch, and usually I'd power through, but it's like..."

His breathing picked up, and he forced himself to press on. "It's like it all came tumbling down. The interview. The animation. My knee. I don't know what I was thinking. I don't even know what I was feeling. I hesitated, and then Denny was getting slammed into the boards, and I was too late, and it looked like I never even tried to get to him. As if I saw it happening...and watched."

Gemma crawled onto his lap and hugged him, and he buried

his face in her shoulder, breathing her in until his heart rate slowed.

"Maybe I *was* jealous," he said. "If I don't know why I did it, then maybe the fans are right. I don't care if they hate me, but I do care…" His chest tightened. "I care whether I did it on purpose, and I care whether Denny thinks I did."

"Have you talked to him?" she said, her voice low.

He shook his head. "The coach didn't think I should, and I…didn't push."

"Denny didn't want to see you?"

Mason hesitated, and then said, "No, the coach just thought it'd add to the problem, and I…jumped on the excuse. I should have reached out, gone to see him or texted or even sent a get-well card. If I'd done that, missing tonight's game wouldn't be such a big deal. Yeah, people might say I skipped it on purpose, but Denny would know better. The team would know better. But I never reached out, and if I miss the game, it'll seem like proof that I intentionally let him get hurt."

She leaned against him, the two of them sitting there, wrapped in each other.

"We'll make this right," Gemma said. "If we can't get you to the game, we'll find a way to fix it later. But getting you to the game is—"

Her head jerked up. "Did you hear that?"

CHAPTER THIRTY-SIX

GEMMA

There was a boat, a small fishing vessel coming from the east. Gemma and Mason did everything to get the crew's attention. Waved their arms. Shouted. Shouted some more. It was too far off to hear them. Gemma kept waiting for it to be in line with their boat, as close as it would get. Surely the crew would hear them then.

And then it stopped. They waved and shouted, but the boat was at least five hundred feet away, with no sign it would get closer. Gemma didn't pause to think. She had no idea how long the boat would stay there, whether it would get any closer once it restarted. Their chance was evaporating, and she knew how important it was to Mason to make the game. And how desperately she wanted to make up for her mistake. So she told Mason to stay where he was, jumped into the ocean, and started to swim.

It was only after jumping in that she realized this was not a pool. It was not the shallow water around their island. It was the open sea. With sharks.

Gemma knew the popularity of shark TV shows. She'd never seen one, which seemed a serious oversight at this moment. Or maybe it was better, leaving her mind unclouded by deadly shark facts.

Oh yes, it was definitely better to only have horror movies about sharks to fall back on.

Gemma reminded herself that the ocean was a very big place. The chance of a shark being nearby was…Okay, it was probably higher than she liked. But the chance of it being nearby *and* hungry *and* choosing her above all the other delicious fish in the sea seemed low.

It had to be low. More people died from lightning strikes than shark attacks, right?

Keep swimming. That was all that mattered.

Swim and think about things that were not sharks.

Her mind went back to Mason's confession. Whether or not there'd been a hint of jealousy in what happened with Denny, Mason wasn't the kind of guy to intentionally allow a young player to get hurt. Just like he wasn't the kind of guy to kiss a girl on a dare. He'd handled things poorly, and the important part was that he knew it.

She suspected there was another layer to the Denny issue, because she also suspected that Mason did not have a retirement plan. Hockey was his life. It had always been his life.

The unfairness of it enraged her. Did she feel "old" at thirty-six? Hell, no. She was starting a new phase of life, and while she wasn't a precociously young debut author, she was at exactly the right age to start this career. At the same age Mason was nearing the end of his.

He'd need to deal with that, and she'd help him deal with that. But not today. Today was about getting him to that game.

So she ignored thoughts of sharks and stingrays and whatever else might be swimming beneath her. She ignored the growing burn in her lungs. She ignored the stitch in her arm. She ignored the fact that she hadn't swum more than a few laps in a decade.

She could do this. She *would* do it. How did she feel about Mason Moretti? She was ready to brave shark-infested waters for him, to foolishly swim so far that if she failed, she might not be able to get back. The depth of that emotion scared her more than the sharks or the risk of drowning. But she was going to get past that fear, and this was how she'd do it. She'd been hurt—by Alan, and by Mason himself—but she wouldn't let that be an excuse for not trying again. She wouldn't use it as an excuse for hiding how she felt, as she had all those years ago with Mason.

In her books, it was always the guy who made the grand gesture. Well, she was doing this differently. She'd get to the damned boat, one way or another and...

And there it was. One moment she was swimming, head down, arms churning, and then the boat was in front of her. A few more long strokes brought her up beside it, where she grabbed on to a net and looked up...

Into the barrel of a rifle.

Everything inside her convulsed as an inner voice screamed that she'd forgotten this part. She'd been worrying about sharks when the real danger was that she was swimming to a boat while having no idea who was on it.

She looked up, but the rising sun meant she couldn't see anything except a figure behind the gun. A man snapped in something that might have been Spanish, might have been Portuguese, oh hell, she couldn't even tell right now, all her attention on that barrel.

"Pl-please," she said, catching her breath. "Our boat..." She waved in the general direction. "Broke down. Radio..." Another gasping breath. "Not working. Stranded."

A murmur of voices. Could they understand her? Why the hell

hadn't she studied a brief smattering of tourist Spanish before going on vacation?

Well, because she thought she'd be traveling to someplace with snow, someplace in Canada.

"Por favor," she said, and that exhausted her Spanish. She couldn't even remember whether she knew the word for help.

"Up," the man's voice said, and a rope ladder descended.

Gemma hesitated. Did she really want to enter a boat bearing men with guns? No, not really, but the alternative was drowning, because she didn't have the strength to swim back.

She grabbed the ladder and began to climb. After two rungs, something jerked the ladder from below, and a babble of angry words shot from above.

Gemma looked down . . . to see Mason's dark head below her as he held the ladder, panting hard, his arms wobbling from the long swim.

Had she really expected him to stay behind? To be honest, she hadn't thought about it, just like she hadn't thought about what to expect from this boat.

"Off!" a man snapped from above. "You! Off!"

Gemma twisted. "Mace? Are you okay staying there?"

"Wh—?" His breath came ragged. "What?"

"I need you to stay down there while I handle this."

He looked up, and that must have been when he saw the gun, because he let out a string of curses and then grabbed her ankle.

"I'll talk to them," he said.

"Yeah, they don't want the big scary guy on their boat, Mace. I need to handle this. Please." She lowered her voice. "Just let me talk to them. You'll be right there."

His eyes narrowed, but his grip eased on her ankle. He never quite let go, as if he couldn't bring himself to do that, yet he did let her pull from his grasp. When she resumed climbing, though, he called up something in Spanish, falteringly, but certainly better than she could have managed.

The man answered, and Mason said something else.

Please don't be threatening him, Mace.

He wasn't. She could tell by his tone that he was calmly explaining, and as she climbed onto the deck, she saw the two people there—a man and a woman, both a little older than her, the man holding an obviously old rifle, the barrel no longer pointed at her but still raised.

Because she was a stranger who'd latched on to the side of their fishing boat.

"Perdón," she said, the word coming to her as she hoped it was right and not just some Spanish word close to "pardon." She added, "I'm sorry. We're stranded."

Mason called up in more broken Spanish. The woman shook her head, rolling her eyes and then saying, "Tourists. You go out into the water without even a working radio."

"It was an emergency," Gemma said. "We were supposed to be picked up this morning for our flight and no one came. May my, uh, boyfriend come up, please? We swam a long way."

The man shook his head, which she feared meant no, but he called down, "Up." The head shake was just for the reckless tourists. Then Mason crested the side, and the man stepped back, gun rising as he realized how big Mason was.

"Stay there," Gemma said, motioning to Mason. "Please."

She turned to the couple. "Is there any way we can convince you to take us to shore?"

"We can pay," Mason said.

Gemma cut him a look. Of course they'd pay, but leading with that could be insulting. For Mason, though, it was his first response because, well, it usually worked.

"We will reimburse you, of course," Gemma said. "We just need to get to shore."

"Your boat?" the woman said.

"Screw the boat," Mason muttered.

Gemma shot him another look, but she swore the woman's lips twitched.

"We can deal with that later," Gemma said. "We urgently need to get home today. It's an emergency. Otherwise, we wouldn't have left the island. Please. I know this is an inconvenience."

The two spoke rapidly, but it seemed more like a conversation than a debate. Was that a good sign? Please let it be a good sign.

"Okay," the woman said. "We can take you as far as the marina. But you will need to pay for our gas."

"Absolutely," Gemma said. "Thank you."

And with that, she could finally breathe again.

MASON

The couple took them to the boat first, to get their belongings. Then they delivered them to the marina. Mason paid them enough that they protested, but it must have been clear how grateful he was, because they finally accepted it and wished them well.

When they walked up the marina steps, it felt like setting foot in

Vancouver, their journey at an end. Of course it was not at an end. It was only starting.

Mason had been on his phone the moment they got service. The vacation planner would tell the owners about the boat, and any charges could be passed on to the company that had stranded them. Mason didn't care who paid for what. He cared about getting home.

Gemma had jumped into the ocean and swum to strangers for him. Now it was up to him to make sure that hadn't been for nothing. And he wasn't relying on the vacation planners for that. Oh, he told them they'd damn well better get him home after this latest fuckup, but what he didn't tell them was that he'd also be making his own plans.

He went straight to the local airport and started asking around, and he'd managed to snag seats on a private charter to Los Angeles just before the planners called to say they could get him one leaving two hours later...paired with a late-night flight to Vancouver. Yeah, that wouldn't work. He still let them arrange it, as a backup.

The charter flight he'd gotten them spots on would arrive in LA just past one. That seemed like plenty of time, but the only flight with available seats would get them into Vancouver just before six. Cutting it extremely close, but he would make the game, and that was all that mattered.

The other passengers on the LA flight were a bunch of guys who reminded Mason of his teammates when they went on vacation... well, if his teammates were rich tech bros instead of pro hockey players. The vibe was the same, a bunch of loud guys who'd already been drinking and had offered the seats to Mason when one of them—a former Calgarian and longtime hockey fan—recognized

Mason. So it was more about having a sports celebrity on their plane than helping two stranded passengers, but whatever. Beggars couldn't be choosers.

The problem with catching a flight with guys like him and his buddies? They were *exactly* like him and his buddies. Entitled assholes with zero respect for the charter company's schedule. Two of their party were delayed, apparently by a late breakfast and a goodbye to some "local senoritas" as their friends winked and guffawed. Okay, Mason stood corrected. These guys were worse than him and his teammates.

By the time the others arrived, they were thirty minutes behind schedule. Still time to catch their flight to Vancouver…until the late departure meant they missed their takeoff window and they were delayed another thirty minutes.

Mason and Gemma arrived in LA over an hour late, which gave them…Fuck, he didn't want to calculate how much time they had. Luckily they had only carry-ons and they had downloaded their boarding passes. They went straight into the security queue, where he may have made the rich-asshole move of handing out twenties to shift them up the line. Eventually, of course, someone decided they were not taking that twenty bucks, but by then they were close enough.

While in line, Gemma mapped out the fastest route to the gate. Once through, they were off and running—literally. They made it to the gate as people were still boarding.

Gemma flung herself into his arms, and he caught her up, laughing.

"We did it," she whispered, smiling at him.

"*You* did it. You swam after that boat."

"But you figured out the rest." She hugged him. "We make a pretty good team."

He hugged her back. "We do."

They joined the line. Being a Vancouver-bound flight meant people turned and looked at him and whispered. Back to being recognized, which was fine. Oh hell, who was he kidding. He liked being recognized. It sometimes made life tougher but—as with those tech bros letting them on their flight—it usually made things easier.

Hands clenched together, they waited their turn to the podium. Then they handed the attendant their tickets.

"Oh," she said. "You don't have seats."

"What?" Gemma looked at her ticket and at the board overhead. "No, we have tickets for this flight."

"But you don't have *seats*. We're overbooked."

"Hold on," Mason said. "No one told me that when I booked."

"See where there's no assigned seat on your boarding pass?" The woman's voice dripped with the faux patience of someone dealing with not-too-clever customers. "That means you don't *have* seats. We offered vouchers to try getting people to switch to later flights, and some took them, but you were the last two left. You've already been rebooked on the six p.m. flight."

"I need to get back by—"

"Please step aside so I can help these other guests. If you'd like to look for alternate routes, speak to customer service."

Gemma turned to him. "Ask around. See if someone recognizes you. Tell them you have a game and you'll pay for their seat."

He hesitated. "Isn't that an asshole move?"

"Only if you hoped someone would give up their seat for free, so you could get home for a poker game."

"No," the gate attendant said, clearly listening in. "I do not care who you are, you are not getting on this flight. We don't do that."

"You just did," Gemma said. "You tried to find volunteers to switch tickets. If we can find them—"

"That's different."

Gemma turned to the waiting passengers. "Sorry, folks, I know everyone really wants to get home—or wherever you're going—and you can say no, obviously, but this is—"

"Mason Moretti," a voice said, and they pulled apart and turned as an elderly woman walked over with her companion following behind. "Aren't you supposed to be playing hockey tonight?"

Gemma gave the woman a rueful smile. "He is, but we're stuck on standby and there aren't any seats. He really needs to get back, and the universe seems to be conspiring against him. If anyone—anyone—could help, I swear we'll pay double whatever the airline offered—"

"No one is giving up their ticket," the attendant cut in, having left her post to advance on them.

"Hush now," the woman said. "You're coming between me and Growler box seats."

"It is not permitted—"

"If you can switch seats, we can switch seats," Gemma said. "And it'll just be him. I'll stay behind to minimize disruption."

Mason opened his mouth, but she cut him off with a look.

"Minimize disruption," she repeated. Then, to the attendant: "If you have a problem, get your manager, but I suspect no one's going to want the flight held up for that, so if it's all the same to you, we'd like to get through this negotiation and get him on that plane."

A few people clapped. Gemma looked up at him with the fiery

determination that had bewitched him thirty years ago, and when his knees wobbled, it wasn't his bad one misbehaving. She looked at him that way, and he wanted to blurt, *Marry me, Gemma.*

I'm about three years from being a has-been hockey player, and I have no idea what's in my future after that, but I know one thing I want there. You. Marry me.

These days, he felt like he was walking on shifting sand where it'd always been solid concrete. He could see what lurked on his horizon: the day when he wouldn't be Mason Moretti anymore. Yes, fine, that'd still be his name, but being "Mason Moretti" was a whole different thing. He'd spent his life chasing a goal, and now it was slipping from his grasp and he wasn't even forty yet. Half a lifetime to go and ...

And fuck it. He'd figure it out. He'd hold on to this job until they ripped it from his fists, but when it went, he'd have a plan, and part of it stood right there in front of him. Because he hadn't just been chasing one goal all his life. He'd been chasing two. Hockey and Gemma Stanton.

"Box seats," the old woman said. "I'll also want a photo op. And a team jersey—signed."

"I can do that," Mason said.

"All right then." She held out her boarding pass to the attendant. "Switch us."

CHAPTER THIRTY-SEVEN

GEMMA

Mason had to board immediately, but he kept up a text conversation long after he should have put his phone in airplane mode. After that, she had a lovely dinner with the woman who'd given up her seat, who turned out to be a retired high school history teacher. They enjoyed a leisurely meal, and by the time it ended, their plane was almost ready to board...and Mason was texting from Vancouver.

Gemma had been surreptitiously following his flight, worried it could be delayed. It wasn't. He landed on time and whipped through customs.

They kept texting while he was in the car and she was boarding. He promised that another driver would be waiting to take her home. They'd discussed whether she'd go to the arena, but she'd be lucky to make it before the game ended, and then he had something else he needed to do, and she wasn't giving him any excuse to skip that.

Her flight was uneventful, and she was following the driver to the car when her phone buzzed with an incoming email. Seeing it was from Mason, she frowned and checked her watch. Nine thirty. The game should still be going. Was something wrong?

She quickly opened the email to find a video. After making sure it was definitely from Mason, she clicked it.

Mason's face filled the screen. The background noise suggested he was in a car, which made her heart pound. Something was wrong. He'd been sent home.

"Don't worry," he said. "I recorded this on the way to the game. It's coming to you now via the magic of scheduled email. I have a proposition for you."

She turned down the volume fast.

"No, not that kind," he said on the screen.

She smiled and shook her head.

On the video, he continued, "I know we discussed the problems with things like surprise parties or being picked up last minute for a trip. So if this doesn't work for you, do not feel obligated to agree. I just thought I'd suggest it. As for what it is . . ." He paused dramatically. "Okay, the email should be there now. Hit pause until you've read it."

She stopped the video and checked her email. Nothing. Had it gone to spam?

A bing as the email appeared. She read it, grinned, and hit Play on the video.

Prerecorded Mason continued, "You've read my suggestion. The driver is prepared for two possible destinations tonight. If you want to go home, tell her you want option A. Otherwise, option B. Either way, it's your choice."

Gemma stopped the video and caught up with the driver.

"Option B, please."

The woman dipped her chin. "Yes, ma'am."

MASON

Gemma had taken him up on his offer. He got that text as soon as he retrieved his phone, and he exhaled in relief. He didn't think his suggestion qualified as an unwelcome surprise—just spontaneity—but he hadn't been sure. Better yet, she'd agreed with a line of exclamation marks. So that was settled, and he couldn't wait to see her. He did, however, have something he needed to do first.

He didn't have a chance to say hi to Denny before the game, and that pissed him off because it felt deliberate, as if everyone was keeping them apart to avoid awkwardness. Which only made the damn game even more awkward.

Could that mean Denny didn't *want* to speak to him? Maybe. A week ago—hell, even yesterday—that would have sent him spiraling into guilt and self-recriminations and, of course, avoidance. But now that he'd opened up to Gemma, he accepted that if there'd been any jealousy behind what he did, it was subconscious. That didn't make it okay. It just meant that he hadn't deliberately let the kid get hurt, but he'd still need to deal with all the stuff that had made him freeze up.

If Denny was angry, Mason would deal with that. Not avoid it. Not pretend he didn't see it. Deal with it.

Denny seemed okay during the game. He'd nodded to Mason and accepted Mason's gruff "good to see you" with a blazing smile. The kid really was a fucking ray of sunshine, and if that made Mason feel old and cranky, well, that was on him. No one needed a team full of assholes.

After the game, he again felt herded, this time kept away from anyone with a camera or other recording device. That was fine. This was Denny's moment. The kid had not only returned but scored the winning goal in the final moments of the last period.

Mason changed and then hung out waiting for Denny. When he appeared, Mason barreled through everyone who seemed to be oh so casually between them. Denny was unlacing his skates while chattering with the goalie. As Mason neared Denny, he thought, for the hundredth time, *Was I ever that young?* The kid looked like he should still be in high school. Fresh-faced and bright-eyed, with brown hair that stuck up every which way after pulling off his helmet.

"Can we talk?" Mason said. "Once you're dressed."

Denny gave that wide smile. "Sure. Just give me a sec."

Mason stepped away and exchanged a few texts with Gemma. Then Denny was at his elbow.

"Where to?" Denny said.

Mason waved toward the door, and Denny followed him. By now, the stands were empty, the Zamboni on the ice. Mason led Denny to the boards and stood there, watching the hypnotic slow progress of the ice cleaner.

Denny leaned on the boards and looked over. "Thanks for the assist."

Mason shrugged. Then he said, "I fucked up."

Denny frowned. "With the assist? It was perfect."

"No, last month. I should have been there to make sure you didn't get hurt."

Denny waved a gloved hand. "I need to learn to take care of myself."

"No," Mason said firmly. "Your job is getting goals. Mine is to make sure you're allowed to get them."

"Was it the animation?" Denny asked.

"What?"

"The animation on the scoreboard. They didn't warn you, did they?"

"No, but that's…" Mason made a face. "It's just an animation. For the crowds. No big deal."

"Uh, yes it was. Only you have one, and then they gave me one without warning either of us. That wasn't right. If I were you, I'd have been pissed." Denny glanced toward the rink. "And I wouldn't be too quick to jump in and save me from a fight."

"That wasn't it." Mason caught Denny's gaze again. "Yeah, the animation caught me off guard. Yeah, it didn't feel great. But I'd never have taken that out on you. I just…I had a lot going on, and I got distracted."

"The retirement-plans interview? I heard something about that. I've seen reporters do that before. Always asking older players what their plans are. It's shitty. Like the animation."

Mason shrugged. "It's not fun. But yeah, there was that, plus a personal issue, and then the animation. My head wasn't on straight, and that's no excuse. I fucked up. But it wasn't intentional, and it won't happen again. I was late seeing him go after you, and I turned to get over there and…"

Mason took a deep breath. *Just do this.* "My knee twinged. It's been giving me trouble. Not much, just normal shit for a guy my age. I haven't said anything because it doesn't slow me down."

Denny grinned. "I saw you skate tonight. I can't do that, and I don't have any knee problems."

"It didn't physically stop me from going after you, but up here?" Mason tapped his forehead. "There was a lot going on up here.

Retirement questions. The animation. My knee. It all reminded me that…" He took another deep breath. "I'm getting too old for this shit, and the kicker is that I don't *feel* old. At all. I've been careful, and I've been lucky, but the end is coming, and I need to deal with that. That night, it all came together and I…I froze up."

Denny opened his mouth, but Mason kept going.

"Did I deliberately let you get hurt?" Mason said. "No. I'm an asshole, but I'm not *that* kind of asshole. You don't deserve it, and the team doesn't deserve it. But that doesn't mean I don't look at you and see…"

Mason leaned against the boards. "You're my replacement. Not as right wing or an enforcer. They can find someone for those easily enough. What's not so easy is finding another star. The fans love you. The press loves you. That animation they chose was dead-on. You're a shooting star…and I'm a falling one, and that has nothing to do with you personally. I need to deal with it."

Denny looked like he was going to argue, but then he nodded and leaned on the boards beside Mason.

"You're dealing with it better than I will," Denny said softly. "I think about that a lot. We spend our life getting here. We give up…" Denny's voice caught. "We give up so much to get here, and then it's over in fifteen years."

Denny glanced over. "Did anyone ever tell you that high school would be over in a flash? Enjoy it while it lasts, because it won't last long?"

"Yeah. In my case, they were *reassuring* me it wouldn't last long."

Denny gave a hollow laugh. "That, too. But a hockey career feels just as short. Fifteen years if I'm *lucky*. And then what?"

Mason shrugged. "And then you lead the part of your life you didn't get before. Make up for what you missed out on. Look at Jesse. He's doing amazing things. Me? I'll probably be the guy playing in three old-timer leagues."

Denny smiled. "Same."

"Hockey is what I do. I want the rest. A wife, kids, time to be a partner and a father, but whatever I do for a living, it'll still be about hockey. It's what I know, but it's also what I love."

A quiet moment passed, and then Denny said, "Can I tell you something?"

"Sure."

"I saw you play when I was a kid. I'd beg my dad to take us to Growler games, even though we lived in Seattle. And it was because...because the time I saw you in Seattle, you were tearing it up, owning the ice, and looking so damn happy. That..."

Denny's cheeks flushed. "It was the first time I saw someone who seemed to feel the same way I did out there, and that was when I decided I wanted to make the NHL. And then I was drafted to the Growlers? I could not believe my luck. I got to play with *Mason Moretti*."

"Who then let you get slammed into the boards and miss weeks of the season."

"That wasn't on you. Yes, you'll say it was your job, and I think you've been beaten up way too much for a simple mistake." He met Mason's eyes. "I know you didn't do it on purpose. You wouldn't do it to the team. If I could ask you to teach me something, that's it. How to put the team first. After juniors, I still feel like everyone is my competition, even my teammates. I know that's wrong, and I need to get over it."

"Sure, I can help with that." Mason straightened. "Are you heading out? Or do you have time for a beer?"

The kid grinned like a fan being asked to join his hockey hero for a drink. Mason thought of what Denny said, about following Mason's games when he was a boy. He pictured young Denny in the stands and, man, did that make him feel old. But he'd been a kid in those stands, too, cheering for players long since retired. And somewhere in the stands tonight, there'd probably been a kid who saw Denny play and said, *I want to do that.*

That was the cycle, and Mason was part of it. A career in pro sports was a Roman candle, a brief blast of brilliance, that you had to enjoy while it lasted. Then it was time to start planning for the next stage. And for the first time in his life, Mason was starting to think it could be just as amazing and shine just as bright...and maybe last a whole lot longer.

CHAPTER THIRTY-EIGHT

GEMMA

Mason had texted two hours ago to say he was going out for a beer with Denny, and he hoped that was okay, and she shouldn't wait up. It was better than okay—a shared drink meant the talk had gone well. As for waiting up, she certainly wasn't going to bed. He'd had a hellishly long and stressful day. She'd be here for him.

Also, she was hoping for sex. Okay, fine, that was probably not on the table after that long and stressful day, capped off by a physically strenuous game. Gemma had already watched the highlights reel, and she'd seen how hard Mason had worked, as if he wasn't already exhausted from the trip. He'd even scored an assist to help Denny win the game.

So probably no sex. But she could hope, right? Either way, there would be lots of time for that, because their getaway had gone into overtime.

Gemma stretched out with her laptop in front of the roaring fire, watched snow drift past the window, and she grinned at her luck. The luck of finding a guy who didn't just listen to her but *heard* her.

They'd had a lazy conversation late last night, where he'd gotten her to admit what she'd wanted for their getaway. And that's what he gave her. A chalet in Whistler for a week.

He'd been careful about the "surprise" this time because, again, he *had* been listening. He told her what he had in mind and asked the driver to stop by her apartment so she could pack. Whistler was only an hour from home, and he'd promised they'd go into the city tomorrow to grab anything she'd forgotten.

This was not the chalet she imagined. It was about three times the size. Two fireplaces. A Jacuzzi. A sauna. A hot tub on the deck. A full kitchen. And both a living room *and* a study for her to write in. Because that's what she was supposed to be doing here. He'd need to come and go, with practices and games, and she'd hole up and write.

What would she be writing? Her new book, apparently. She flipped to her work email and reread the message. Yesterday, she'd written a proposal for her editor. She'd said she'd still finish the promised book two if they wanted it, but she had this other idea that might work better, given the success—however humble—of *Fling*.

She'd written the email, attached the proposal, and hit Send while they were on the island without cell service. Once they had service, she let it and several other emails go...and then forgot about them in the chaos of the flights. It was only once she reached the chalet, settled in, and cracked open her laptop that she realized she had a reply.

Love the new direction! We'd need to rework
the schedule, but I hadn't presented the

new book to sales yet, so we're fine. Let's
chat when you're home. We can talk due dates
and get you back on the schedule. Hope you
had a great trip!

And that was it. All her worrying that she'd torpedo her nascent career, and her editor gave her an enthusiastic thumbs-up. The other email from her editor might have helped. It congratulated her on hitting the *USA Today* list. Gemma had forgotten all about that. Her editor—and the imprint—was thrilled that she'd debuted on the list and that her sales were going strong into the second week.

Then there was the email from Daphne.

Congrats on hitting the list!!! I'm so
thrilled for you. And before you credit
Hockey Guy and the publicity, you're holding above four stars on Goodreads. The extra
publicity only helped people find your book.
That's what Chris reminded me every time I
fretted that Edge only sold because it had
your hot brother playing the author :)
  On a related note, my agent would like to
speak to you about representation. No, I did
not ask him. I know you didn't want that.
I mentioned months ago that my sister-in-
law had a romance coming out, but now that
he's had a chance to read it, he's eager
to talk to you. Whether you go with him or

```
someone else, I really think you're going
to need representation. It'll also help
having someone to talk to about issues with
deadlines, hint, hint.
```

Gemma had replied to Daphne and said yes to a meeting with Lawrence. He was her dream agent, naturally, but he didn't represent romance, and she'd been terrified of him taking her on as a favor to his biggest-selling client.

Gemma had spent the last two hours working on her new book, and she already had a first chapter. Her new hero wasn't exactly warm and fuzzy, but he wasn't an asshole. Nor did he particularly remind her of anyone she knew, which was good. And being in Lilias's point of view made the words flow like water. These were the sorts of characters Gemma wanted to write—capable women and the not-entirely-assholes who loved them.

When the front door opened, she scrambled up and ran like a twenty-year-old newlywed. She skidded barefoot into the hall just as Mason flicked on the light and saw her. He grinned, any exhaustion falling away as he swept her up in his arms.

"Did it go well?" she asked. "With Denny?"

"Very well." He hugged her, still holding her aloft. "Thank you. I needed to do that."

"And thank you for all this." She waved a hand around. "It's perfect."

"Good semi-surprise then?"

She answered with a kiss that told him everything.

EPILOGUE

GEMMA

Six Months Later

It was their six-month anniversary, and Mason was cooking dinner in Nonna Jean's. The restaurant was closed Mondays, and they often commandeered it for a private dinner for two. Sometimes, his grandmother insisted on making the meal so they could properly enjoy their romantic dinner, which was lovely, but Gemma actually preferred this—sitting on a stool in the kitchen watching Mason cook.

Today, she was only half watching him, her attention pulled to the papers spread on the counter. Papers for launching the adoption process…and papers for launching the process to become foster parents. They'd been planning the adoption route until Jesse convinced them to consider fostering.

Gemma had broached the possibility of surrogacy, if Mason wanted a child with his own DNA, but he didn't give a damn, and that was…Her eyes prickled. That was an amazing feeling, to know all the options were on the table. Almost as amazing as knowing he was as eager to start the process as she was.

They weren't married yet, which, yes, was the traditional first step. But she had the ring and he wanted a big wedding and, honestly, so did she. For now, she'd moved into his condo, and they were making wedding plans, but this came first—starting a family. It wouldn't be right for everyone, but it was right for them.

"Fostering might be good," Gemma said as she moved around the papers. "If we don't mind not having an infant…"

"I don't," Mason said as he chopped tomatoes, the knife flying. "I'm not sure how good I'd be with babies. I think I'd be good with kids, though."

She leaned over to kiss his cheek. "You will be awesome with kids. And probably awesome with babies, too, but if we don't have a strong preference, maybe this is the answer. Fostering with an eye to adoption. Would that work?"

He stopped chopping, took her chin in his hand, and kissed her, long and slow. "Anything that involves starting a family with you works. You know that. But, yeah, fostering an older kid with hopes of adopting, sounds really good. If we want to adopt or foster a baby later, we can do it once I'm out of the NHL and you can count on me being around full-time."

She nodded. He wouldn't be out of the Growlers anytime soon. They'd discussed that ad nauseam—should he start making plans to retire before he was pushed out? They'd decided no. Screw dignity. He was staying right up until they escorted him from the arena, and maybe not even then, as he already had his eye on coaching. For some players, retirement meant leaving hockey behind. Mason wasn't ever doing that. He was just going to slow down and expand his horizons to include things like a wife, kids, coaching…

Mason went back to chopping. "Nonna Jean wants to take over the wedding plans."

Gemma sighed. "Of course she does."

"With your Grandma Dot. They have been conspiring, apparently. Since I'm heading back into the hockey season and you're writing book three, with book two out this fall, they have graciously offered to plan everything."

"Graciously, huh?"

He grinned. "Out of the goodness of their hearts. However, if you really want to plan the wedding…"

She shuddered. "I do not. They can have it, and I'll take this." She waved at the papers. "Oh, and I spoke to administration at the college. I'm dropping to a half schedule, so I can focus on my writing and some hockey player."

"Pro athletes are very demanding."

"Almost as demanding as new novelists."

He grinned at her. "Well, you get a break tonight. The only thing I'll be demanding is that you eat dinner."

"That's the only thing?"

His grin grew. "The rest isn't a demand." His eyes twinkled. "Unless you want it to be."

She laughed and popped one piece of fried artichoke in her mouth and another in his. "We'll see. For now, just get cooking."

"Yes, ma'am."

ABOUT THE AUTHOR

#1 *New York Times* bestselling author **Kelley Armstrong** believes experience is the best teacher, though she's been told this shouldn't apply to writing her murder scenes. To craft her books, she has studied aikido, archery, and fencing. She sucks at all of them. She has also crawled through very shallow cave systems and climbed half a mountain before chickening out. She is, however, an expert coffee drinker and a true connoisseur of chocolate chip cookies.

Find out more, at:
  KelleyArmstrong.com
  Facebook.com/KelleyArmstrongAuthor
  Threads.com/KelleyArmstrongAuthor
  Instagram.com/KelleyArmstrongAuthor